CW01370743

The Collected Works of Ambrose Bierce,
Volume 1

Ambrose Bierce

The Collected Works of Ambrose Bierce, Volume 1
Copyright © 2023 Bibliotech Press
All rights reserved

The present edition is a reproduction of previous publication of this classic work. Minor typographical errors may have been corrected without note; however, for an authentic reading experience the spelling, punctuation, and capitalization have been retained from the original text.

ISBN: 979-8-88830-375-7

CONTENTS

Ashes of the Beacon 1

The Land Beyond the Blow

Thither 32
Sons of the Fair Star 32
An Interview with Gnarmag-Zote 38
The Tamtonians 43
Marooned on Ug 50
The Dog in Gangewag 56
A Conflagration in Ghargaroo 58
An Execution in Batrugia 61
The Jumjum of Gokeetle-Guk 66
The Kingdom of Tortirra 70
Hither 77

For the Ahkoond 78
John Smith, Liberator 85

Bits of Autobiography

On a Mountain 88
What I Saw of Shiloh 92
A Little of Chickamauga 108
The Crime at Pickett's Mill 111
Four Days in Dixie 119
What Occurred at Franklin 127
'Way Down in Alabam' 132
Working for an Empress 141
Across the Plains 146
The Mirage 150
A Sole Survivor 155

ASHES OF THE BEACON

AN HISTORICAL MONOGRAPH WRITTEN IN 4930

Of the many causes that conspired to bring about the lamentable failure of "self-government" in ancient America the most general and comprehensive was, of course, the impracticable nature of the system itself. In the light of modern culture, and instructed by history, we readily discern the folly of those crude ideas upon which the ancient Americans based what they knew as "republican institutions," and maintained, as long as maintenance was possible, with something of a religious fervor, even when the results were visibly disastrous. To us of to-day it is clear that the word "self-government" involves a contradiction, for government means control by something other than the thing to be controlled. When the thing governed is the same as the thing governing there is no government, though for a time there may be, as in the case under consideration there was, a considerable degree of forbearance, giving a misleading appearance of public order. This, however, soon must, as in fact it soon did, pass away with the delusion that gave it birth. The habit of obedience to written law, inculcated by generations of respect for actual government able to enforce its authority, will persist for a long time, with an ever lessening power upon the imagination of the people; but there comes a time when the tradition is forgotten and the delusion exhausted. When men perceive that nothing is restraining them but their consent to be restrained, then at last there is nothing to obstruct the free play of that selfishness which is the dominant characteristic and fundamental motive of human nature and human action respectively. Politics, which may have had something of the character of a contest of principles, becomes a struggle of interests, and its methods are frankly serviceable to personal and class advantage. Patriotism and respect for law pass like a tale that is told. Anarchy, no longer disguised as "government by consent," reveals his hidden hand, and in the words of our greatest living poet,

lets the curtain fall,
And universal darkness buries all!

The ancient Americans were a composite people; their blood was a blend of all the strains known in their time. Their government, while they had one, being merely a loose and mutable expression of the desires and caprices of the majority—that is to say, of the ignorant, restless and reckless—gave the freest rein and play to all the primal instincts and elemental passions of the race. In so far and for so long as it had any restraining force, it was only the restraint of the present over the power of the past—that of a new habit over an old and insistent tendency ever seeking expression in large liberties and indulgences impatient of control. In the history of that unhappy people, therefore, we see unveiled the workings of the human will in its most lawless state, without fear of authority or care of consequence. Nothing could be more instructive.

Of the American form of government, although itself the greatest of evils afflicting the victims of those that it entailed, but little needs to be said here; it has perished from the earth, a system discredited by an unbroken record of failure in all parts of the world, from the earliest historic times to its final extinction. Of living students of political history not one professes to see in it anything but a mischievous creation of theorists and visionaries—persons whom our gracious sovereign has deigned to brand for the world's contempt as "dupes of hope purveying to sons of greed." The political philosopher of to-day is spared the trouble of pointing out the fallacies of republican government, as the mathematician is spared that of demonstrating the absurdity of the convergence of parallel lines; yet the ancient Americans not only clung to their error with a blind, unquestioning faith, even when groaning under its most insupportable burdens, but seem to have believed it of divine origin. It was thought by them to have been established by the god Washington, whose worship, with that of such dii minores as Gufferson, Jaxon and Lincon (identical probably with the Hebru Abrem) runs like a shining thread through all the warp and woof of the stuff that garmented their moral nakedness. Some stones, very curiously inscribed in many tongues, were found by the explorer Droyhors in the wilderness bordering the river Bhitt (supposed by him to be the ancient Potomac) as lately as the reign of Barukam IV. These stones appear to be fragments of a monument or temple erected to the glory of Washington in his divine character of Founder and Preserver of republican institutions. If this tutelary deity of the ancient Americans really invented representative government they were not the first by many to whom he imparted the malign secret of its inauguration and denied that of its maintenance.

Although many of the causes which finally, in combination,

brought about the downfall of the great American republic were in operation from the beginning—being, as has been said, inherent in the system—it was not until the year 1995 (as the ancients for some reason not now known reckoned time) that the collapse of the vast, formless fabric was complete. In that year the defeat and massacre of the last army of law and order in the lava beds of California extinguished the final fires of enlightened patriotism and quenched in blood the monarchical revival. Thenceforth armed opposition to anarchy was confined to desultory and insignificant warfare waged by small gangs of mercenaries in the service of wealthy individuals and equally feeble bands of prescripts fighting for their lives. In that year, too, "the Three Presidents" were driven from their capitals, Cincinnati, New Orleans and Duluth, their armies dissolving by desertion and themselves meeting death at the hands of the populace.

The turbulent period between 1920 and 1995, with its incalculable waste of blood and treasure, its dreadful conflicts of armies and more dreadful massacres by passionate mobs, its kaleidoscopic changes of government and incessant effacement and redrawing of boundaries of states, its interminable tale of political assassinations and proscriptions—all the horrors incident to intestinal wars of a naturally lawless race—had so exhausted and dispirited the surviving protagonists of legitimate government that they could make no further head against the inevitable, and were glad indeed and most fortunate to accept life on any terms that they could obtain.

But the purpose of this sketch is not bald narration of historic fact, but examination of antecedent germinal conditions; not to recount calamitous events familiar to students of that faulty civilization, but to trace, as well as the meager record will permit, the genesis and development of the causes that brought them about. Historians in our time have left little undone in the matter of narration of political and military phenomena. In Golpek's "Decline and Fall of the American Republics," in Soseby's "History of Political Fallacies," in Holobom's "Monarchical Renasence," and notably in Gunkux's immortal work, "The Rise, Progress, Failure and Extinction of The Connected States of America" the fruits of research have been garnered, a considerable harvest. The events are set forth with such conscientiousness and particularity as to have exhausted the possibilities of narration. It remains only to expound causes and point the awful moral.

To a delinquent observation it may seem needless to point out the inherent defects of a system of government which the logic of events has swept like political rubbish from the face of the earth, but we must not forget that ages before the inception of the American republics and that of France and Ireland this form of government had been discredited by emphatic failures among the most enlightened and powerful nations of antiquity: the Greeks, the Romans, and long before them (as we now know) the Egyptians and the Chinese. To the lesson of these failures the founders of the eighteenth and nineteenth century republics were blind and deaf. Have we then reason to believe that our posterity will be wiser because instructed by a greater number of examples? And is the number of examples which they will have in memory really greater? Already the instances of China, Egypt, Greece and Rome are almost lost in the mists of antiquity; they are known, except by infrequent report, to the archæologist only, and but dimly and uncertainly to him. The brief and imperfect record of yesterdays which we call History is like that traveling vine of India which, taking new root as it advances, decays at one end while it grows at the other, and so is constantly perishing and finally lost in all the spaces which it has over-passed.

From the few and precious writings that have descended to us from the early period of the American republic we get a clear if fragmentary view of the disorders and lawlessness affecting that strange and unhappy nation. Leaving the historically famous "labor troubles" for more extended consideration, we may summarize here a few of the results of hardly more than a century and a quarter of "self-government" as it existed on this continent just previously to the awful end. At the beginning of the "twentieth century" a careful study by trustworthy contemporary statisticians of the public records and those apparently private ones known as "newspapers" showed that in a population of about 80,000,000 the annual number of homicides was not less than 10,000; and this continued year after year to increase, not only absolutely, but proportionately, until, in the words of Dumbleshaw, who is thought to have written his famous "Memoirs of a Survivor" in the year 1908 of their era, "it would seem that the practice of suicide is a needless custom, for if a man but have patience his neighbor is sure to put him out of his misery." Of the 10,000 assassins less than three per cent. were punished, further than by incidental imprisonment if unable to give bail while awaiting trial. If the chief end of government is the citizen's security of life and his protection from aggression, what kind of government do these appalling figures disclose? Yet so infatuated with their imaginary "liberty" were these singular people that the contemplation of all this crime abated nothing of the volume and persistence of their patriotic ululations, and affected not their faith in the perfection of their system. They were like a man standing on a rock already submerged by the rising tide, and calling to his neighbors on adjacent cliffs to observe his superior security.

When three men engage in an undertaking in which they have an equal interest, and in the direction of which they have equal power, it necessarily results that any action approved by two of them, with or without the assent of the third, will be taken. This is called—or was called when it was an accepted principle in political and other affairs—"the rule of the majority." Evidently, under the malign conditions supposed, it is the only practicable plan of getting anything done. A and B rule and overrule C, not because they ought, but because they can; not because they are wiser, but because they are stronger. In order to avoid a conflict in which he is sure to be worsted, C submits as soon as the vote is taken. C is as likely to be right as A and B; nay, that eminent ancient philosopher, Professor Richard A. Proctor (or Proroctor, as the learned now spell the name), has clearly shown by the law of probabilities that any one of the three, all being of the same intelligence, is far likelier to be right than the other two.

It is thus that the "rule of the majority" as a political system is established. It is in essence nothing but the discredited and discreditable principle that "might makes right"; but early in the life of a republic this essential character of government by majority is not seen. The habit of submitting all questions of policy to the arbitrament of counting noses and assenting without question to the result invests the ordeal with a seeming sanctity, and what was at first obeyed as the command of power comes to be revered as the oracle of wisdom. The innumerable instances—such as the famous ones of Galileo and Keeley—in which one man has been right and all the rest of the race wrong, are overlooked, or their significance missed, and "public opinion" is followed as a divine and infallible guide through every bog into which it blindly stumbles and over every precipice in its fortuitous path. Clearly, sooner or later will be encountered a bog that will smother or a precipice that will crush. Thoroughly to apprehend the absurdity of the ancient faith in the wisdom of majorities let the loyal reader try to fancy our gracious Sovereign by any possibility wrong, or his unanimous Ministry by any possibility right!

During the latter half of the "nineteenth century" there arose in the Connected States a political element opposed to all government, which frankly declared its object to be anarchy. This astonishing heresy was not of indigenous growth: its seeds were imported from Europe by the emigration or banishment thence of criminals congenitally incapable of understanding and valuing the blessings of monarchical institutions, and whose method of protest was murder. The governments against which they conspired in their native lands were too strong in authority and too enlightened in policy for them to overthrow. Hundreds of them were put to death, thousands imprisoned and sent into exile. But in America, whither those who escaped fled for safety, they found conditions entirely favorable to the prosecution of their designs.

A revered fetish of the Americans was "freedom of speech": it was believed that if bad men were permitted to proclaim their evil wishes they would go no further in the direction of executing them—that if they might say what they would like to do they would not care to do it. The close relation between speech and action was not understood. Because the Americans themselves had long been accustomed, in their own political debates and discussions, to the use of unmeaning declamations and threats which they had no intention of executing, they reasoned that others were like them, and attributed to the menaces of these desperate and earnest outcasts no greater importance than to their own. They thought also that the foreign anarchists, having exchanged the tyranny of kings for that of majorities, would be content with their new and better lot and become in time good and law-abiding citizens.

The anarchist of that far day (thanks to the firm hands of our gracious sovereigns the species is now extinct) was a very different person from what our infatuated ancestors imagined him. He struck at government, not because it was bad, but because it was government. He hated authority, not for its tyranny, but for its power. And in order to make this plain to observation he frequently chose his victim from amongst those whose rule was most conspicuously benign.

Of the seven early Presidents of the American republic who perished by assassination no fewer than four were slain by anarchists with no personal wrongs to impel them to the deed—nothing but an implacable hostility to law and authority. The fifth victim, indeed, was a notorious demagogue who had pardoned the assassin of the fourth.

The field of the anarchist's greatest activity was always a republic, not only to emphasize his impartial hatred of all government, but because of the inherent feebleness of that form of government, its inability to protect itself against any kind of aggression by any considerable number of its people having a common malevolent purpose. In a republic the crust that confined the fires of violence and sedition was thinnest.

No improvement in the fortunes of the original anarchists through immigration to what was then called the New World would have made them good citizens. From centuries of secret war against particular forms of authority in their own countries they had inherited a bitter antagonism to all authority, even the most beneficent. In their new home they were worse than in their old. In the sunshine of opportunity the rank and sickly growth of their perverted natures became hardy, vigorous, bore fruit. They surrounded themselves with proselytes from the ranks of the idle, the vicious, the unsuccessful. They stimulated and organized discontent. Every one of them became a center of moral and political contagion. To those as yet unprepared to accept anarchy was offered the milder dogma of Socialism, and to those even weaker in the faith something vaguely called Reform. Each was initiated into that degree to which the induration of his conscience and the character of his discontent made him eligible, and in which he could be most serviceable, the body of the people still cheating themselves with the false sense of security begotten of the belief that they were somehow exempt from the operation of all agencies inimical to their national welfare and integrity. Human nature, they thought, was different in the West from what it was in the East: in the New World the old causes would not have the old effects: a republic had some inherent vitality of its own, entirely independent of any action intended to keep it alive. They felt that words and phrases had some talismanic power, and charmed themselves asleep by repeating "liberty," "all men equal before the law," "dictates of conscience," "free speech" and all manner of such incantation to exorcise the spirits of the night. And when they could no longer close their eyes to the dangers environing them; when they saw at last that what they had mistaken for the magic power of their form of government and its assured security was really its radical weakness and subjective peril—they found their laws inadequate to repression of the enemy, the enemy too strong to permit the enactment of adequate laws. The belief that a malcontent armed with freedom of speech, a newspaper, a vote and a rifle is less dangerous than a malcontent with a still tongue in his head, empty hands and under police surveillance was abandoned, but all too late. From its fatuous dream the nation was awakened by the noise of arms, the shrieks of women and the red glare of burning cities.

Beginning with the slaughter at St. Louis on a night in the year 1920, when no fewer than twenty-two thousand citizens were slain in the streets and half the city destroyed, massacre followed massacre with frightful rapidity. New York fell in the month following, many thousands of its inhabitants escaping fire and sword only to be driven into the bay and drowned, "the roaring of the water in their ears," says Bardeal, "augmented by the hoarse clamor of their red-handed pursuers, whose blood-thirst was unsated by the sea." A week later Washington was destroyed, with all its public buildings and archives; the President and his Ministry were slain, Congress was dispersed, and an unknown number of officials and private citizens perished. Of all the principal cities only Chicago and San Francisco escaped. The people of the former were all anarchists and the latter was valorously and successfully defended by the Chinese.

The urban anarchists were eventually subdued and some semblance of order was restored, but greater woes and sharper shames awaited this unhappy nation, as we shall see.

In turning from this branch of our subject to consider the causes of the failure and bloody disruption of the great American republic other than those inherent in the form of government, it may not be altogether unprofitable to glance briefly at what seems to a superficial view the inconsistent phenomenon of great material prosperity. It is not to be denied that this unfortunate people was at one time singularly prosperous, in so far as national wealth is a measure and proof of prosperity. Among nations it was the richest nation. But at how great a sacrifice of better things was its wealth obtained! By the neglect of all education except that crude, elementary sort which fits men for the coarse delights of business and affairs but confers no capacity of rational enjoyment; by exalting the worth of wealth and making it the test and touchstone of merit; by ignoring art, scorning literature and despising science, except as these might contribute to the glutting of the purse; by setting up and maintaining an artificial standard of morals which condoned all offenses against the property and peace of every one but the condoner; by pitilessly crushing out of their natures every sentiment and aspiration unconnected with accumulation of property, these civilized savages and commercial barbarians attained their sordid end. Before they had rounded the first half-century of their existence as a nation they had sunk so low in the scale of morality that it was considered nothing discreditable to take the hand and even visit the house of a man who had grown rich by means notoriously corrupt and dishonorable; and Harley declares that even the editors and writers of newspapers, after fiercely assailing such men in their journals, would be seen "hobnobbing" with them in public places. (The nature of the social ceremony named the "hobnob" is not now understood, but it is known that it was a sign of amity and favor.) When men or nations devote all the powers of their minds and bodies to the heaping up of wealth, wealth is heaped up. But what avails it? It may not be amiss to quote here the words of one of the greatest of the ancients whose works—fragmentary, alas—have come down to us.

"Wealth has accumulated itself into masses; and poverty, also in accumulation enough, lies impassably separated from it; opposed, uncommunicating, like forces in positive and negative poles. The gods of this lower world sit aloft on glittering thrones, less happy than Epicurus's gods, but as indolent, as impotent; while the boundless living chaos of ignorance and hunger welters, terrific in its dark fury, under their feet. How much among us might be likened to a whited sepulcher: outwardly all pomp and strength, but inwardly full of horror and despair and dead men's bones! Iron highways, with their wains fire-winged, are uniting all the ends of the land; quays and moles, with their innumerable stately fleets, tame the ocean into one pliant bearer of burdens; labor's thousand arms, of sinew and of metal, all-conquering everywhere, from the tops of the mount down to the depths of the mine and the caverns of the sea, ply unweariedly for the service of man; yet man remains unserved. He has subdued this planet, his habitation and inheritance, yet reaps no profit from the victory. Sad to look upon: in the highest stage of civilization nine-tenths of mankind have to struggle in the lowest battle of savage or even animal man—the battle against famine. Countries are rich, prosperous in all manner of increase, beyond example; but the men of these countries are poor, needier than ever of all sustenance, outward and inward; of belief, of knowledge, of money, of food."

To this somber picture of American "prosperity" in the nineteenth century nothing of worth can be added by the most inspired artist. Let us simply inscribe upon the gloomy canvas the memorable words of an illustrious poet of the period:

> That country speeds to an untoward fate,
> Where men are trivial and gold is great.

One of the most "sacred" rights of the ancient American was the trial of an accused person by "a jury of his peers." This, in America, was a right secured to him by a written constitution. It was almost universally believed to have had its origin in Magna Carta, a famous document which certain rebellious noblemen of another country had compelled their sovereign to sign under a threat of death. That celebrated "bill of rights" has not all come down to us, but researches of the learned have made it certain that it contained no mention of trial by jury, which, indeed, was unknown to its authors. The words judicium parium meant to them something entirely different—the judgment of the entire community of freemen. The words and the practice they represented antedated Magna Carta by many centuries and were common to the Franks and other Germanic nations, amongst whom a trial "jury" consisted of persons having a knowledge of the matter to be determined—persons who in later times were called "witnesses" and rigorously excluded from the seats of judgment.

It is difficult to conceive a more clumsy and ineffective machinery for ascertaining truth and doing justice than a jury of twelve men of the average intelligence, even among ourselves. What, then, must this device have been among the half-civilized tribes of the Connected States of America! Nay, the case is worse than that, for it was the practice to prevent men of even the average intelligence from serving as jurors. Jurors had to be residents of the locality of the crime charged, and every crime was made a matter of public notoriety long before the accused was brought to trial; yet, as a rule, he who had read or talked about the trial was held disqualified to serve. This in a country where, when a man who could read was not reading about local crimes he was talking about them, or if doing neither was doing something worse!

To the twelve men so chosen the opposing lawyers addressed their disingenuous pleas and for their consideration the witnesses presented their carefully rehearsed testimony, most of it false. So unintelligent were these juries that a great part of the time in every trial was consumed in keeping from them certain kinds of evidence with which they could not be trusted; yet the lawyers were permitted to submit to them any kind of misleading argument that they pleased and fortify it with innuendoes without relevancy and logic without sense. Appeals to their passions, their sympathies, their prejudices, were regarded as legitimate influences and tolerated by the judges on the theory that each side's offenses would about offset those of the other. In a criminal case it was expected that the prosecutor would declare repeatedly and in the most solemn manner his belief in the guilt of the person accused, and that the attorney for the defense would affirm with equal gravity his conviction of his client's innocence. How could they impress the jury with a belief which they did not themselves venture to affirm? It is not recorded that any lawyer ever rebelled against the iron authority of these conditions and stood for truth and conscience. They were, indeed, the conditions of his existence as a lawyer, a fact which they easily persuaded themselves mitigated the baseness of their obedience to them, or justified it altogether.

The judges, as a rule, were no better, for before they could become judges they must have been advocates, with an advocate's fatal disabilities of judgment. Most of them depended for their office upon the favor of the people, which, also, was fatal to the independence, the dignity and the impartiality to which they laid so solemn claim. In their decisions they favored, so far as they dared, every interest, class or person powerful enough to help or hurt them in an election. Holding their high office by so precarious a tenure, they were under strong temptation to enrich themselves from the serviceable purses of wealthy litigants, and in disregard of justice to cultivate the favor of the attorneys practicing before them, and before whom they might soon be compelled themselves to practice.

In the higher courts of the land, where juries were unknown and appointed judges held their seats for life, these awful conditions did not obtain, and there Justice might have been content to dwell, and there she actually did sometimes set her foot. Unfortunately, the great judges had the consciences of their education. They had crept to place through the slime of the lower courts and their robes of office bore the damnatory evidence. Unfortunately, too, the attorneys, the jury habit strong upon them, brought into the superior tribunals the moral characteristics and professional methods acquired in the lower. Instead of assisting the judges to ascertain the truth and the law, they cheated in argument and took liberties with fact, deceiving the court whenever they deemed it to the interest of their cause to do so, and as willingly won by a technicality or a trick as by the justice of their contention and their ability in supporting it. Altogether, the entire judicial system of the Connected States of America was inefficient, disreputable, corrupt.

The result might easily have been foreseen and doubtless was predicted by patriots whose admonitions have not come down to us. Denied protection of the law, neither property nor life was safe. Greed filled his coffers from the meager hoards of Thrift, private vengeance took the place of legal redress, mad multitudes rioted and slew with virtual immunity from punishment or blame, and the land was red with crime.

A singular phenomenon of the time was the immunity of criminal women. Among the Americans woman held a place unique in the history of nations. If not actually worshiped as a deity, as some historians, among them the great Sagab-Joffoy, have affirmed, she was at least regarded with feelings of veneration which the modern mind has a difficulty in comprehending. Some degree of compassion for her mental inferiority, some degree of forbearance toward her infirmities of temper, some degree of immunity for the offenses which these peculiarities entail—these are common to all peoples above the grade of barbarians. In ancient America these chivalrous sentiments found open and lawful expression only in relieving woman of the burden of participation in political and military service; the laws gave her no express exemption from responsibility for crime. When she murdered, she was arrested; when arrested, brought to trial—though the origin and meaning of those observances are not now known. Gunkux, whose researches into the jurisprudence of antiquity enable him to speak with commanding authority of many things, gives us here nothing better than the conjecture that the trial of women for murder, in the nineteenth century and a part of the twentieth, was the survival of an earlier custom of actually convicting and punishing them, but it seems extremely improbable that a people that once put its female assassins to death would ever have relinquished the obvious advantages of the practice while retaining with purposeless tenacity some of its costly preliminary forms. Whatever may have been the reason, the custom was observed with all the gravity of a serious intention. Gunkux professes knowledge of one or two instances (he does not name his authorities) where matters went so far as conviction and sentence, and adds that the mischievous sentimentalists who had always lent themselves to the solemn jest by protestations of great vraisemblance against "the judicial killing of women," became really alarmed and filled the land with their lamentations. Among the phenomena of brazen effrontery he classes the fact that some of these loud protagonists of the right of women to assassinate unpunished were themselves women! Howbeit, the sentences, if ever pronounced, were never executed, and during the first quarter of the twentieth century the meaningless custom of bringing female assassins to trial was abandoned. What the effect was of their exemption from this considerable inconvenience we have not the data to conjecture, unless we understand as an allusion to it some otherwise obscure words of the famous Edward Bok, the only writer of the period whose work has survived. In his monumental essay on barbarous penology, entitled "Slapping the Wrist," he couples "woman's emancipation from the trammels of law" and "man's better prospect of death" in a way that some have construed as meaning that he regarded them as cause and effect. It must be said, however, that this interpretation finds no support in the general character of his writing, which is exceedingly humane, refined and womanly.

It has been said that the writings of this great man are the only surviving work of his period, but of that we are not altogether sure. There exists a fragment of an anonymous essay on woman's legal responsibility which many Americologists think belongs to the beginning of the twentieth century. Certainly it could not have been written later than the middle of it, for at that time woman had been definitely released from any responsibility to any law but that of her own will. The essay is an argument against even such imperfect exemption as she had in its author's time.

"It has been urged," the writer says, "that women, being less rational and more emotional than men, should not be held accountable in the same degree. To this it may be answered that punishment for crime is not intended to be retaliatory, but admonitory and deterrent. It is, therefore, peculiarly necessary to those not easily reached by other forms of warning and dissuasion. Control of the wayward is not to be sought in reduction of restraints, but in their multiplication. One who cannot be curbed by reason may be curbed by fear, a familiar truth which lies at the foundation of all penological systems. The argument for exemption of women is equally cogent for exemption of habitual criminals, for they too are abnormally inaccessible to reason, abnormally disposed to obedience to the suasion of their unregulated impulses and passions. To free them from the restraints of the fear of punishment would be a bold innovation which has as yet found no respectable proponent outside their own class.

"Very recently this dangerous enlargement of the meaning of the phrase 'emancipation of woman' has been fortified with a strange advocacy by the female 'champions of their sex.' Their argument runs this way: 'We are denied a voice in the making of the laws relating to infliction of the death penalty; it is unjust to hold us to an accountability to which we have not assented.' Of course this argument is as broad as the entire body of law; it amounts to nothing less than a demand for general immunity from all laws, for to none of them has woman's assent been asked or given. But let us consider this amazing claim with reference only to the proposal in the service and promotion of which it is now urged: exemption of women from the death penalty for murder. In the last analysis it is seen to be a simple demand for compensation. It says: 'You owe us a solatium. Since you deny us the right to vote, you should give us the right to assassinate. We do not appraise it at so high a valuation as the other franchise, but we do value it.'

"Apparently they do: without legal, but with virtual, immunity from punishment, the women of this country take an average of one thousand lives annually, nine in ten being the lives of men. Juries of men, incited and sustained by public opinion, have actually deprived every adult male American of the right to live. If the death of any man is desired by any woman for any reason he is without protection. She has only to kill him and say that he wronged or insulted her. Certain almost incredible recent instances prove that no woman is too base for immunity, no crime against life sufficiently rich in all the elements of depravity to compel a conviction of the assassin, or, if she is convicted and sentenced, her punishment by the public executioner."

In this interesting fragment, quoted by Bogul in his "History of an Extinct Civilization," we learn something of the shame and peril of American citizenship under institutions which, not having run their foreordained course to the unhappy end, were still in some degree supportable. What these institutions became afterward is a familiar story. It is true that the law of trial by jury was repealed. It had broken down, but not until it had sapped the whole nation's respect for all law, for all forms of authority, for order and private virtues. The people whose rude forefathers in another land it had served roughly to protect against their tyrants, it had lamentably failed to protect against themselves, and when in madness they swept it away, it was not as one renouncing an error, but as one impatient of the truth which the error is still believed to contain. They flung it away, not as an ineffectual restraint, but as a restraint; not because it was no longer an instrument of justice for the determination of truth, but because they feared that it might again become such. In brief, trial by jury was abolished only when it had provoked anarchy.

Before turning to another phase of this ancient civilization I cannot forbear to relate, after the learned and ingenious Gunkux, the only known instance of a public irony expressing itself in the sculptor's noble art. In the ancient city of Hohokus once stood a monument of colossal size and impressive dignity. It was erected by public subscription to the memory of a man whose only distinction consisted in a single term of service as a juror in a famous murder trial, the details of which have not come down to us. This occupied the court and held public attention for many weeks, being bitterly contested by both prosecution and defense. When at last it was given to the jury by the judge in the most celebrated charge that had ever been delivered from the bench, a ballot was taken at once. The jury stood eleven for acquittal to one for conviction. And so it stood at every ballot of the more than fifty that were taken during the fortnight that the jury was locked up for deliberation. Moreover, the dissenting juror would not argue the matter; he would listen with patient attention while his eleven indignant opponents thundered their opinions into his ears, even when they supported them with threats of personal violence; but not a word would he say. At last a disagreement was formally entered, the jury discharged and the obstinate juror chased from the city by the maddened populace. Despairing of success in another trial and privately admitting his belief in the prisoner's innocence, the public prosecutor moved for his release, which the judge ordered with remarks plainly implying his own belief that the wrong man had been tried.

Years afterward the accused person died confessing his guilt, and a little later one of the jurors who had been sworn to try the case admitted that he had attended the trial on the first day only, having been personated during the rest of the proceedings by a twin brother, the obstinate member, who was a deaf-mute.

The monument to this eminent public servant was overthrown and destroyed by an earthquake in the year 2342.

One of the causes of that popular discontent which brought about the stupendous events resulting in the disruption of the great republic, historians and archæologists are agreed in reckoning "insurance." Of the exact nature of that factor in the problem of the national life of that distant day we are imperfectly informed; many of its details have perished from the record, yet its outlines loom large through the mist of ages and can be traced with greater precision than is possible in many more important matters.

In the monumental work of Professor Golunk-Dorsto ("Some Account of the Insurance Delusion in Ancient America") we have its most considerable modern exposition; and Gakler's well-known volume, "The Follies of Antiquity," contains much interesting matter relating to it. From these and other sources the student of human unreason can reconstruct that astounding fallacy of insurance as, from three joints of its tail, the great naturalist Bogramus restored the ancient elephant, from hoof to horn.

The game of insurance, as practiced by the ancient Americans (and, as Gakler conjectures, by some of the tribesmen of Europe), was gambling, pure and simple, despite the sentimental character that its proponents sought to impress upon some forms of it for the greater prosperity of their dealings with its dupes. Essentially, it was a bet between the insurer and the insured. The number of ways in which the wager was made—all devised by the insurer—was almost infinite, but in none of them was there a departure from the intrinsic nature of the transaction as seen in its simplest, frankest form, which we shall here expound.

To those unlearned in the economical institutions of antiquity it is necessary to explain that in ancient America, long prior to the disastrous Japanese war, individual ownership of property was unrestricted; every person was permitted to get as much as he was able, and to hold it as his own without regard to his needs, or whether he made any good use of it or not. By some plan of distribution not now understood even the habitable surface of the earth, with the minerals beneath, was parceled out among the favored few, and there was really no place except at sea where children of the others could lawfully be born. Upon a part of the dry land that he had been able to acquire, or had leased from another for the purpose, a man would build a house worth, say, ten thousand drusoes. (The ancient unit of value was the "dollar," but nothing is now known as to its actual worth.) Long before the building was complete the owner was beset by "touts" and "cappers" of the insurance game, who poured into his ears the most ingenious expositions of the advantages of betting that it would burn down— for with incredible fatuity the people of that time continued, generation after generation, to build inflammable habitations. The persons whom the capper represented—they called themselves an "insurance company"—stood ready to accept the bet, a fact which seems to have generated no suspicion in the mind of the house-owner. Theoretically, of course, if the house did burn payment of the wager would partly or wholly recoup the winner of the bet for the loss of his house, but in fact the result of the transaction was commonly very different. For the privilege of betting that his property would be destroyed by fire the owner had to pay to the gentleman betting that it would not be, a certain percentage of its value every year, called a "premium." The amount of this was determined by the company, which employed statisticians and actuaries to fix it at such a sum that, according to the law of probabilities, long before the house was "due to burn," the company would have received more than the value of it in premiums. In other words, the owner of the house would himself supply the money to pay his bet, and a good deal more.

But how, it may be asked, could the company's actuary know that the man's house would last until he had paid in more than its insured value in premiums—more, that is to say, than the company would have to pay back? He could not, but from his statistics he could know how many houses in ten thousand of that kind burned in their first year, how many in their second, their third, and so on. That was all that he needed to know, the house-owners knowing nothing about it. He fixed his rates according to the facts, and the occasional loss of a bet in an individual instance did not affect the certainty of a general winning. Like other professional gamblers, the company expected to lose sometimes, yet knew that in the long run it must win; which meant that in any special case it would probably win. With a thousand gambling games open to him in which the chances were equal, the infatuated dupe chose to "sit into" one where they were against him! Deceived by the cappers' fairy tales, dazed by the complex and incomprehensible "calculations" put forth for his undoing, and having ever in the ear of his imagination the crackle and roar of the impoverishing flames, he grasped at the hope of beating—in an unwelcome way, it is true—"the man that kept the table." He must have known for a certainty that if the company could afford to insure him he could not afford to let it. He must have known that the whole body of the insured paid to the insurers more than the insurers paid to them; otherwise the business could not have been conducted. This they cheerfully admitted; indeed, they proudly affirmed it. In fact, insurance companies were the only professional gamblers that had the incredible hardihood to parade their enormous winnings as an inducement to play against their game. These winnings ("assets," they called them) proved their ability, they said, to pay when they lost; and that was indubitably true. What they did not prove, unfortunately, was the will to pay, which from the imperfect court records of the period that have come down to us, appears frequently to have been lacking. Gakler relates that in the instance of the city of San Francisco (somewhat doubtfully identified by Macronus as the modern fishing-village of Gharoo) the disinclination of the insurance companies to pay their bets had the most momentous consequences.

In the year 1906 San Francisco was totally destroyed by fire. The conflagration was caused by the friction of a pig scratching itself against an angle of a wooden building. More than one hundred thousand persons perished, and the loss of property is estimated by Kobo-Dogarque at one and a half million drusoes. On more than two-thirds of this enormous sum the insurance companies had laid bets, and the greater part of it they refused to pay. In justification they pointed out that the deed performed by the pig was "an act of God," who in the analogous instance of the express companies had been specifically forbidden to take any action affecting the interests of parties to a contract, or the result of an agreed undertaking.

In the ensuing litigation their attorneys cited two notable precedents. A few years before the San Francisco disaster, another American city had experienced a similar one through the upsetting of a lamp by the kick of a cow. In that case, also, the insurance companies had successfully denied their liability on the ground that the cow, manifestly incited by some supernatural power, had unlawfully influenced the result of a wager to which she was not a party. The companies defendant had contended that the recourse of the property-owners was against, not them, but the owner of the cow. In his decision sustaining that view and dismissing the case, a learned judge (afterward president of one of the defendant companies) had in the legal phraseology of the period pronounced the action of the cow an obvious and flagrant instance of unwarrantable intervention. Kobo-Dogarque believes that this decision was afterward reversed by an appellate court of contrary political complexion and the companies were compelled to compromise, but of this there is no record. It is certain that in the San Francisco case the precedent was urged.

Another precedent which the companies cited with particular emphasis related to an unfortunate occurrence at a famous millionaires' club in London, the capital of the renowned king, John Bui. A gentleman passing in the street fell in a fit and was carried into the club in convulsions. Two members promptly made a bet upon his life. A physician who chanced to be present set to work upon the patient, when one of the members who had laid the wager came forward and restrained him, saying: "Sir, I beg that you will attend to your own business. I have my money on that fit."

Doubtless these two notable precedents did not constitute the entire case of the defendants in the San Francisco insurance litigation, but the additional pleas are lost to us.

Of the many forms of gambling known as insurance that called life insurance appears to have been the most vicious. In essence it was the same as fire insurance, marine insurance, accident insurance and so forth, with an added offensiveness in that it was a betting on human lives—commonly by the policy-holder on lives that should have been held most sacred and altogether immune from the taint of traffic. In point of practical operation this ghastly business was characterized by a more fierce and flagrant dishonesty than any of its kindred pursuits. To such lengths of robbery did the managers go that at last the patience of the public was exhausted and a comparatively trivial occurrence fired the combustible elements of popular indignation to a white heat in which the entire insurance business of the country was burned out of existence, together with all the gamblers who had invented and conducted it. The president of one of the companies was walking one morning in a street of New York, when he had the bad luck to step on the tail of a dog and was bitten in retaliation. Frenzied by the pain of the wound, he gave the creature a savage kick and it ran howling toward a group of idlers in front of a grocery store. In ancient America the dog was a sacred animal, worshiped by all sorts and conditions of tribesmen. The idlers at once raised a great cry, and setting upon the offender beat him so that he died.

Their act was infectious: men, women and children trooped out of their dwellings by thousands to join them, brandishing whatever weapons they could snatch, and uttering wild cries of vengeance. This formidable mob overpowered the police, and marching from one insurance office to another, successively demolished them all, slew such officers as they could lay hands on, and chased the fugitive survivors into the sea, "where," says a quaint chronicle of the time, "they were eaten by their kindred, the sharks." This carnival of violence continued all the day, and at set of sun not one person connected with any form of insurance remained alive.

Ferocious and bloody as was the massacre, it was only the beginning. As the news of it went blazing and coruscating along the wires by which intelligence was then conveyed across the country, city after city caught the contagion. Everywhere, even in the small hamlets and the agricultural districts, the dupes rose against their dupers. The smoldering resentment of years burst into flame, and within a week all that was left of insurance in America was the record of a monstrous and cruel delusion written in the blood of its promoters.

A remarkable feature of the crude and primitive civilization of the Americans was their religion. This was polytheistic, as is that of all backward peoples, and among their minor deities were their own women. This has been disputed by respectable authorities, among them Gunkux and the younger Kekler, but the weight of archæological testimony is against them, for, as Sagab-Joffy ingeniously points out, none of less than divine rank would by even the lowest tribes be given unrestricted license to kill. Among the Americans woman, as already pointed out, indubitably had that freedom, and exercised it with terrible effect, a fact which makes the matter of their religion pertinent to the purpose of this monograph. If ever an American woman was punished by law for murder of a man no record of the fact is found; whereas, such American literature as we possess is full of the most enthusiastic adulation of the impossible virtues and imaginary graces of the human female. One writer even goes to the length of affirming that respect for the sex is the foundation of political stability, the cornerstone of civil and religious liberty! After the break-up of the republic and the savage intertribal wars that followed, Gyneolatry was an exhausted cult and woman was relegated to her old state of benign subjection.

Unfortunately, we know little of the means of travel in ancient America, other than the names. It seems to have been done mainly by what were called "railroads," upon which wealthy associations of men transported their fellow-citizens in some kind of vehicle at a low speed, seldom exceeding fifty or sixty miles an hour, as distance and time were then reckoned—about equal to seven kaltabs a grillog. Notwithstanding this slow movement of the vehicles, the number and fatality of accidents were incredible. In the Zopetroq Museum of Archæology is preserved an official report (found in the excavations made by Droyhors on the supposed site of Washington) of a Government Commission of the Connected States. From that document we learn that in the year 1907 of their era the railroads of the country killed 5,000 persons and wounded 72,286—a mortality which is said by the commissioners to be twice that of the battle of Gettysburg, concerning which we know nothing but the name. This was about the annual average of railroad casualties of the period, and if it provoked comment it at least led to no reform, for at a later period we find the mortality even greater. That it was preventable is shown by the fact that in the same year the railroads of Great Britain, where the speed was greater and the intervals between vehicles less, killed only one passenger. It was a difference of government: Great Britain had a government that governed; America had not. Happily for humanity, the kind of government that does not govern, self-government, "government of the people, by the people and for the people" (to use a meaningless paradox of that time) has perished from the face of the earth.

An inherent weakness in republican government was that it assumed the honesty and intelligence of the majority, "the masses," who were neither honest nor intelligent. It would doubtless have been an excellent government for a people so good and wise as to need none. In a country having such a system the leaders, the politicians, must necessarily all be demagogues, for they can attain to place and power by no other method than flattery of the people and subserviency to the will of the majority. In all the ancient American political literature we look in vain for a single utterance of truth and reason regarding these matters. In none of it is a hint that the multitude was ignorant and vicious, as we know it to have been, and as it must necessarily be in any country, to whatever high average of intelligence and morality the people attain; for "intelligence" and "morality" are comparative terms, the standard of comparison being the intelligence and morality of the wisest and best, who must always be the few. Whatever general advance is made, those not at the head are behind—are ignorant and immoral according to the new standard, and unfit to control in the higher and broader policies demanded by the progress made. Where there is true and general progress the philosopher of yesterday would be the ignoramus of to-day, the honorable of one generation the vicious of another. The peasant of our time is incomparably superior to the statesman of ancient America, yet he is unfit to govern, for there are others more fit.

That a body of men can be wiser than its wisest member seems to the modern understanding so obvious and puerile an error that it is inconceivable that any people, even the most primitive, could ever have entertained it; yet we know that in America it was a fixed and steadfast political faith. The people of that day did not, apparently, attempt to explain how the additional wisdom was acquired by merely assembling in council, as in their "legislatures"; they seem to have assumed that it was so, and to have based their entire governmental system upon that assumption, with never a suspicion of its fallacy. It is like assuming that a mountain range is higher than its highest peak. In the words of Golpek, "The early Americans believed that units of intelligence were addable quantities," or as Soseby more wittily puts it, "They thought that in a combination of idiocies they had the secret of sanity."

The Americans, as has been said, never learned that even among themselves majorities ruled, not because they ought, but because they could—not because they were wise, but because they were strong. The count of noses determined, not the better policy, but the more powerful party. The weaker submitted, as a rule, for it had to or risk a war in which it would be at a disadvantage. Yet in all the early years of the republic they seem honestly to have dignified their submission as "respect for the popular verdict." They even quoted from the Latin language the sentiment that "the voice of the people is the voice of God." And this hideous blasphemy was as glib upon the lips of those who, without change of mind, were defeated at the polls year after year as upon those of the victors.

Of course, their government was powerless to restrain any aggression or encroachment upon the general welfare as soon as a considerable body of voters had banded together to undertake it. A notable instance has been recorded by Bamscot in his great work, "Some Evil Civilizations." After the first of America's great intestinal wars the surviving victors formed themselves into an organization which seems at first to have been purely social and benevolent, but afterward fell into the hands of rapacious politicians who in order to preserve their power corrupted their followers by distributing among them enormous sums of money exacted from the government by threats of overturning it. In less than a half century after the war in which they had served, so great was the fear which they inspired in whatever party controlled the national treasury that the total sum of their exactions was no less annually than seventeen million prastams! As Dumbleshaw naïvely puts it, "having saved their country, these gallant gentlemen naturally took it for themselves." The eventual massacre of the remnant of this hardy and impenitent organization by the labor unions more accustomed to the use of arms is beyond the province of this monograph to relate. The matter is mentioned at all only because it is a typical example of the open robbery that marked that period of the republic's brief and inglorious existence; the Grand Army, as it called itself, was no worse and no better than scores of other organizations having no purpose but plunder and no method but menace. A little later nearly all classes and callings became organized conspiracies, each seeking an unfair advantage through laws which the party in power had not the firmness to withhold, nor the party hoping for power the courage to oppose. The climax of absurdity in this direction was reached in 1918, when an association of barbers, known as Noblemen of the Razor, procured from the parliament of the country a law giving it a representative in the President's Cabinet, and making it a misdemeanor to wear a beard.

In Soseby's "History of Popular Government" he mentions "a monstrous political practice known as 'Protection to American Industries.'" Modern research has not ascertained precisely what it was; it is known rather from its effects than in its true character, but from what we can learn of it to-day I am disposed to number it among those malefic agencies concerned in the destruction of the American republics, particularly the Connected States, although it appears not to have been peculiar to "popular government." Some of the contemporary monarchies of Europe were afflicted with it, but by the divine favor which ever guards a throne its disastrous effects were averted. "Protection" consisted in a number of extraordinary expedients, the purposes of which and their relations to one another cannot with certainty be determined in the present state of our knowledge. Debrethin and others agree that one feature of it was the support, by general taxation, of a few favored citizens in public palaces, where they passed their time in song and dance and all kinds of revelry. They were not, however, altogether idle, being required out of the sums bestowed upon them, to employ a certain number of men each in erecting great piles of stone and pulling them down again, digging holes in the ground and then filling them with earth, pouring water into casks and then drawing it off, and so forth. The unhappy laborers were subject to the most cruel oppressions, but the knowledge that their wages came from the pockets of those whom their work nowise benefited was so gratifying to them that nothing could induce them to leave the service of their heartless employers to engage in lighter and more useful labor.

Another characteristic of "Protection" was the maintenance at the principal seaports of "customs-houses," which were strong fortifications armed with heavy guns for the purpose of destroying or driving away the trading ships of foreign nations. It was this that caused the Connected States to be known abroad as the "Hermit Republic," a name of which its infatuated citizens were strangely proud, although they had themselves sent armed ships to open the ports of Japan and other Oriental countries to their own commerce.

In their own case, if a foreign ship came empty and succeeded in evading the fire of the "customs-house," as sometimes occurred, she was permitted to take away a cargo.

It is obvious that such a system was distinctly evil, but it must be confessed our uncertainty regarding the whole matter of "Protection" does not justify us in assigning it a definite place among the causes of national decay. That in some way it produced an enormous revenue is certain, and that the method was dishonest is no less so; for this revenue—known as a "surplus"—was so abhorred while it lay in the treasury that all were agreed upon the expediency of getting rid of it, two great political parties existing for apparently no other purpose than the patriotic one of taking it out.

But how, it may be asked, could people so misgoverned get on, even as well as they did?

From the records that have come down to us it does not appear that they got on very well. They were preyed upon by all sorts of political adventurers, whose power in most instances was limited only by the contemporaneous power of other political adventurers equally unscrupulous. A full half of the taxes wrung from them was stolen. Their public lands, millions of square miles, were parceled out among banded conspirators. Their roads and the streets of their cities were nearly impassable. Their public buildings, conceived in abominable taste and representing enormous sums of money, which never were used in their construction, began to tumble about the ears of the workmen before they were completed. The most delicate and important functions of government were intrusted to men with neither knowledge, heart nor experience, who by their corruption imperiled the public interest and by their blundering disgraced the national name. In short, all the train of evils inseparable from government of any kind beset this unhappy people with tenfold power, together with hundreds of worse ones peculiar to their own faulty and unnatural system. It was thought that their institutions would give them peace, yet in the first three-quarters of a century of their existence they fought three important wars: one of revenge, one of aggression and one—the bloodiest and most wasteful known up to that time—among themselves. And before a century and a half had passed they had the humiliation to see many of their seaport cities destroyed by the Emperor of Japan in a quarrel which they had themselves provoked by their greed of Oriental dominion.

By far the most important factor concerned in bringing about the dissolution of the republic and the incredible horrors that followed it was what was known as "the contest between capital and labor." This momentous struggle began in a rather singular way through an agitation set afoot by certain ambitious women who preached at first to inattentive and inhospitable ears, but with ever increasing acceptance, the doctrine of equality of the sexes, and demanded the "emancipation" of woman. True, woman was already an object of worship and had, as noted before, the right to kill. She was treated with profound and sincere deference, because of certain humble virtues, the product of her secluded life. Men of that time appear to have felt for women, in addition to religious reverence, a certain sentiment known as "love." The nature of this feeling is not clearly known to us, and has been for ages a matter of controversy evolving more heat than light. This much is plain: it was largely composed of good will, and had its root in woman's dependence. Perhaps it had something of the character of the benevolence with which we regard our slaves, our children and our domestic animals—everything, in fact, that is weak, helpless and inoffensive.

Woman was not satisfied; her superserviceable advocates taught her to demand the right to vote, to hold office, to own property, to enter into employment in competition with man. Whatever she demanded she eventually got. With the effect upon her we are not here concerned; the predicted gain to political purity did not ensue, nor did commercial integrity receive any stimulus from her participation in commercial pursuits. What indubitably did ensue was a more sharp and bitter competition in the industrial world through this increase of more than thirty per cent, in its wage-earning population. In no age nor country has there ever been sufficient employment for those requiring it. The effect of so enormously increasing the already disproportionate number of workers in a single generation could be no other than disastrous. Every woman employed displaced or excluded some man, who, compelled to seek a lower employment, displaced another, and so on, until the least capable or most unlucky of the series became a tramp—a nomadic mendicant criminal! The number of these dangerous vagrants in the beginning of the twentieth century of their era has been estimated by Holobom at no less than seven and a half blukuks! Of course, they were as tow to the fires of sedition, anarchy and insurrection. It does not very nearly relate to our present purpose, but it is impossible not to note in passing that this unhappy result, directly flowing from woman's invasion of the industrial field, was unaccompanied by any material advantage to herself. Individual women, here and there one, may themselves have earned the support that they would otherwise not have received, but the sex as a whole was not benefited. They provided for themselves no better than they had previously been provided for, and would still have been provided for, by the men whom they displaced. The whole somber incident is unrelieved by a single gleam of light.

Previously to this invasion of the industrial field by woman there had arisen conditions that were in themselves peculiarly menacing to the social fabric. Some of the philosophers of the period, rummaging amongst the dubious and misunderstood facts of commercial and industrial history, had discovered what they were pleased to term "the law of supply and demand"; and this they expounded with so ingenious a sophistry, and so copious a wealth of illustration and example that what is at best but a faulty and imperfectly applicable principle, limited and cut into by all manner of other considerations, came to be accepted as the sole explanation and basis of material prosperity and an infallible rule for the proper conduct of industrial affairs. In obedience to this "law"—for, interpreting it in its straitest sense they understood it to be mandatory—employers and employees alike regulated by its iron authority all their dealings with one another, throwing off the immemorial relations of mutual dependence and mutual esteem as tending to interfere with beneficent operation. The employer came to believe conscientiously that it was not only profitable and expedient, but under all circumstances his duty, to obtain his labor for as little money as possible, even as he sold its product for as much. Considerations of humanity were not banished from his heart, but most sternly excluded from his business. Many of these misguided men would give large sums to various charities; would found universities, hospitals, libraries; would even stop on their way to relieve beggars in the street; but for their own work-people they had no care. Straman relates in his "Memoirs" that a wealthy manufacturer once said to one of his mill-hands who had asked for an increase of his wages because unable to support his family on the pay that he was getting: "Your family is nothing to me. I cannot afford to mix benevolence with my business." Yet this man, the author adds, had just given a thousand drusoes to a "sea-man's home." He could afford to care for other men's employees, but not for his own. He could not see that the act which he performed as truly, and to the same degree, cut down his margin of profit in his business as the act which he refused to perform would have done, and had not the advantage of securing him better service from a grateful workman.

On their part the laborers were no better. Their relations to their employers being "purely commercial," as it was called, they put no heart into their work, seeking ever to do as little as possible for their money, precisely as their employers sought to pay as little as possible for the work they got. The interests of the two classes being thus antagonized, they grew to distrust and hate each other, and each accession of ill feeling produced acts which tended to broaden the breach more and more. There was neither cheerful service on the one side nor ungrudging payment on the other.

The harder industrial conditions generated by woman's irruption into a new domain of activity produced among laboring men a feeling of blind discontent and concern. Like all men in apprehension, they drew together for mutual protection, they knew not clearly against what. They formed "labor unions," and believed them to be something new and effective in the betterment of their condition; whereas, from the earliest historical times, in Rome, in Greece, in Egypt, in Assyria, labor unions with their accepted methods of "striking" and rioting had been discredited by an almost unbroken record of failure. One of the oldest manuscripts then in existence, preserved in a museum at Turin, but now lost, related how the workmen employed in the necropolis at Thebes, dissatisfied with their allowance of corn and oil, had refused to work, broken out of their quarters and, after much rioting, been subdued by the arrows of the military. And such, despite the sympathies and assistance of brutal mobs of the populace, was sometimes the end of the American "strike." Originally organized for self-protection, and for a time partly successful, these leagues became great tyrannies, so reasonless in their demands and so unscrupulous in their methods of enforcing them that the laws were unable to deal with them, and frequently the military forces of the several States were ordered out for the protection of life and property; but in most cases the soldiers fraternized with the leagues, ran away, or were easily defeated. The cruel and mindless mobs had always the hypocritical sympathy and encouragement of the newspapers and the politicians, for both feared their power and courted their favor. The judges, dependent for their offices not only on "the labor vote," but, to obtain it, on the approval of the press and the politicians, boldly set aside the laws against conspiracy and strained to the utmost tension those relating to riot, arson and murder. To such a pass did all this come that in the year 1931 an inn-keeper's denial of a half-holiday to an under-cook resulted in the peremptory closing of half the factories in the country, the stoppage of all railroad travel and movement of freight by land and water and a general paralysis of the industries of the land. Many thousands of families, including those of the "strikers" and their friends, suffered from famine; armed conflicts occurred in every State; hundreds were slain and incalculable amounts of property wrecked and destroyed.

Failure, however, was inherent in the method, for success depended upon unanimity, and the greater the membership of the unions and the more serious their menace to the industries of the country, the higher was the premium for defection; and at last strike-breaking became a regular employment, organized, officered and equipped for the service required by the wealth and intelligence that directed it. From that moment the doom of labor unionism was decreed and inevitable. But labor unionism did not live long enough to die that way.

Naturally combinations of labor entailed combinations of capital. These were at first purely protective. They were brought into being by the necessity of resisting the aggressions of the others. But the trick of combination once learned, it was seen to have possibilities of profit in directions not dreamed of by its early promoters; its activities were not long confined to fighting the labor unions with their own weapons and with superior cunning and address. The shrewd and energetic men whose capacity and commercial experience had made them rich while the laborers remained poor were not slow to discern the advantages of coöperation over their own former method of competition among themselves. They continued to fight the labor unions, but ceased to fight one another. The result was that in the brief period of two generations almost the entire business of the country fell into the hands of a few gigantic corporations controlled by bold and unscrupulous men, who, by daring and ingenious methods, made the body of the people pay tribute to their greed.

In a country where money was all-powerful the power of money was used without stint and without scruple. Judges were bribed to do their duty, juries to convict, newspapers to support and legislators to betray their constituents and pass the most oppressive laws. By these corrupt means, and with the natural advantage of greater skill in affairs and larger experience in concerted action, the capitalists soon restored their ancient reign and the state of the laborer was worse than it had ever been before. Straman says that in his time two millions of unoffending workmen in the various industries were once discharged without warning and promptly arrested as vagrants and deprived of their ears because a sulking canal-boatman had kicked his captain's dog into the water. And the dog was a retriever.

Had the people been honest and intelligent, as the politicians affirmed them to be, the combination of capital could have worked no public injury—would, in truth, have been a great public benefit. It enormously reduced the expense of production and distribution, assured greater permanency of employment, opened better opportunities to general and special aptitude, gave an improved product, and at first supplied it at a reduced price. Its crowning merit was that the industries of the country, being controlled by a few men from a central source, could themselves be easily controlled by law if law had been honestly administered. Under the old order of scattered jurisdictions, requiring a multitude of actions at law, little could be done, and little was done, to put a check on commercial greed; under the new, much was possible, and at times something was accomplished. But not for long; the essential dishonesty of the American character enabled these capable and conscienceless managers—"captains of industry" and "kings of finance"—to buy with money advantages and immunities superior to those that the labor unions could obtain by menaces and the promise of votes. The legislatures, the courts, the executive officers, all the sources of authority and springs of control, were defiled and impested until right and justice fled affrighted from the land, and the name of the country became a stench in the nostrils of the world.

Let us pause in our narrative to say here that much of the abuse of the so-called "trusts" by their victims took no account of the folly, stupidity and greed of the victims themselves. A favorite method by which the great corporations crushed out the competition of the smaller ones and of the "individual dealers" was by underselling them—a method made possible by nothing but the selfishness of the purchasing consumers who loudly complained of it. These could have stood by their neighbor, the "small dealer," if they had wanted to, and no underselling could, have been done. When the trust lowered the price of its product they eagerly took the advantage offered, then cursed the trust for ruining the small dealer. When it raised the price they cursed it for ruining themselves. It is not easy to see what the trust could have done that would have been acceptable, nor is it surprising that it soon learned to ignore their clamor altogether and impenitently plunder those whom it could not hope to appease.

Another of the many sins justly charged against the "kings of finance" was this: They would buy properties worth, say, ten millions of "dollars" (the value of the dollar is now unknown) and issue stock upon it to the face value of, say, fifty millions. This their clamorous critics called "creating" for themselves forty millions of dollars. They created nothing; the stock had no dishonest value unless sold, and even at the most corrupt period of the government nobody was compelled by law to buy. In nine cases in ten the person who bought did so in the hope and expectation of getting much for little and something for nothing. The buyer was no better than the seller. He was a gambler. He "played against the game of the man who kept the table" (as the phrase went), and naturally he lost.

Naturally, too, he cried out, but his lamentations, though echoed shrilly by the demagogues, seem to have been unavailing. Even the rudimentary intelligence of that primitive people discerned the impracticability of laws forbidding the seller to set his own price on the thing he would sell and declare it worth that price. Then, as now, nobody had to believe him. Of the few who bought these "watered" stocks in good faith as an investment in the honest hope of dividends it seems sufficient to say, in the words of an ancient Roman, "Against stupidity the gods themselves are powerless." Laws that would adequately protect the foolish from the consequence of their folly would put an end to all commerce. The sin of "over-capitalization" differed in magnitude only, not in kind, from the daily practice of every salesman in every shop. Nevertheless, the popular fury that it aroused must be reckoned among the main causes contributory to the savage insurrections that accomplished the downfall of the republic.

With the formation of powerful and unscrupulous trusts of both labor and capital to subdue each other the possibilities of combination were not exhausted; there remained the daring plan of combining the two belligerents! And this was actually effected. The laborer's demand for an increased wage was always based upon an increased cost of living, which was itself chiefly due to increased cost of production from reluctant concessions of his former demands. But in the first years of the twentieth century observers noticed on the part of capital a lessening reluctance. More frequent and more extortionate and reasonless demands encountered a less bitter and stubborn resistance; capital was apparently weakening just at the time when, with its strong organizations of trained and willing strike-breakers, it was most secure. Not so; an ingenious malefactor, whose name has perished from history, had thought out a plan for bringing the belligerent forces together to plunder the rest of the population. In the accounts that have come down to us details are wanting, but we know that, little by little, this amazing project was accomplished. Wages rose to incredible rates. The cost of living rose with them, for employers—their new allies wielding in their service the weapons previously used against them, intimidation, the boycott, and so forth—more than recouped themselves from the general public. Their employees got rebates on the prices of products, but for consumers who were neither laborers nor capitalists there was no mercy. Strikes were a thing of the past; strike-breakers threw themselves gratefully into the arms of the unions; "industrial discontent" vanished, in the words of a contemporary poet, "as by the stroke of an enchanter's wand." All was peace, tranquillity and order! Then the storm broke.

A man in St. Louis purchased a sheep's kidney for seven-and-a-half dollars. In his rage at the price he exclaimed: "As a public man I have given twenty of the best years of my life to bringing about a friendly understanding between capital and labor. I have succeeded, and may God have mercy on my meddlesome soul!"

The remark was resented, a riot ensued, and when the sun went down that evening his last beams fell upon a city reeking with the blood of a hundred millionaires and twenty thousand citizens and sons of toil!

Students of the history of those troublous times need not to be told what other and more awful events followed that bloody reprisal. Within forty-eight hours the country was ablaze with insurrection, followed by intestinal wars which lasted three hundred and seventy years and were marked by such hideous barbarities as the modern historian can hardly bring himself to relate. The entire stupendous edifice of popular government, temple and citadel of fallacies and abuses, had crashed to ruin. For centuries its fallen columns and scattered stones sheltered an ever diminishing number of skulking anarchists, succeeded by hordes of skin-clad savages subsisting on offal and raw flesh—the race-remnant of an extinct civilization. All finally vanished from history into a darkness impenetrable to conjecture.

In concluding this hasty and imperfect sketch I cannot forbear to relate an episode of the destructive and unnatural contest between labor and capital, which I find recorded in the almost forgotten work of Antrolius, who was an eye-witness to the incident.

At a time when the passions of both parties were most inflamed and scenes of violence most frequent it was somehow noised about that at a certain hour of a certain day some one—none could say who—would stand upon the steps of the Capitol and speak to the people, expounding a plan for reconciliation of all conflicting interests and pacification of the quarrel. At the appointed hour thousands had assembled to hear—glowering capitalists attended by hireling body-guards with firearms, sullen laborers with dynamite bombs concealed in their clothing. All eyes were directed to the specified spot, where suddenly appeared (none saw whence—it seemed as if he had been there all the time, such his tranquillity) a tall, pale man clad in a long robe, bare-headed, his hair falling lightly upon his shoulders, his eyes full of compassion, and with such majesty of face and mien that all were awed to silence ere he spoke. Stepping slowly forward toward the throng and raising his right hand from the elbow, the index finger extended upward, he said, in a voice ineffably sweet and serious: "Whatsoever ye would that men should do unto you, even so do ye also unto them."

These strange words he repeated in the same solemn tones three times; then, as the expectant multitude waited breathless for his discourse, stepped quietly down into the midst of them, every one afterward declaring that he passed within a pace of where himself had stood. For a moment the crowd was speechless with surprise and disappointment, then broke into wild, fierce cries: "Lynch him, lynch him!" and some have testified that they heard the word "crucify." Struggling into looser order, the infuriated mob started in mad pursuit; but each man ran a different way and the stranger was seen again by none of them.

THE LAND BEYOND THE BLOW

(After the method of Swift, who followed Lucian, and was himself followed by Voltaire and many others.)

THITHER

A crowd of men were assisting at a dog-fight. The scene was one of indescribable confusion. In the center of the tumult the dogs, obscure in a cloud of dust, rolled over and over, howling, yarring, tearing each other with sickening ferocity. About them the hardly less ferocious men shouted, cursed and struck, encouraged the animals with sibilant utterances and threatened with awful forms of death and perdition all who tried to put an end to the combat. Caught in the thick of this pitiless mob I endeavored to make my way to a place of peace, when a burly blackguard, needlessly obstructing me, said derisively:

"I guess you are working pockets."

"You are a liar!" I retorted hotly.

That is all the provocation that I remember to have given.

SONS OF THE FAIR STAR

When consciousness returned the sun was high in the heavens, yet the light was dim, and had that indefinable ghastly quality that is observed during a partial eclipse. The sun itself appeared singularly small, as if it were at an immensely greater distance than usual. Rising with some difficulty to my feet, I looked about me. I was in an open space among some trees growing on the slope of a mountain range whose summit on the one hand was obscured by a mist of a strange pinkish hue, and on the other rose into peaks glittering with snow. Skirting the base at a distance of two or three miles flowed a wide river, and beyond it a nearly level plain stretched away to the horizon, dotted with villages and farmhouses and apparently in a high state of cultivation. All was unfamiliar in its every aspect. The trees were unlike any that I had ever seen or even imagined, the trunks being mostly square and the foliage consisting of slender filaments resembling hair, in many instances long enough to reach the earth. It was of many colors, and I could not perceive that there was any prevailing one, as green is in the vegetation to which I was accustomed. As far as I could see there were no grass, no weeds, no flowers; the earth was covered with a kind of lichen, uniformly blue. Instead of rocks, great masses of metals protruded here and there, and above me on the mountain were high cliffs of what seemed to be bronze veined with brass. No animals were visible, but a few birds as uncommon in appearance as their surroundings glided through the air or perched upon the rocks. I say glided, for their motion was not true flight, their wings being mere membranes extended parallel to their sides, and having no movement independent of the body. The bird was, so to say, suspended between them and moved forward by quick strokes of a pair of enormously large webbed feet, precisely as a duck propels itself in water. All these things excited in me no surprise, nor even curiosity; they were merely unfamiliar. That which most interested me was what appeared to be a bridge several miles away, up the river, and to this I directed my steps, crossing over from the barren and desolate hills to the populous plain.

For a full history of my life and adventures in Mogon-Zwair, and a detailed description of the country, its people, their manners and customs, I must ask the reader to await the publication of a book, now in the press, entitled A Blackened Eye; in this brief account I can give only a few of such particulars as seem instructive by contrast with our own civilization.

The inhabitants of Mogon-Zwair call themselves Golampis, a word signifying Sons of the Fair Star. Physically they closely resemble ourselves, being in all respects the equals of the highest Caucasian type. Their hair, however, has a broader scheme of color, hair of every hue known to us, and even of some imperceptible to my eyes but brilliant to theirs, being too common to excite remark. A Golampian assemblage with uncovered heads resembles, indeed, a garden of flowers, vivid and deep in color, no two alike. They wear no clothing of any kind, excepting for adornment and protection from the weather, resembling in this the ancient Greeks and the Japanese of yesterday; nor was I ever able to make them comprehend that clothing could be worn for those reasons for which it is chiefly worn among ourselves. They are destitute of those feelings of delicacy and refinement which distinguish us from the lower animals, and which, in the opinion of our acutest and most pious thinkers, are evidences of our close relation to the Power that made us.

Among this people certain ideas which are current among ourselves as mere barren faiths expressed in disregarded platitudes receive a practical application to the affairs of life. For example, they hold, with the best, wisest and most experienced of our own race, and one other hereafter to be described, that wealth does not bring happiness and is a misfortune and an evil. None but the most ignorant and depraved, therefore, take the trouble to acquire or preserve it. A rich Golampi is naturally regarded with contempt and suspicion, is shunned by the good and respectable and subjected to police surveillance. Accustomed to a world where the rich man is profoundly and justly respected for his goodness and wisdom (manifested in part by his own deprecatory protests against the wealth of which, nevertheless, he is apparently unable to rid himself) I was at first greatly pained to observe the contumelious manner of the Golampis toward this class of men, carried in some instances to the length of personal violence; a popular amusement being the pelting them with coins. These the victims would carefully gather from the ground and carry away with them, thus increasing their hoard and making themselves all the more liable to popular indignities.

When the cultivated and intelligent Golampi finds himself growing too wealthy he proceeds to get rid of his surplus riches by some one of many easy expedients. One of these I have just described; another is to give his excess to those of his own class who have not sufficient to buy employment and so escape leisure, which is considered the greatest evil of all. "Idleness," says one of their famous authors, "is the child of poverty and the parent of discontent"; and another great writer says: "No one is without employment; the indolent man works for his enemies."

In conformity to these ideas the Golampis—all but the ignorant and vicious rich—look upon labor as the highest good, and the man who is so unfortunate as not to have enough money to purchase employment in some useful industry will rather engage in a useless one than not labor at all. It is not unusual to see hundreds of men carrying water from a river and pouring it into a natural ravine or artificial channel, through which it runs back into the stream. Frequently a man is seen conveying stones—or the masses of metal which there correspond to stones—from one pile to another. When all have been heaped in a single place he will convey them back again, or to a new place, and so proceed until darkness puts an end to the work. This kind of labor, however, does not confer the satisfaction derived from the consciousness of being useful, and is never performed by any person having the means to hire another to employ him in some beneficial industry. The wages usually paid to employers are from three to six balukan a day. This statement may seem incredible, but I solemnly assure the reader that I have known a bad workman or a feeble woman to pay as high as eight; and there have been instances of men whose incomes had outgrown their desires paying even more.

Labor being a luxury which only those in easy circumstances can afford, the poor are the more eager for it, not only because it is denied them, but because it is a sign of respectability. Many of them, therefore, indulge in it on credit and soon find themselves deprived of what little property they had to satisfy their hardfisted employers. A poor woman once complained to me that her husband spent every rylat that he could get in the purchase of the most expensive kinds of employment, while she and the children were compelled to content themselves with such cheap and coarse activity as dragging an old wagon round and round in a small field which a kind-hearted neighbor permitted them to use for the purpose. I afterward saw this improvident husband and unnatural father. He had just squandered all the money he had been able to beg or borrow in buying six tickets, which entitled the holder to that many days' employment in pitching hay into a barn. A week later I met him again. He was broken in health, his limbs trembled, his walk was an uncertain shuffle. Clearly he was suffering from overwork. As I paused by the wayside to speak to him a wagon loaded with hay was passing. He fixed his eyes upon it with a hungry, wolfish glare, clutched a pitchfork and leaned eagerly forward, watching the vanishing wagon with breathless attention and heedless of my salutation. That night he was arrested, streaming with perspiration, in the unlawful act of unloading that hay and putting it into its owner's barn. He was tried, convicted and sentenced to six months' detention in the House of Indolence.

The whole country is infested by a class of criminal vagrants known as strambaltis, or, as we should say, "tramps." These persons prowl about among the farms and villages begging for work in the name of charity. Sometimes they travel in groups, as many as a dozen together, and then the farmer dares not refuse them; and before he can notify the constabulary they will have performed a great deal of the most useful labor that they can find to do and escaped without paying a rylat. One trustworthy agriculturist assured me that his losses in one year from these depredations amounted to no less a sum than seven hundred balukan! On nearly all the larger and more isolated farms a strong force of guards is maintained during the greater part of the year to prevent these outrages, but they are frequently overpowered, and sometimes prove unfaithful to their trust by themselves working secretly by night.

The Golampi priesthood has always denounced overwork as a deadly sin, and declared useless and apparently harmless work, such as carrying water from the river and letting it flow in again, a distinct violation of the divine law, in which, however, I could never find any reference to the matter; but there has recently risen a sect which holds that all labor being pleasurable, each kind in its degree is immoral and wicked. This sect, which embraces many of the most holy and learned men, is rapidly spreading and becoming a power in the state. It has, of course, no churches, for these cannot be built without labor, and its members commonly dwell in caves and live upon such roots and berries as can be easily gathered, of which the country produces a great abundance though all are exceedingly unpalatable. These Gropoppsu (as the members of this sect call themselves) pass most of their waking hours sitting in the sunshine with folded hands, contemplating their navels; by the practice of which austerity they hope to obtain as reward an eternity of hard labor after death.

The Golampis are an essentially pious and religious race. There are few, indeed, who do not profess at least one religion. They are nearly all, in a certain sense, polytheists: they worship a supreme and beneficent deity by one name or another, but all believe in the existence of a subordinate and malevolent one, whom also, while solemnly execrating him in public rites, they hold at heart in such reverence that needlessly to mention his name or that of his dwelling is considered sin of a rank hardly inferior to blasphemy. I am persuaded that this singular tenderness toward a being whom their theology represents as an abominable monster, the origin of all evil and the foe to souls, is a survival of an ancient propitiatory adoration. Doubtless this wicked deity was once so feared that his conciliation was one of the serious concerns of life. He is probably as greatly feared now as at any former time, but is apparently less hated, and is by some honestly admired.

It is interesting to observe the important place held in Golampian affairs by religious persecution. The Government is a pure theocracy, all the Ministers of State and the principal functionaries in every department of control belonging to the priesthood of the dominant church. It is popularly believed in Mogon-Zwair that persecution, even to the extent of taking life, is in the long run beneficial to the cause enduring it. This belief has, indeed, been crystallized into a popular proverb, not capable of accurate translation into our tongue, but to the effect that martyrs fertilize religion by pouring out their blood about its roots. Acting upon this belief with their characteristically logical and conscientious directness, the sacerdotal rulers of the country mercilessly afflict the sect to which themselves belong. They arrest its leading members on false charges, throw them into loathsome and unwholesome dungeons, subject them to the crudest tortures and sometimes put them to death. The provinces in which the state religion is especially strong are occasionally raided and pillaged by government soldiery, recruited for the purpose by conscription among the dissenting sects, and are sometimes actually devastated with fire and sword. The result is not altogether confirmatory of the popular belief and does not fulfil the pious hope of the governing powers who are cruel to be kind. The vitalizing efficacy of persecution is not to be doubted, but the persecuted of too feeble faith frequently thwart its beneficent intent and happy operation by apostasy.

Having in mind the horrible torments which a Golampian general had inflicted upon the population of a certain town I once ventured to protest to him that so dreadful a sum of suffering, seeing that it did not accomplish its purpose, was needless and unwise.

"Needless and unwise it may be," said he, "and I am disposed to admit that the result which I expected from it has not followed; but why do you speak of the sum of suffering? I tortured those people in but a single, simple way—by skinning their legs."

"Ah, that is very true," said I, "but you skinned the legs of one thousand."

"And what of that?" he asked. "Can one thousand, or ten thousand, or any number of persons suffer more agony than one? A man may have his leg broken, then his nails pulled out, then be seared with a hot iron. Here is suffering added to suffering, and the effect is really cumulative. In the true mathematical sense it is a sum of suffering. A single person can experience it. But consider, my dear sir. How can you add one man's agony to another's? They are not addable quantities. Each is an individual pain, unaffected by the other. The limit of anguish which ingenuity can inflict is that utmost pang which one man has the vitality to endure."

I was convinced but not silenced.

The Golampians all believe, singularly enough, that truth possesses some inherent vitality and power that give it an assured prevalence over falsehood; that a good name cannot be permanently defiled and irreparably ruined by detraction, but, like a star, shines all the brighter for the shadow through which it is seen; that justice cannot be stayed by injustice; that vice is powerless against virtue. I could quote from their great writers hundreds of utterances affirmative of these propositions. One of their poets, for example, has some striking and original lines, of which the following is a literal but unmetrical translation:

> A man who is in the right has three arms,
> But he whose conscience is rotten with wrong
> Is stripped and confined in a metal cell.

Imbued with these beliefs, the Golampis think it hardly worth while to be truthful, to abstain from slander, to do justice and to avoid vicious actions. "The practice," they say, "of deceit, calumniation, oppression and immorality cannot have any sensible and lasting injurious effect, and it is most agreeable to the mind and heart. Why should there be personal self-denial without commensurate general advantage?"

In consequence of these false views, affirmed by those whom they regard as great and wise, the people of Mogon-Zwair are, as far as I have observed them, the most conscienceless liars, cheats, thieves, rakes and all-round, many-sided sinners that ever were created to be damned. It was, therefore, with inexpressible joy that I received one day legal notification that I had been tried in the High Court of Conviction and sentenced to banishment to Lalugnan. My offense was that I had said that I regarded consistency as the most detestable of all vices.

AN INTERVIEW WITH GNARMAG-ZOTE

Mogon-Zwair and Lalugnan, having the misfortune to lie on opposite sides of a line, naturally hate each other; so each country sends its dangerous political criminals into the other, where they usually enjoy high honors and are sometimes elevated to important office under the crown. I was therefore received in Lalugnan with hospitality and given every encouragement in prosecuting my researches into the history and intellectual life of the people. They are so extraordinary a people, inhabiting so marvelous a country, that everything which the traveler sees, hears or experiences makes a lively and lasting impression upon his mind, and the labor of a lifetime would be required to relate the observation of a single year. I shall notice here only one or two points of national character—

those which differ most conspicuously from ours, and in which, consequently, they are least worthy.

With a fatuity hardly more credible than creditable, the Lalugwumps, as they call themselves, deny the immortality of the soul. In all my stay in their country I found only one person who believed in a life "beyond the grave," as we should say, though as the Lalugwumps are cannibals they would say "beyond the stomach." In testimony to the consolatory value of the doctrine of another life, I may say that this one true believer had in this life a comparatively unsatisfactory lot, for in early youth he had been struck by a flying stone from a volcano and had lost a considerable part of his brain.

I cannot better set forth the nature and extent of the Lalugwumpian error regarding this matter than by relating a conversation that occurred between me and one of the high officers of the King's household—a man whose proficiency in all the vices of antiquity, together with his service to the realm in determining the normal radius of curvature in cats' claws, had elevated him to the highest plane of political preferment. His name was Gnarmag-Zote.

"You tell me," said he, "that the soul is immaterial. Now, matter is that of which we can have knowledge through one or more of our senses. Of what is immaterial—not matter—we can gain no knowledge in that way. How, then, can we know anything about it?"

Perceiving that he did not rightly apprehend my position I abandoned it and shifted the argument to another ground. "Consider," I said, "the analogous case of a thought. You will hardly call thought material, yet we know there are thoughts."

"I beg your pardon, but we do not know that. Thought is not a thing, therefore cannot be in any such sense, for example, as the hand is. We use the word 'thought' to designate the result of an action of the brain, precisely as we use the word 'speed' to designate the result of an action of a horse's legs. But can it be said that speed exists in the same way as the legs which produce it exist, or in any way? Is it a thing?"

I was about to disdain to reply, when I saw an old man approaching, with bowed head, apparently in deep distress. As he drew near he saluted my distinguished interlocutor in the manner of the country, by putting out his tongue to its full extent and moving it slowly from side to side. Gnarmag-Zote acknowledged the civility by courteously spitting, and the old man, advancing, seated himself at the great officer's feet, saying: "Exalted Sir, I have just lost my wife by death, and am in a most melancholy frame of mind. He who has mastered all the vices of the ancients and wrested from nature the secret of the normal curvature of cats' claws can surely spare from his wisdom a few rays of philosophy to cheer an old man's gloom. Pray tell me what I shall do to assuage my grief."

The reader can, perhaps, faintly conceive my astonishment when Gnarmag-Zote gravely replied: "Kill yourself."

"Surely," I cried, "you would not have this honest fellow procure oblivion (since you think that death is nothing else) by so rash an act!"

"An act that Gnarmag-Zote advises," he said, coldly, "is not rash."

"But death," I said, "death, whatever else it may be, is an end of life. This old man is now in sorrow almost insupportable. But a few days and it will be supportable; a few months and it will have become no more than a tender melancholy. At last it will disappear, and in the society of his friends, in the skill of his cook, the profits of avarice, the study of how to be querulous and in the pursuit of loquacity, he will again experience the joys of age. Why for a present grief should he deprive himself of all future happiness?"

Gnarmag-Zote looked upon me with something like compassion. "My friend," said he, "guest of my sovereign and my country, know that in any circumstances, even those upon which true happiness is based and conditioned, death is preferable to life. The sum of miseries in any life (here in Lalugnan at least) exceeds the sum of pleasures; but suppose that it did not. Imagine an existence in which happiness, of whatever intensity, is the rule, and discomfort, of whatever moderation, the exception. Still there is some discomfort. There is none in death, for (as it is given to us to know) that is oblivion, annihilation. True, by dying one loses his happiness as well as his sorrows, but he is not conscious of the loss. Surely, a loss of which one will never know, and which, if it operate to make him less happy, at the same time takes from him the desire and capacity and need of happiness, cannot be an evil. That is so intelligently understood among us here in Lalugnan that suicide is common, and our word for sufferer is the same as that for fool. If this good man had not been an idiot he would have taken his life as soon as he was bereaved."

"If what you say of the blessing of death is true," I said, smilingly, for I greatly prided myself on the ingenuity of my thought, "it is unnecessary to commit suicide through grief for the dead; for the more you love the more glad you should be that the object of your affection has passed into so desirable a state as death."

"So we are—those of us who have cultivated philosophy, history and logic; but this poor fellow is still under the domination of feelings inherited from a million ignorant and superstitious ancestors—for Lalugnan was once as barbarous a country as your own. The most grotesque and frightful conceptions of death, and life after death, were current; and now many of even those whose understandings are emancipated wear upon their feelings the heavy chain of heredity."

"But," said I, "granting for the sake of the argument which I am about to build upon the concession" (I could not bring myself to use the idiotic and meaningless phrase, "for the sake of argument") "that death, especially the death of a Lalugwump, is desirable, yet the act of dying, the transition state between living and being dead, may be accompanied by the most painful physical, and most terrifying mental phenomena. The moment of dissolution may seem to the exalted sensibilities of the moribund a century of horrors."

The great man smiled again, with a more intolerable benignity than before. "There is no such thing as dying," he said; "the 'transition state' is a creation of your fancy and an evidence of imperfect reason. One is at any time either alive or dead. The one condition cannot shade off into the other. There is no gradation like that between waking and sleeping. By the way, do you recognize a certain resemblance between death and a dreamless sleep?"

"Yes—death as you conceive it to be."

"Well, does any one fear sleep? Do we not seek it, court it, wish that it may be sound—that is to say, dreamless? We desire occasional annihilation—wish to be dead for eight and ten hours at a time. True, we expect to awake, but that expectation, while it may account for our alacrity in embracing sleep, cannot alter the character of the state that we cheerfully go into. Suppose we did not wake in the morning, never did wake! Would our mental and spiritual condition be in any respect different through all eternity from what it was during the first few hours? After how many hours does oblivion begin to be an evil? The man who loves to sleep yet hates to die might justly be granted everlasting life with everlasting insomnia."

Gnarmag-Zote paused and appeared to be lost in the profundity of his thoughts, but I could easily enough see that he was only taking breath. The old man whose grief had given this turn to the conversation had fallen asleep and was roaring in the nose like a beast. The rush of a river near by, as it poured up a hill from the ocean, and the shrill singing of several kinds of brilliant quadrupeds were the only other sounds audible. I waited deferentially for the great antiquarian, scientist and courtier to resume, amusing myself meantime by turning over the leaves of an official report by the Minister of War on a new and improved process of making thunder from snail slime. Presently the oracle spoke.

"You have been born," he said, which was true. "There was, it follows, a time when you had not been born. As we reckon time, it was probably some millions of ages. Of this considerable period you are unable to remember one unhappy moment, and in point of fact there was none. To a Lalugwump that is entirely conclusive as to the relative values of consciousness and oblivion, existence and nonexistence, life and death. This old man lying here at my feet is now, if not dreaming, as if he had never been born. Would not it be cruel and inhuman to wake him back to grief? Is it, then, kind to permit him to wake by the natural action of his own physical energies? I have given him the advice for which he asked. Believing it good advice, and seeing him too irresolute to act, it seems my clear duty to assist him."

Before I could interfere, even had I dared take the liberty to do so, Gnarmag-Zote struck the old man a terrible blow upon the head with his mace of office. The victim turned upon his back, spread his fingers, shivered convulsively and was dead.

"You need not be shocked," said the distinguished assassin, coolly: "I have but performed a sacred duty and religious rite. The religion (established first in this realm by King Skanghutch, the sixty-second of that name) consists in the worship of Death. We have sacred books, some three thousand thick volumes, said to be written by inspiration of Death himself, whom no mortal has ever seen, but who is described by our priests as having the figure of a fat young man with a red face and wearing an affable smile. In art he is commonly represented in the costume of a husbandman sowing seeds.

"The priests and sacred books teach that death is the supreme and only good—that the chief duties of man are, therefore, assassination and suicide. Conviction of these cardinal truths is universal among us, but I am sorry to say that many do not honestly live up to the faith. Most of us are commendably zealous in assassination, but slack and lukewarm in suicide. Some justify themselves in this half-hearted observance of the Law and imperfect submission to the Spirit by arguing that if they destroy themselves their usefulness in destroying others will be greatly abridged. 'I find,' says one of our most illustrious writers, not without a certain force, it must be confessed, 'that I can slay many more of others than I can of myself.'

"There are still others, more distinguished for faith than works, who reason that if A kill B, B cannot kill C. So it happens that although many Lalugwumps die, mostly by the hands of others, though some by their own, the country is never wholly depopulated."

"In my own country," said I, "is a sect holding somewhat Lalugwumpian views of the evil of life; and among the members it is considered a sin to bestow it. The philosopher Schopenhauer taught the same doctrine, and many of our rulers have shown strong sympathetic leanings toward it by procuring the destruction of many of their own people and those of other nations in what is called war."

"They are greatly to be commended," said Gnarmag-Zote, rising to intimate that the conversation was at an end. I respectfully protruded my tongue while he withdrew into his palace, spitting politely and with unusual copiousness in acknowledgment. A few minutes later, but before I had left the spot, two lackeys in livery emerged from the door by which he had entered, and while one shouldered the body of the old man and carried it into the palace kitchen the other informed me that his Highness was graciously pleased to desire my company at dinner that evening. With many expressions of regret I declined the invitation, unaware that to do so was treason. With the circumstances of my escape to the island of Tamtonia the newspapers have made the world already familiar.

THE TAMTONIANS

In all my intercourse with the Tamtonians I was treated with the most distinguished consideration and no obstacles to a perfect understanding of their social and political life were thrown in my way. My enforced residence on the island was, however, too brief to enable me to master the whole subject as I should have liked to do.

The government of Tamtonia is what is known in the language of the island as a gilbuper. It differs radically from any form known in other parts of the world and is supposed to have been invented by an ancient chief of the race, named Natas, who was for many centuries after his death worshiped as a god, and whose memory is still held in veneration. The government is of infinite complexity, its various functions distributed among as many officers as possible, multiplication of places being regarded as of the greatest importance, and not so much a means as an end. The Tamtonians seem to think that the highest good to which a human being can attain is the possession of an office; and in order that as many as possible may enjoy that advantage they have as many offices as the country will support, and make the tenure brief and in no way dependent on good conduct and intelligent administration of official duty. In truth, it occurs usually that a man is turned out of his office (in favor of an incompetent successor) before he has acquired sufficient experience to perform his duties with credit to himself or profit to the country. Owing to this incredible folly, the affairs of the island are badly mismanaged. Complaints are the rule, even from those who have had their way in the choice of officers. Of course there can be no such thing as a knowledge of the science of government among such a people, for it is to nobody's interest to acquire it by study of political history. There is, indeed, a prevalent belief that nothing worth knowing is to be learned from the history of other nations—not even from the history of their errors—such is this extraordinary people's national vanity! One of the most notable consequences of this universal and voluntary ignorance is that Tamtonia is the home of all the discreditable political and fiscal heresies from which many other nations, and especially our own, emancipated themselves centuries ago. They are there in vigorous growth and full flower, and believed to be of purely Tamtonian origin.

It needs hardly to be stated that in their personal affairs these people pursue an entirely different course, for if they did not there could be no profitable industries and professions among them, and no property to tax for the support of their government. In his private business a Tamtonian has as high appreciation of fitness and experience as anybody, and having secured a good man keeps him in service as long as possible.

The ruler of the nation, whom they call a Tnediserp, is chosen every five years but may be rechosen for five more. He is supposed to be selected by the people themselves, but in reality they have nothing to do with his selection. The method of choosing a man for Tnediserp is so strange that I doubt my ability to make it clear.

The adult male population of the island divides itself into two or more seitrap[1]. Commonly there are three or four, but only two ever have any considerable numerical strength, and none is ever strong morally or intellectually. All the members of each ytrap profess the same political opinions, which are provided for them by their leaders every five years and written down on pieces of paper so

---

[1] The Tamtonian language forms its plurals most irregularly, but usually by an initial inflection. It has a certain crude and primitive grammar, but in point of orthoepy is extremely difficult. With our letters I can hardly hope to give an accurate conception of its pronunciation. As nearly as possible I write its words as they sounded to my ear when carefully spoken for my instruction by intelligent natives. It is a harsh tongue.

that they will not be forgotten. The moment that any Tamtonian has read his piece of paper, or mroftalp, he unhesitatingly adopts all the opinions that he finds written on it, sometimes as many as forty or fifty, although these may be altogether different from, or even antagonistic to, those with which he was supplied five years before and has been advocating ever since. It will be seen from this that the Tamtonian mind is a thing whose processes no American can hope to respect, or even understand. It is instantaneously convinced without either fact or argument, and when these are afterward presented they only confirm it in its miraculous conviction; those which make against that conviction having an even stronger confirmatory power than the others. I have said any Tamtonian, but that is an overstatement. A few usually persist in thinking as they did before; or in altering their convictions in obedience to reason instead of authority, as our own people do; but they are at once assailed with the most opprobrious names, accused of treason and all manner of crimes, pelted with mud and stones and in some instances deprived of their noses and ears by the public executioner. Yet in no country is independence of thought so vaunted as a virtue, and in none is freedom of speech considered so obvious a natural right or so necessary to good government.

At the same time that each ytrap is supplied with its political opinions for the next five years, its leaders—who, I am told, all pursue the vocation of sharpening axes—name a man whom they wish chosen for the office of Tnediserp. He is usually an idiot from birth, the Tamtonians having a great veneration for such, believing them to be divinely inspired. Although few members of the ytrap have ever heard of him before, they at once believe him to have been long the very greatest idiot in the country; and for the next few months they do little else than quote his words and point to his actions to prove that his idiocy is of entirely superior quality to that of his opponent—a view that he himself, instructed by his discoverers, does and says all that he can to confirm. His inarticulate mumblings are everywhere repeated as utterances of profound wisdom, and the slaver that drools from his chin is carefully collected and shown to the people, evoking the wildest enthusiasm of his supporters. His opponents all this time are trying to blacken his character by the foulest conceivable falsehoods, some even going so far as to assert that he is not an idiot at all! It is generally agreed among them that if he were chosen to office the most dreadful disasters would ensue, and that, therefore, he will not be chosen.

To this last mentioned conviction, namely that the opposing

sometimes actually putting themselves into uniform and marching in procession with banners, music and torchlights.

I feel that this last statement will be hardly understood without explanation. Among the agencies employed by the Tamtonians to prove that one set of candidates is better than another, or to show that one political policy is more likely than another to promote the general prosperity, a high place is accorded to colored rags, flames of fire, noises made upon brass instruments, inarticulate shouts, explosions of gunpowder and lines of men walking and riding through the streets in cheap and tawdry costumes more or less alike. Vast sums of money are expended to procure these strange evidences of the personal worth of candidates and the political sanity of ideas. It is very much as if a man should paint his nose pea-green and stand on his head to convince his neighbors that his pigs are fed on acorns. Of course the money subscribed for these various controversial devices is not all wasted; the greater part of it is pocketed by the ax-grinders by whom it is solicited, and who have invented the system. That they have invented it for their own benefit seems not to have occurred to the dupes who pay for it. In the universal madness everybody believes whatever monstrous and obvious falsehood is told by the leaders of his own ytrap, and nobody listens for a moment to the exposures of their rascality. Reason has flown shrieking from the scene; Caution slumbers by the wayside with unbuttoned pocket. It is the opportunity of thieves!

With a view to abating somewhat the horrors of this recurring season of depravity, it has been proposed by several wise and decent Tamtonians to extend the term of office of the Tnediserp to six years instead of five, but the sharpeners of axes are too powerful to be overthrown. They have made the people believe that if the man whom the country chooses to rule it because it thinks him wise and good were permitted to rule it too long it would be impossible to displace him in punishment for his folly and wickedness. It is, indeed, far more likely that the term of office will be reduced to four years than extended to six. The effect can be no less than hideous!

In Tamtonia there is a current popular saying dating from many centuries back and running this way: "Eht eciffo dluohs kees eht nam, ton eht nam eht eciffo"—which may be translated thus: "No citizen ought to try to secure power for himself, but should be selected by others for his fitness to exercise it." The sentiment which this wise and decent phrase expresses has long ceased to have a place in the hearts of those who are everlastingly repeating it, but with regard to the office of Tnediserp it has still a remnant of the vitality of habit. This, however, is fast dying out, and a few years ago one of the congenital idiots who was a candidate for the highest dignity boldly broke the inhibition and made speeches to the people in advocacy of himself, all over the country. Even more recently another has uttered his preferences in much the same way, but with this difference: he did his speechmaking at his own home, the axgrinders in his interest rounding up audiences for him and herding them before his door. One of the two corpses, too, was galvanized into a kind of ghastly activity and became a talking automaton; but the other had been too long dead. In a few years more the decent tradition that a man should not blow his own horn will be obsolete in its application to the high office, as it is to all the others, but the popular saying will lose none of its currency for that.

To the American mind nothing can be more shocking than the Tamtonian practice of openly soliciting political preferment and even paying money to assist in securing it. With us such immodesty would be taken as proof of the offender's unfitness to exercise the power which he asks for, or bear the dignity which, in soliciting it, he belittles. Yet no Tamtonian ever refused to take the hand of a man guilty of such conduct, and there have been instances of fathers giving these greedy vulgarians the hands of their daughters in marriage and thereby assisting to perpetuate the species. The kind of government given by men who go about begging for the right to govern can be more easily imagined than endured. In short, I cannot help thinking that when, unable longer to bear with patience the evils entailed by the vices and follies of its inhabitants, I sailed away from the accursed island of Tamtonia, I left behind me the most pestilent race of rascals and ignoramuses to be found anywhere in the universe; and I never can sufficiently thank the divine Power who spared me the disadvantage and shame of being one of them, and cast my lot in this favored land of goodness and right reason, the blessed abode of public morality and private worth—of liberty, conscience and common sense.

I was not, however, to reach it without further detention in barbarous countries. After being at sea four days I was seized by my mutinous crew, set ashore upon an island, and having been made insensible by a blow upon the head was basely abandoned.

MAROONED ON UG

When I regained my senses I found myself lying on the strand a short remove from the margin of the sea. It was high noon and an insupportable itching pervaded my entire frame, that being the effect of sunshine in that country, as heat is in ours. Having observed that the discomfort was abated by the passing of a light cloud between me and the sun, I dragged myself with some difficulty to a clump of trees near by and found permanent relief in their shade. As soon as I was comfortable enough to examine my surroundings I saw that the trees were of metal, apparently copper, with leaves of what resembled pure silver, but may have contained alloy. Some of the trees bore burnished flowers shaped like bells, and in a breeze the tinkling as they clashed together was exceedingly sweet. The grass with which the open country was covered as far as I could see amongst the patches of forest was of a bright scarlet hue, excepting along the water-courses, where it was white. Lazily cropping it at some little distance away, or lying in it, indolently chewing the cud and attended by a man half-clad in skins and bearing a crook, was a flock of tigers. My travels in New Jersey having made me proof against surprise, I contemplated these several visible phenomena without emotion, and with a merely expectant interest in what might be revealed by further observation.

The tigerherd having perceived me, now came striding forward, brandishing his crook and shaking his fists with great vehemence, gestures which I soon learned were, in that country, signs of amity and good-will. But before knowing that fact I had risen to my feet and thrown myself into a posture of defense, and as he approached I led for his head with my left, following with a stiff right upon his solar plexus, which sent him rolling on the grass in great pain. After learning something of the social customs of the country I felt extreme mortification in recollecting this breach of etiquette, and even to this day I cannot think upon it without a blush.

Such was my first meeting with Jogogle-Zadester, Pastor-King of Ug, the wisest and best of men. Later in our acquaintance, when I had for a long time been an honored guest at his court, where a thousand fists were ceremoniously shaken under my nose daily, he explained that my luke-warm reception of his hospitable advances gave him, for the moment, an unfavorable impression of my breeding and culture.

The island of Ug, upon which I had been marooned, lies in the Southern Hemisphere, but has neither latitude nor longitude. It has an area of nearly seven hundred square samtains and is peculiar in shape, its width being considerably greater than its length. Politically it is a limited monarchy, the right of succession to the throne being vested in the sovereign's father, if he have one; if not in his grandfather, and so on upward in the line of ascent. (As a matter of fact there has not within historic times been a legitimate succession, even the great and good Jogogle-Zadester being a usurper chosen by popular vote.) To assist him in governing, the King is given a parliament, the Uggard word for which is gabagab, but its usefulness is greatly circumscribed by the Blubosh, or Constitution, which requires that every measure, in order to become a law, shall have an affirmative majority of the actual members, yet forbids any member to vote who has not a distinct pecuniary interest in the result. I was once greatly amused by a spirited contest over a matter of harbor improvement, each of two proposed harbors having its advocates. One of these gentlemen, a most eloquent patriot, held the floor for hours in advocacy of the port where he had an interest in a projected mill for making dead kittens into cauliflower pickles; while other members were being vigorously persuaded by one who at the other place had a clam ranch. In a debate in the Uggard gabagab no one can have a "standing" except a party in interest; and as a consequence of this enlightened policy every bill that is passed is found to be most intelligently adapted to its purpose.

The original intent of this requirement was that members having no pecuniary interest in a proposed law at the time of its inception should not embarrass the proceedings and pervert the result; but the inhibition is now thought to be sufficiently observed by formal public acceptance of a nominal bribe to vote one way or the other. It is of course understood that behind the nominal bribe is commonly a more substantial one of which there is no record. To an American accustomed to the incorrupt methods of legislation in his own country the spectacle of every member of the Uggard gabagab qualifying himself to vote by marching up, each in his turn as his name is called, to the proponent of the bill, or to its leading antagonist, and solemnly receiving a tonusi (the smallest coin of the realm) is exceedingly novel. When I ventured to mention to the King my lack of faith in the principle upon which this custom is founded, he replied:

"Heart of my soul, if you and your compatriots distrust the honesty and intelligence of an interested motive why is it that in your own courts of law, as you describe them, no private citizen can institute a civil action to right the wrongs of anybody but himself?"

I had nothing to say and the King proceeded: "And why is it

that your judges will listen to no argument from any one who has not acquired a selfish concern in the matter?"

"O, your Majesty," I answered with animation, "they listen to attorneys-general, district attorneys and salaried officers of the law generally, whose prosperity depends in no degree upon their success; who prosecute none but those whom they believe to be guilty; who are careful to present no false nor misleading testimony and argument; who are solicitous that even the humblest accused person shall be accorded every legal right and every advantage to which he is entitled; who, in brief, are animated by the most humane sentiments and actuated by the purest and most unselfish motives."

The King's discomfiture was pitiful: he retired at once from the capital and passed a whole year pasturing his flock of tigers in the solitudes beyond the River of Wine. Seeing that I would henceforth be persona non grata at the palace, I sought obscurity in the writing and publication of books. In this vocation I was greatly assisted by a few standard works that had been put ashore with me in my sea-chest.

The literature of Ug is copious and of high merit, but consists altogether of fiction—mainly history, biography, theology and novels. Authors of exceptional excellence receive from the state marks of signal esteem, being appointed to the positions of laborers in the Department of Highways and Cemeteries. Having been so fortunate as to win public favor and attract official attention by my locally famous works, "The Decline and Fall of the Roman Empire," "David Copperfield," "Pilgrim's Progress," and "Ben Hur," I was myself that way distinguished and my future assured. Unhappily, through ignorance of the duties and dignities of the position I had the mischance to accept a gratuity for sweeping a street crossing and was compelled to flee for my life.

Disguising myself as a sailor I took service on a ship that sailed due south into the unknown Sea.

It is now many years since my marooning on Ug, but my recollection of the country, its inhabitants and their wonderful manners and customs is exceedingly vivid. Some small part of what most interested me I shall here set down.

The Uggards are, or fancy themselves, a warlike race: nowhere in those distant seas are there any islanders so vain of their military power, the consciousness of which they acquired chiefly by fighting one another. Many years ago, however, they had a war with the people of another island kingdom, called Wug. The Wuggards held dominion over a third island, Scamadumclitchclitch, whose people had tried to throw off the yoke. In order to subdue them—at least to tears—it was decided to deprive them of garlic, the sole article of diet known to them and the Wuggards, and in that country dug out of the ground like coal. So the Wuggards in the rebellious island stopped up all the garlic mines, supplying their own needs by purchase from foreign trading proas. Having few cowrie shells, with which to purchase, the poor Scamadumclitchclitchians suffered a great distress, which so touched the hearts of the compassionate Uggards—a most humane and conscientious people—that they declared war against the Wuggards and sent a fleet of proas to the relief of the sufferers. The fleet established a strict blockade of every port in Scamadumclitchclitch, and not a clove of garlic could enter the island. That compelled the Wuggard army of occupation to reopen the mines for its own subsistence.

All this was told to me by the great and good and wise Jogogle-Zadester, King of Ug.

"But, your Majesty," I said, "what became of the poor Scamadumclitchclitchians?"

"They all died," he answered with royal simplicity.

"Then your Majesty's humane intervention," I said, "was not entirely—well, fattening?"

"The fortune of war," said the King, gravely, looking over my head to signify that the interview was at an end; and I retired from the Presence on hands and feet, as is the etiquette in that country.

As soon as I was out of hearing I threw a stone in the direction of the palace and said: "I never in my life heard of such a cold-blooded scoundrel!"

In conversation with the King's Prime Minister, the famous Grumsquutzy, I asked him how it was that Ug, being a great military power, was apparently without soldiers.

"Sir," he replied, courteously shaking his fist under my nose in sign of amity, "know that when Ug needs soldiers she enlists them. At the end of the war they are put to death."

"Visible embodiment of a great nation's wisdom," I said, "far be it from me to doubt the expediency of that military method; but merely as a matter of economy would it not be better to keep an army in time of peace than to be compelled to create one in time of war?"

"Ug is rich," he replied; "we do not have to consider matters of economy. There is among our people a strong and instinctive distrust of a standing army."

"What are they afraid of," I asked—what do they fear that it will do?"

"It is not what the army may do," answered the great man, "but what it may prevent others from doing. You must know that we have in this land a thing known as Industrial Discontent."

"Ah, I see," I exclaimed, interrupting—"the industrial classes fear that the army may destroy, or at least subdue, their discontent."

The Prime Minister reflected profoundly, standing the while, in order that he might assist his faculties by scratching himself, even as we, when thinking, scratch our heads.

"No," he said presently; "I don't think that is quite what they apprehend—they and the writers and statesmen who speak for them. As I said before, what is feared in a case of industrial discontent is the army's preventive power. But I am myself uncertain what it is that these good souls dislike to have the army prevent. I shall take the customary means to learn."

Having occasion on the next day to enter the great audience hall of the palace I observed in gigantic letters running across the entire side opposite the entrance this surprising inscription:

"In a strike, what do you fear that the army will prevent which ought to be done?"

Facing the entrance sat Grumsquutzy, in his robes of office and surrounded by an armed guard. At a little distance stood two great black slaves, each bearing a scourge of thongs. All about them the floor was slippery with blood. While I wondered at all this two policemen entered, having between them one whom I recognized as a professional Friend of the People, a great orator, keenly concerned for the interests of Labor. Shown the inscription and unable or unwilling to answer, he was given over to the two blacks and, being stripped to the skin, was beaten with the whips until he bled copiously and his cries resounded through the palace. His ears were then shorn away and he was thrown into the street. Another Friend of the People was brought in, and treated in the same way; and the inquiry was continued, day after day, until all had been interrogated. But Grumsquutzy got no answer.

A most extraordinary and interesting custom of the Uggards is called the Naganag and has existed, I was told, for centuries. Immediately after every war, and before the returned army is put to death, the chieftains who have held high command and their official head, the Minister of National Displeasure, are conducted with much pomp to the public square of Nabootka, the capital. Here all are stripped naked, deprived of their sight with a hot iron and armed with a club each. They are then locked in the square, which has an inclosing wall thirty clowgebs high. A signal is given and they begin to fight. At the end of three days the place is entered and searched. If any of the dead bodies has an unbroken bone in it the survivors are boiled in wine; if not they are smothered in butter.

Upon the advantages of this custom—which surely has not its like in the whole world—I could get little light. One public official told me its purpose was "peace among the victorious"; another said it was "for gratification of the military instinct in high places," though if that is so one is disposed to ask "What was the war for?" The Prime Minister, profoundly learned in all things else, could not enlighten me, and the commander-in-chief in the Wuggard war could only tell me, while on his way to the public square, that it was "to vindicate the truth of history."

In all the wars in which Ug has engaged in historic times that with Wug was the most destructive of life. Excepting among the comparatively few troops that had the hygienic and preservative advantage of personal collision with the enemy, the mortality was appalling. Regiments exposed to the fatal conditions of camp life in their own country died like flies in a frost. So pathetic were the pleas of the sufferers to be led against the enemy and have a chance to live that none hearing them could forbear to weep. Finally a considerable number of them went to the seat of war, where they began an immediate attack upon a fortified city, for their health; but the enemy's resistance was too brief materially to reduce the death rate and the men were again in the hands of their officers. On their return to Ug they were so few that the public executioners charged with the duty of reducing the army to a peace footing were themselves made ill by inactivity.

As to the navy, the war with Wug having shown the Uggard sailors to be immortal, their government knows not how to get rid of them, and remains a great sea power in spite of itself. I ventured to suggest mustering out, but neither the King nor any Minister of State was able to form a conception of any method of reduction and retrenchment but that of the public headsman.

It is said—I do not know with how much truth—that the defeat of Wug was made easy by a certain malicious prevision of the Wuggards themselves: something of the nature of heroic self-sacrifice, the surrender of a present advantage for a terrible revenge in the future. As an instance, the commander of the fortified city already mentioned is reported to have ordered his garrison to kill as few of their assailants as possible.

"It is true," he explained to his subordinates, who favored a defense to the death—"it is true this will lose us the place, but there are other places; you have not thought of that."

They had not thought of that.

"It is true, too, that we shall be taken prisoners, but"—and he smiled grimly—"we have fairly good appetites, and we must be fed. That will cost something, I take it. But that is not the best of it. Look at that vast host of our enemies—each one of them a future pensioner on a fool people. If there is among us one man who would willingly deprive the Uggard treasury of a single dependent—who would spare the Uggard pigs one gukwam of expense, let the traitor stand forth."

No traitor stood forth, and in the ensuing battles the garrison, it is said, fired only blank cartridges, and such of the assailants as were killed incurred that mischance by falling over their own feet.

It is estimated by Wuggard statisticians that in twenty years from the close of the war the annual appropriation for pensions in Ug will amount to no less than one hundred and sixty gumdums to every enlisted man in the kingdom. But they know not the Uggard customs of exterminating the army.

THE DOG IN GANEGWAG

A about the end of the thirty-seventh month of our voyage due south from Ug we sighted land, and although the coast appeared wild and inhospitable, the captain decided to send a boat ashore in search of fresh water and provisions, of which we were in sore need. I was of the boat's crew and thought myself fortunate in being able to set foot again upon the earth. There were seven others in the landing party, including the mate, who commanded.

Selecting a sheltered cove, which appeared to be at the mouth of a small creek, we beached the boat, and leaving two men to guard it started inland toward a grove of trees. Before we reached it an animal came out of it and advanced confidently toward us, showing no signs of either fear or hostility. It was a hideous creature, not altogether like anything that we had ever seen, but on its close approach we recognized it as a dog, of an unimaginably loathsome breed. As we were nearly famished one of the sailors shot it for food. Instantly a great crowd of persons, who had doubtless been watching us from among the trees, rushed upon us with fierce exclamations and surrounded us, making the most threatening gestures and brandishing unfamiliar weapons. Unable to resist such odds we were seized, bound with cords and dragged into the forest almost before we knew what had happened to us. Observing the nature of our reception the ship's crew hastily weighed anchor and sailed away. We never again saw them.

Beyond the trees concealing it from the sea was a great city, and thither we were taken. It was Gumammam, the capital of Ganegwag, whose people are dog-worshipers. The fate of my companions I never learned, for although I remained in the country for seven years, much of the time as a prisoner, and learned to speak its language, no answer was ever given to my many inquiries about my unfortunate friends.

The Ganegwagians are an ancient race with a history covering a period of ten thousand supintroes. In stature they are large, in color blue, with crimson hair and yellow eyes. They live to a great age, sometimes as much as twenty supintroes, their climate being so wholesome that even the aged have to sail to a distant island in order to die. Whenever a sufficient number of them reach what they call "the age of going away" they embark on a government ship and in the midst of impressive public rites and ceremonies set sail for "the Isle of the Happy Change." Of their strange civilization, their laws, manners and customs, their copper clothing and liquid houses I have written—at perhaps too great length—in my famous book, "Ganegwag the Incredible." Here I shall confine myself to their religion, certainly the most amazing form of superstition in the world.

Nowhere, it is believed, but in Ganegwag has so vile a creature as the dog obtained general recognition as a deity. There this filthy beast is considered so divine that it is freely admitted to the domestic circle and cherished as an honored guest. Scarcely a family that is able to support a dog is without one, and some have as many as a half-dozen. Indeed, the dog is the special deity of the poor, those families having most that are least able to maintain them. In some sections of the country, particularly the southern and southwestern provinces, the number of dogs is estimated to be greater than that of the children, as is the cost of their maintenance. In families of the rich they are fewer in number, but more sacredly cherished, especially by the female members, who lavish upon them a wealth of affection not always granted to the husband and children, and distinguish them with indescribable attentions and endearments.

Nowhere is the dog compelled to make any other return for all this honor and benefaction than a fawning and sycophantic demeanor toward those who bestow them and an insulting and injurious attitude toward strangers who have dogs of their own, and toward other dogs. In any considerable town of the realm not a day passes but the public newsman relates in the most matter-of-fact and unsympathetic way to his circle of listless auditors painful instances of human beings, mostly women and children, bitten and mangled by these ferocious animals without provocation.

In addition to these ravages of the dog in his normal state are a vastly greater number of outrages committed by the sacred animal in the fury of insanity, for he has an hereditary tendency to madness, and in that state his bite is incurable, the victim awaiting in the most horrible agony the sailing of the next ship to the Isle of the Happy Change, his suffering imperfectly medicined by expressions of public sympathy for the dog.

A cynical citizen of Gumammam said to the writer of this narrative: "My countrymen have three hundred kinds of dogs, and only one way to hang a thief." Yet all the dogs are alike in this, that none is respectable.

Withal, it must be said of this extraordinary people that their horrible religion is free from the hollow forms and meaningless ceremonies in which so many superstitions of the lower races find expression. It is a religion of love, practical, undemonstrative, knowing nothing of pageantry and spectacle. It is hidden in the lives and hearts of the people; a stranger would hardly know of its existence as a distinct faith. Indeed, other faiths and better ones (one of them having some resemblance to a debased form of Christianity) co-exist with it, sometimes in the same mind. Cynolatry is tolerant so long as the dog is not denied an equal divinity with the deities of other faiths. Nevertheless, I could not think of the people of Ganegwag without contempt and loathing; so it was with no small joy that I sailed for the contiguous island of Ghargaroo to consult, according to my custom, the renowned statesman and philosopher, Juptka-Getch, who was accounted the wisest man in all the world, and held in so high esteem that no one dared speak to him without the sovereign's permission, countersigned by the Minister of Morals and Manners.

A CONFLAGRATION IN GHARGAROO

Through the happy accident of having a mole on the left side of my nose, as had also a cousin of the Prime Minister, I obtained a royal rescript permitting me to speak to the great Juptka-Getch, and went humbly to his dwelling, which, to my astonishment, I found to be an unfurnished cave in the side of a mountain. Inexpressibly surprised to observe that a favorite of the sovereign and the people was so meanly housed, I ventured, after my salutation, to ask how this could be so. Regarding me with an indulgent smile, the venerable man, who was about two hundred and fifty years old and entirely bald, explained.

"In one of our Sacred Books, of which we have three thousand," said he, "it is written, 'Golooloo ek wakwah betenka,' and in another, 'Jebeb uq seedroy im aboltraqu ocrux ti smelkit.'"

Translated, these mean, respectively, "The poor are blessed," and, "Heaven is not easily entered by those who are rich."

I asked Juptka-Getch if his countrymen really gave to these texts a practical application in the affairs of life.

"Why, surely," he replied, "you cannot think us such fools as to disregard the teachings of our gods! That would be madness. I cannot imagine a people so mentally and morally depraved as that! Can you?"

Observing me blushing and stammering, he inquired the cause of my embarrassment. "The thought of so incredible a thing confuses me," I managed to reply. "But tell me if in your piety and wisdom you really stripped yourself of all your property in order to obey the gods and get the benefit of indigence."

"I did not have to do so," he replied with a smile; "my King attended to that. When he wishes to distinguish one of his subjects by a mark of his favor, he impoverishes him to such a degree as will attest the exact measure of the royal approbation. I am proud to say that he took from me all that I had."

"But, pardon me," I said; "how does it occur that among a people which regards poverty as the greatest earthly good all are not poor? I observe here as much wealth and 'prosperity' as in my own country."

Juptka-Getch smiled and after a few moments answered: "The only person in this country that owns anything is the King; in the service of his people he afflicts himself with that burden. All property, of whatsoever kind, is his, to do with as he will. He divides it among his subjects in the ratio of their demerit, as determined by the waguks—local officers—whose duty it is to know personally every one in their jurisdiction. To the most desperate and irreclaimable criminals is allotted the greatest wealth, which is taken from them, little by little, as they show signs of reformation."

"But what," said I, "is to prevent the wicked from becoming poor at any time? How can the King and his officers keep the unworthy, suffering the punishment and peril of wealth, from giving it away?"

"To whom, for example?" replied the illustrious man, taking the forefinger of his right hand into his mouth, as is the fashion in Ghargaroo when awaiting an important communication. The respectful formality of the posture imperfectly concealed the irony of the question, but I was not of the kind to be easily silenced.

"One might convert one's property into money," I persisted, "and throw the money into the sea."

Juptka-Getch released the finger and gravely answered: "Every person in Ghargaroo is compelled by law to keep minute accounts of his income and expenditures, and must swear to them. There is an annual appraisement by the waguk, and any needless decrease in the value of an estate is punished by breaking the offender's legs. Expenditures for luxuries and high living are, of course, approved, for it is universally known among us, and attested by many popular proverbs, that the pleasures of the rich are vain and disappointing. So they are considered a part of the punishment, and not only allowed but required. A man sentenced to wealth who lives frugally, indulging in only rational and inexpensive delights, has his ears cut off for the first offense, and for the second is compelled to pass six months at court, participating in all the gaieties, extravagances and pleasures of the capital, and——"

"Most illustrious of mortals," I said, turning a somersault—the Ghargarese manner of interrupting a discourse without offense—"I am as the dust upon your beard, but in my own country I am esteemed no fool, and right humbly do I perceive that you are ecxroptug nemk puttog peleemy."

This expression translates, literally, "giving me a fill," a phrase without meaning in our tongue, but in Ghargarese it appears to imply incredulity.

"The gaieties of the King's court," I continued, "must be expensive. The courtiers of the sovereign's entourage, the great officers of the realm—surely they are not condemned to wealth, like common criminals!"

"My son," said Juptka-Getch, tearing out a handful of his beard to signify his tranquillity under accusation, "your doubt of my veracity is noted with satisfaction, but it is not permitted to you to impeach my sovereign's infallible knowledge of character. His courtiers, the great officers of the realm, as you truly name them, are the richest men in the country because he knows them to be the greatest rascals. After each annual reapportionment of the national wealth he settles upon them the unallotted surplus."

Prostrating myself before the eminent philosopher, I craved his pardon for my doubt of his sovereign's wisdom and consistency, and begged him to cut off my head.

"Nay," he said, "you have committed the unpardonable sin and I cannot consent to bestow upon you the advantages of death. You shall continue to live the thing that you are."

"What!" I cried, remembering the Lalugwumps and Gnarmag-Zote, "is it thought in Ghargaroo that death is an advantage, a blessing?"

"Our Sacred Books," he said, "are full of texts affirming the vanity of life."

"Then," I said, "I infer that the death penalty is unknown to your laws!"

"We have the life penalty instead. Convicted criminals are not only enriched, as already explained, but by medical attendance kept alive as long as possible. On the contrary, the very righteous, who have been rewarded with poverty, are permitted to die whenever it pleases them.

"Do not the Sacred Books of your country teach the vanity of life, the blessedness of poverty and the wickedness of wealth?"

"They do, O Most Illustrious, they do."

"And your countrymen believe?"

"Surely—none but the foolish and depraved entertain a doubt."

"Then I waste my breath in expounding laws and customs already known to you. You have, of course, the same."

At this I averted my face and blushed so furiously that the walls of the cave were illuminated with a wavering crimson like the light of a great conflagration! Thinking that the capital city was ablaze, Juptka-Getch ran from the cave's mouth, crying, "Fire, fire!" and I saw him no more.

AN EXECUTION IN BATRUGIA

My next voyage was not so prosperous. By violent storms lasting seven weeks, during which we saw neither the sun nor the stars, our ship was driven so far out of its course that the captain had no knowledge of where we were. At the end of that period we were blown ashore and wrecked on a coast so wild and desolate that I had never seen anything so terrifying. Through a manifest interposition of Divine Providence I was spared, though all my companions perished miserably in the waves that had crushed the ship among the rocks.

As soon as I was sufficiently recovered from my fatigue and bruises, and had rendered thanks to merciful Heaven for my deliverance, I set out for the interior of the country, taking with me a cutlas for protection against wild beasts and a bag of sea-biscuit for sustenance. I walked vigorously, for the weather was then cool and pleasant, and after I had gone a few miles from the inhospitable coast I found the country open and level. The earth was covered with a thick growth of crimson grass, and at wide intervals were groups of trees. These were very tall, their tops in many instances invisible in a kind of golden mist, or haze, which proved to be, not a transient phenomenon, but a permanent one, for never in that country has the sun been seen, nor is there any night. The haze seems to be self-luminous, giving a soft, yellow light, so diffused that shadows are unknown. The land is abundantly supplied with pools and rivulets, whose water is of a beautiful orange color and has a pleasing perfume somewhat like attar of rose. I observed all this without surprise and with little apprehension, and went forward, feeling that anything, however novel and mysterious, was better than the familiar terrors of the sea and the coast.

After traveling a long time, though how long I had not the means to determine, I arrived at the city of Momgamwo, the capital of the kingdom of Batrugia, on the mainland of the Hidden Continent, where it is always twelve o'clock.

The Batrugians are of gigantic stature, but mild and friendly disposition. They offered me no violence, seeming rather amused by my small stature. One of them, who appeared to be a person of note and consequence, took me to his house (their houses are but a single story in height and built of brass blocks), set food before me, and by signs manifested the utmost good will. A long time afterward, when I had learned the language of the country, he explained that he had recognized me as an American pigmy, a race of which he had some little knowledge through a letter from a brother, who had been in my country. He showed me the letter, of which the chief part is here presented in translation:

"You ask me, my dear Tgnagogu, to relate my adventures among the Americans, as they call themselves. My adventures were very brief, lasting altogether not more than three gumkas, and most of the time was passed in taking measures for my own safety.

"My skyship, which had been driven for six moons before an irresistible gale, passed over a great city just at daylight one morning, and rather than continue the voyage with a lost reckoning I demanded that I be permitted to disembark. My wish was respected, and my companions soared away without me. Before night I had escaped from the city, by what means you know, and with my remarkable experiences in returning to civilization all Batrugia is familiar. The description of the strange city I have reserved for you, by whom only could I hope to be believed. Nyork, as its inhabitants call it, is a city of inconceivable extent—not less, I should judge, than seven square glepkeps! Of the number of its inhabitants I can only say that they are as the sands of the desert. They wear clothing—of a hideous kind, 'tis true—speak an apparently copious though harsh language, and seem to have a certain limited intelligence. They are puny in stature, the tallest of them being hardly higher than my breast.

"Nevertheless, Nyork is a city of giants. The magnitude of all things artificial there is astounding! My dear Tgnagogu, words can give you no conception of it. Many of the buildings, I assure you, are as many as fifty sprugas in height, and shelter five thousand persons each. And these stupendous structures are so crowded together that to the spectator in the narrow streets below they seem utterly devoid of design and symmetry—mere monstrous aggregations of brick, stone and metal—mountains of masonry, cliffs and crags of architecture hanging in the sky!

"A city of giants inhabited by pigmies! For you must know, oh friend of my liver, that the rearing of these mighty structures could not be the work of the puny folk that swarm in ceaseless activity about their bases. These fierce little savages invaded the island in numbers so overwhelming that the giant builders had to flee before them. Some escaped across great bridges which, with the help of their gods, they had suspended in the air from bank to bank of a wide river parting the island from the mainland, but many could do no better than mount some of the buildings that they had reared, and there, in these inaccessible altitudes, they dwell to-day, still piling stone upon stone. Whether they do this in obedience to their instinct as builders, or in hope to escape by way of the heavens, I had not the means to learn, being ignorant of the pigmy tongue and in continual fear of the crowds that followed me.

"You can see the giants toiling away up there in the sky, laying in place the enormous beams and stones which none but they could handle. They look no bigger than beetles, but you know that they are many sprugas in stature, and you shudder to think what would ensue if one should lose his footing. Fancy that great bulk whirling down to earth from so dizzy an altitude!...

"May birds ever sing above your grave.
                                                "JOQUOLK WAK MGAPY."

By my new friend, Tgnagogu, I was presented to the King, a most enlightened monarch, who not only reigned over, but ruled absolutely, the most highly civilized people in the world. He received me with gracious hospitality, quartered me in the palace of his Prime Minister, gave me for wives the three daughters of his

Lord Chamberlain, and provided me with an ample income from the public revenues. Within a year I had made a fair acquaintance with the Batrugian language, and was appointed royal interpreter, with a princely salary, although no one speaking any other tongue, myself and two native professors of rhetoric excepted, had ever been seen in the kingdom.

One day I heard a great tumult in the street, and going to a window saw, in a public square opposite, a crowd of persons surrounding some high officials who were engaged in cutting off a man's head. Just before the executioner delivered the fatal stroke, the victim was asked if he had anything to say. He explained with earnestness that the deed for which he was about to suffer had been inspired and commanded by a brass-headed cow and four bushels of nightingales' eggs!

"Hold! hold!" I shouted in Batrugian, leaping from the window and forcing a way through the throng; "the man is obviously insane!"

"Friend," said a man in a long blue robe, gently restraining me, "it is not proper for you to interrupt these high proceedings with irrelevant remarks. The luckless gentleman who, in accordance with my will as Lord Chief Justice, has just had the happiness to part with his head was so inconsiderate as to take the life of a fellow-subject."

"But he was insane," I persisted, "clearly and indisputably ptig nupy uggydug!"—a phrase imperfectly translatable, meaning, as near as may be, having flitter-mice in his campanile.

"Am I to infer," said the Lord Chief Justice, "that in your own honorable country a person accused of murder is permitted to plead insanity as a reason why he should not be put to death?"

"Yes, illustrious one," I replied, respectfully, "we regard that as a good defense."

"Well," said he slowly, but with extreme emphasis, "I'll be Gook swottled!"

("Gook," I may explain, is the name of the Batrugian chief deity; but for the verb "to swottle" the English tongue has no equivalent. It seems to signify the deepest disapproval, and by a promise to be "swottled" a Batrugian denotes acute astonishment.)

"Surely," I said, "so wise and learned a person as you cannot think it just to punish with death one who does not know right from wrong. The gentleman who has just now renounced his future believed himself to have been commanded to do what he did by a brass-headed cow and four bushels of nightingales' eggs—powers to which he acknowledged a spiritual allegiance. To have disobeyed would have been, from his point of view, an infraction of a law higher than that of man."

"Honorable but erring stranger," replied the famous jurist, "if we permitted the prisoner in a murder trial to urge such a consideration as that—if our laws recognized any other justification than that he believed himself in peril of immediate death or great bodily injury—nearly all assassins would make some such defense. They would plead insanity of some kind and degree, and it would be almost impossible to establish their guilt. Murder trials would be expensive and almost interminable, defiled with perjury and sentiment. Juries would be deluded and confused, justice baffled, and red-handed man-killers turned loose to repeat their crimes and laugh at the law. Even as the law is, in a population of only one hundred million we have had no fewer than three homicides in less than twenty years! With such statutes and customs as yours we should have had at least twice as many. Believe me, I know my people; they have not the American respect for human life."

As blushing is deemed in Batrugia a sign of pride, I turned my back upon the speaker—an act which, fortunately, signifies a desire to hear more.

"Law," he continued, "is for the good of the greatest number. Execution of an actual lunatic now and then is not an evil to the community, nor, when rightly considered, to the lunatic himself. He is better off when dead, and society is profited by his removal. We are spared the cost of exposing imposture, the humiliation of acquitting the guilty, the peril of their freedom, the contagion of their evil example."

"In my country," I said, "we have a saying to the effect that it is better that ninety-nine guilty escape than that one innocent be punished."

"It is better," said he, "for the ninety-nine guilty, but distinctly worse for everybody else. Sir," he concluded with chilling austerity, "I infer from their proverb that your countrymen are the most offensive blockheads in existence."

By way of refutation I mentioned the English, indignantly withdrew from the country and set sail for Gokeetle-guk, or, as we should translate the name, Trustland.

THE JUMJUM OF GOKEETLE-GUK

Arriving at the capital of the country after many incredible adventures, I was promptly arrested by the police and taken before the Jumjum. He was an exceedingly affable person, and held office by appointment, "for life or fitness," as their laws express it. With one necessary exception all offices are appointive and the tenure of all except that is the same. The Panjandrum, or, as we should call him, King, is elected for a term of ten years, at the expiration of which he is shot. It is held that any man who has been so long in high authority will have committed enough sins and blunders to deserve death, even if none can be specifically proved.

Brought into the presence of the Jumjum, who graciously saluted me, I was seated on a beautiful rug and told in broken English by an interpreter who had escaped from Kansas that I was at liberty to ask any questions that I chose.

"Your Highness," I said, addressing the Jumjum through the interpreting Populist, "I fear that I do not understand; I expected, not to ask questions, but to have to answer them. I am ready to give such an account of myself as will satisfy you that I am an honest man—neither a criminal nor a spy."

"The gentleman seems to regard himself with a considerable interest," said the Jumjum, aside to an officer of his suite—a remark which the interpreter, with characteristic intelligence, duly repeated to me. Then addressing me the Jumjum said:

"Doubtless your personal character is an alluring topic, but it is relevant to nothing in any proceedings that can be taken here. When a foreigner arrives in our capital he is brought before me to be instructed in whatever he may think it expedient for him to know of the manners, customs, laws, and so forth, of the country that he honors with his presence. It matters nothing to us what he is, but much to him what we are. You are at liberty to inquire."

I was for a moment overcome with emotion by so noble an example of official civility and thoughtfulness, then, after a little reflection, I said: "May it please your Highness, I should greatly like to be informed of the origin of the name of your esteemed country."

"Our country," said the Jumjum, acknowledging the compliment by a movement of his ears, "is called Trustland because all its industries, trades and professions are conducted by great aggregations of capital known as 'trusts.' They do the entire business of the country."

"Good God!" I exclaimed; "what a terrible state of affairs that is!

I know about trusts. Why do your people not rise and throw off the yoke?"

"You are pleased to be unintelligible," said the great man, with a smile. "Would you mind explaining what you mean by 'the yoke'?"

"I mean," said I, surprised by his ignorance of metaphor, but reflecting that possibly the figures of rhetoric were not used in that country—"I mean the oppression, the slavery under which your people groan, their bond-age to the tyrannical trusts, entailing poverty, unrequited toil and loss of self-respect."

"Why, as to that," he replied, "our people are prosperous and happy. There is very little poverty and what there is is obviously the result of vice or improvidence. Our labor is light and all the necessaries of life, many of the comforts and some of the luxuries are abundant and cheap. I hardly know what you mean by the tyranny of the trusts; they do not seem to care to be tyrannous, for each having the entire market for what it produces, its prosperity is assured and there is none of the strife and competition which, as I can imagine, might breed hardness and cruelty. Moreover, we should not let them be tyrannous. Why should we?"

"But, your Highness, suppose, for example, the trust that manufactures safety pins should decide to double the price of its product. What is to prevent great injury to the consumer?"

"The courts. Having but one man—the responsible manager—to deal with, protective legislation and its enforcement would be a very simple matter. If there were a thousand manufacturers of safety pins, scattered all over the country in as many jurisdictions, there would be no controlling them at all. They would cheat, not only one another but the consumers, with virtual immunity. But there is no disposition among our trusts to do any such thing. Each has the whole market, as I said, and each has learned by experience what the manager of a large business soon must learn, and what the manager of a small one probably would not learn and could not afford to apply if he knew it—namely, that low prices bring disproportionately large sales and therefore profits. Prices in this country are never put up except when some kind of scarcity increases the cost of production. Besides, nearly all the consumers are a part of the trusts, the stock of which is about the best kind of property for investment."

"What!" I cried,—"do not the managers so manipulate the stock by 'watering' it and otherwise as to fool and cheat the small investors?"

"We should not permit them. That would be dishonest."

"So it is in my country," I replied, rather tartly, for I believed his apparent naïveté assumed for my confusion, "but we are unable to prevent it."

He looked at me somewhat compassionately, I thought. "Perhaps," he said, "not enough of you really wish to prevent it. Perhaps your people are—well, different from mine—not worse, you understand—just different."

I felt the blood go into my cheeks and hot words were upon my tongue's end, but I restrained them; the conditions for a quarrel were not favorable to my side of it. When I had mastered my chagrin and resentment I said:

"In my country when trusts are formed a great number of persons suffer, whether the general consumer does or not—many small dealers, middle men, drummers and general employees. The small dealer is driven out of the business by underselling. The middle man is frequently ignored, the trust dealing directly, or nearly so, with the consumer. The drummer is discharged because, competition having disappeared, custom must come without solicitation. Consolidation lets out swarms of employees of the individual concerns consolidated, for it is nearly as easy to conduct one large concern as a dozen smaller ones. These people get great sympathy from the public and the newspapers and their case is obviously pitiable. Was it not so in this country during the transition stage, and did not these poor gentlemen have to"—the right words would not come; I hardly knew how to finish. "Were they not compelled to go to work?" I finally asked, rather humbly.

The great official was silent for several minutes. Then he spoke.

"I am not sure that I understand you about our transition state. So far as our history goes matters with us have always been as they are to-day. To suppose them to have been otherwise would be to impugn the common sense of our ancestors. Nor do I quite know what you mean by 'small dealers,' 'middle men,' 'drummers,' and so forth."

He paused and fell into meditation, when suddenly his face was suffused with the light of a happy thought. It so elated him that he sprang to his feet and with his staff of office broke the heads of his Chief Admonisher of the Inimical and his Second Assistant Audible Sycophant. Then he said:

"I think I comprehend. Some eighty-five years ago, soon after my induction into office, there came to the court of the Panjandrum a man of this city who had been cast upon the island of Chicago (which I believe belongs to the American archipelago) and had passed many years there in business with the natives. Having learned all their customs and business methods he returned to his own country and laid before the Panjandrum a comprehensive scheme of commercial reform. He and his scheme were referred to me, the Panjandrum being graciously pleased to be unable to make head or tail of it. I may best explain it in its application to a single industry—the manufacture and sale of gootles."

"What is a gootle?" I asked.

"A metal weight for attachment to the tail of a donkey to keep him from braying," was the answer. "It is known in this country that a donkey cannot utter a note unless he can lift his tail. Then, as now, gootles were made by a single concern having a great capital invested and an immense plant, and employing an army of workmen. It dealt, as it does to-day, directly with consumers. Afflicted with a sonant donkey a man would write to the trust and receive his gootle by return mail, or go personally to the factory and carry his purchase home on his shoulder—according to where he lived. The reformer said this was primitive, crude and injurious to the interests of the public and especially the poor. He proposed that the members of the gootle trust divide their capital and each member go into the business of making gootles for himself—I do not mean for his personal use—in different parts of the country. But none of them was to sell to consumers, but to other men, who would sell in quantity to still other men, who would sell single gootles for domestic use. Each manufacturer would of course require a full complement of officers, clerks and so forth, as would the other men—everybody but the consumer—and each would have to support them and make a profit himself. Competition would be so sharp that solicitors would have to be employed to make sales; and they too must have a living out of the business. Honored stranger, am I right in my inference that the proposed system has something in common with the one which obtains in your own happy, enlightened and prosperous country, and which you would approve?"

I did not care to reply.

"Of course," the Jumjum continued, "all this would greatly have enhanced the cost of gootles, thereby lessening the sales, thereby reducing the output, thereby throwing a number of workmen out of employment. You see this, do you not, O guest of my country?"

"Pray tell me," I said, "what became of the reformer who proposed all this change?"

"All this change? Why, sir, the one-thousandth part is not told: he proposed that his system should be general: not only in the gootle trust, but every trust in the country was to be broken up in the same way! When I had him before me, and had stated my objections to the plan, I asked him what were its advantages.

"'Sir,' he replied, 'I speak for millions of gentlemen in

uncongenial employments, mostly manual and fatiguing. This would give them the kind of activity that they would like—such as their class enjoys in other countries where my system is in full flower, and where it is deemed so sacred that any proposal for its abolition or simplification by trusts is regarded with horror, especially by the working men.'

"Having reported to the Panjandrum (whose vermiform appendix may good angels have in charge) and received his orders, I called the reformer before me and addressed him thus:

"'Illustrious economist, I have the honor to inform you that in the royal judgment your proposal is the most absurd, impudent and audacious ever made; that the system which you propose to set up is revolutionary and mischievous beyond the dreams of treason; that only in a nation of rogues and idiots could it have a moment's toleration.'

"He was about to reply, but cutting his throat to intimate that the hearing was at an end, I withdrew from the Hall of Audience, as under similar circumstances I am about to do now."

I withdrew first by way of a window, and after a terrible journey of six years in the Dolorous Mountains and on the Desert of Despair came to the western coast. Here I built a ship and after a long voyage landed on one of the islands constituting the Kingdom of Tortirra.

THE KINGDOM OF TORTIRRA

Of this unknown country and its inhabitants I have written a large volume which nothing but the obstinacy of publishers has kept from the world, and which I trust will yet see the light. Naturally, I do not wish to publish at this time anything that will sate public curiosity, and this brief sketch will consist of such parts only of the work as I think can best be presented in advance without abating interest in what is to follow when Heaven shall have put it into the hearts of publishers to square their conduct with their interests. I must, however, frankly confess that my choice has been partly determined by other considerations. I offer here those parts of my narrative which I conceive to be the least credible—those which deal with the most monstrous and astounding follies of a strange people. Their ceremony of marriage by decapitation; their custom of facing to the rear when riding on horseback; their practice of walking on their hands in all ceremonial processions; their selection of the blind for military command; their pig-worship—these and many other comparatively natural particulars of their religious, political, intellectual and social life I reserve for treatment in the great work for which I shall soon ask public favor and acceptance.

In Tortirran politics, as in Tamtonian, the population is always divided into two, and sometimes three or four "parties," each having a "policy" and each conscientiously believing the policy of the other, or others, erroneous and destructive. In so far as these various and varying policies can be seen to have any relation whatever to practical affairs they can be seen also to be the result of purely selfish considerations. The self-deluded people flatter themselves that their elections are contests of principles, whereas they are only struggles of interests. They are very fond of the word slagthrit, "principle"; and when they believe themselves acting from some high moral motive they are capable of almost any monstrous injustice or stupid folly. This insane devotion to principle is craftily fostered by their political leaders who invent captivating phrases intended to confirm them in it; and these deluding aphorisms are diligently repeated until all the people have them in memory, with no knowledge of the fallacies which they conceal. One of these phrases is "Principles, not men." In the last analysis this is seen to mean that it is better to be governed by scoundrels professing one set of principles than by good men holding another. That a scoundrel will govern badly, regardless of the principles which he is supposed somehow to "represent," is a truth which, however obvious to our own enlightened intelligence, has never penetrated the dark understandings of the Tortirrans. It is chiefly through the dominance of the heresy fostered by this popular phrase that the political leaders are able to put base men into office to serve their own nefarious ends.

I have called the political contests of Tortirra struggles of interests. In nothing is this more clear (to the looker-on at the game) than in the endless disputes concerning restrictions on commerce. It must be understood that lying many leagues to the southeast of Tortirra are other groups of islands, also wholly unknown to people of our race. They are known by the general name of Gropilla-Stron (a term signifying "the Land of the Daydawn"), though it is impossible to ascertain why, and are inhabited by a powerful and hardy race, many of whom I have met in the capital of Tanga. The Stronagu, as they are called, are bold navigators and traders, their proas making long and hazardous voyages in all the adjacent seas to exchange commodities with other tribes. For many years they were welcomed in Tortirra with great hospitality and their goods eagerly purchased. They took back with them all manner of Tortirran products and nobody thought of questioning the mutual advantages of the exchange. But early in the present century a powerful Tortirran demagogue named Pragam began to persuade the people that commerce was piracy—that true prosperity consisted in consumption of domestic products and abstention from foreign. This extraordinary heresy soon gathered such head that Pragam was appointed Regent and invested with almost dictatorial powers. He at once distributed nearly the whole army among the seaport cities, and whenever a Stronagu trading proa attempted to land, the soldiery, assisted by the populace, rushed down to the beach, and with a terrible din of gongs and an insupportable discharge of stink-pots—the only offensive weapon known to Tortirran warfare—drove the laden vessels to sea, or if they persisted in anchoring destroyed them and smothered their crews in mud. The Tortirrans themselves not being a sea-going people, all communication between them and the rest of their little world soon ceased. But with it ceased the prosperity of Tortirra. Deprived of a market for their surplus products and compelled to forego the comforts and luxuries which they had obtained from abroad, the people began to murmur at the effect of their own folly. A reaction set in, a powerful opposition to Pragam and his policy was organized, and he was driven from power.

But the noxious tree that Pragam had planted in the fair garden of his country's prosperity had struck root too deeply to be altogether eradicated. It threw up shoots everywhere, and no sooner was one cut down than from roots underrunning the whole domain of political thought others sprang up with a vigorous and baleful growth. While the dictum that trade is piracy no longer commands universal acceptance, a majority of the populace still hold a modified form of it, and that "importation is theft" is to-day a cardinal political "principle" of a vast body of Tortirra's people. The chief expounders and protagonists of this doctrine are all directly or indirectly engaged in making or growing such articles as were formerly got by exchange with the Stronagu traders. The articles are generally inferior in quality, but consumers, not having the benefit of foreign competition, are compelled to pay extortionate prices for them, thus maintaining the unscrupulous producers in needless industries and a pernicious existence. But these active and intelligent rogues are too powerful to be driven out. They persuade their followers, among whom are many ignorant consumers, that this vestigial remnant of the old Pragam policy is all that keeps the nation from being desolated by small-pox and an epidemic of broken legs. It is impossible within these limits to give a full history of the strange delusion whose origin I have related. It has undergone many modifications and changes, as it is the nature of error to do, but the present situation is about this. The trading proas of the Stronagu are permitted to enter certain ports, but when one arrives she must anchor at a little distance from shore. Here she is boarded by an officer of the government, who ascertains the thickness of her keel, the number of souls on board and the amount and character of the merchandise she brings. From these data—the last being the main factor in the problem—the officer computes her unworthiness and adjudges a suitable penalty. The next day a scow manned by a certain number of soldiers pushes out and anchors within easy throw of her, and there is a frightful beating of gongs. When this has reached its lawful limit as to time it is hushed and the soldiers throw a stated number of stink-pots on board the offending craft. These, exploding as they strike, stifle the captain and crew with an intolerable odor. In the case of a large proa having a cargo of such commodities as the Tortirrans particularly need, this bombardment is continued for hours. At its conclusion the vessel is permitted to land and discharge her cargo without further molestation. Under these hard conditions importers find it impossible to do much business, the exorbitant wages demanded by seamen consuming most of the profit. No restrictions are now placed on the export trade, and vessels arriving empty are subjected to no penalties; but the Stronagu having other markets, in which they can sell as well as buy, cannot afford to go empty handed to Tortirra.

It will be obvious to the reader that in all this no question of "principle" is involved. A well-informed Tortirran's mental attitude with regard to the matter may be calculated with unfailing accuracy from a knowledge of his interests. If he produces anything which his countrymen want, and which in the absence of all restriction they could get more cheaply from the Stronagu than they can from him, he is in politics a Gakphew, or "Stinkpotter"; if not he is what that party derisively calls a Shokerbom, which signifies "Righteous Man"—for there is nothing which the Gakphews hold in so holy detestation as righteousness.

Nominally, Tortirra is an hereditary monarchy; virtually it is a democracy, for under a peculiar law of succession there is seldom an occupant of the throne, and all public affairs are conducted by a Supreme Legislature sitting at Felduchia, the capital of Tanga, to which body each island of the archipelago, twenty-nine in number, elects representatives in proportion to its population, the total membership being nineteen hundred and seventeen. Each island has a Subordinate Council for the management of local affairs and a

Head Chief charged with execution of the laws. There is also a Great Court at Felduchia, whose function it is to interpret the general laws of the Kingdom, passed by the Supreme Council, and a Minor Great Court at the capital of each island, with corresponding duties and powers. These powers are very loosely and vaguely defined, and are the subject of endless controversy everywhere, and nowhere more than in the courts themselves—such is the multiplicity of laws and so many are the contradictory decisions upon them, every decision constituting what is called a lantrag, or, as we might say, "precedent." The peculiarity of a lantrag, or previous decision, is that it is, or is not, binding, at the will of the honorable judge making a later one on a similar point. If he wishes to decide in the same way he quotes the previous decision with all the gravity that he would give to an exposition of the law itself; if not, he either ignores it altogether, shows that it is not applicable to the case under consideration (which, as the circumstances are never exactly the same, he can always do), or substitutes a contradictory lantrag and fortifies himself with that. There is a precedent for any decision that a judge may wish to make, but sometimes he is too indolent to search it out and cite it. Frequently, when the letter and intent of the law under which an action is brought are plainly hostile to the decision which it pleases him to render, the judge finds it easier to look up an older law, with which it is compatible, and which the later one, he says, does not repeal, and to base his decision on that; and there is a law for everything, just as there is a precedent. Failing to find, or not caring to look for, either precedent or statute to sustain him, he can readily show that any other decision than the one he has in will would be tokoli impelly; that is to say, contrary to public morals, and this, too, is considered a legitimate consideration, though on another occasion he may say, with public assent and approval, that it is his duty, not to make the law conform to justice, but to expound and enforce it as he finds it. In short, such is the confusion of the law and the public conscience that the courts of Tortirra do whatever they please, subject only to overruling by higher courts in the exercise of their pleasure; for great as is the number of minor and major tribunals, a case originating in the lowest is never really settled until it has gone through all the intermediate ones and been passed upon by the highest, to which it might just as well have been submitted at first. The evils of this astonishing system could not be even baldly catalogued in a lifetime. They are infinite in number and prodigious in magnitude. To the trained intelligence of the American observer it is incomprehensible how any, even the most barbarous, nation can endure them.

An important function of the Great Court and the Minor Great

Court is passing upon the validity of all laws enacted by the Supreme Council and the Subordinate Councils, respectively. The nation as a whole, as well as each separate island, has a fundamental law called the Trogodal, or, as we should say, the Constitution; and no law whatever that may be passed by the Council is final and determinate until the appropriate court has declared that it conforms to the Trogodal. Nevertheless every law is put in force the moment it is perfected and before it is submitted to the court. Indeed, not one in a thousand ever is submitted at all, that depending upon the possibility of some individual objecting to its action upon his personal interests, which few, indeed, can afford to do. It not infrequently occurs that some law which has for years been rigorously enforced, even by fines and imprisonment, and to which the whole commercial and social life of the nation has adjusted itself with all its vast property interests, is brought before the tribunal having final jurisdiction in the matter and coolly declared no law at all. The pernicious effect may be more easily imagined than related, but those who by loyal obedience to the statute all those years have been injured in property, those who are ruined by its erasure and those who may have suffered the severest penalties for its violation are alike without redress. It seems not to have occurred to the Tortirrans to require the court to inspect the law and determine its validity before it is put in force. It is, indeed, the traditional practice of these strange tribunals, when a case is forced upon them, to decide, not as many points of law as they can, but as few as they may; and this dishonest inaction is not only tolerated but commended as the highest wisdom. The consequence is that only those who make a profession of the law and live by it and find their account in having it as little understood by others as is possible can know which acts and parts of acts are in force and which are not. The higher courts, too, have arrogated to themselves the power of declaring unconstitutional even parts of the Constitution, frequently annulling most important provisions of the very instrument creating them!

A popular folly in Tortirra is the selection of representatives in the Councils from among that class of men who live by the law, whose sole income is derived from its uncertainties and perplexities. Obviously, it is to the interest of these men to make laws which shall be uncertain and perplexing—to confuse and darken legislation as much as they can. Yet in nearly all the Councils these men are the most influential and active element, and it is not uncommon to find them in a numerical majority. It is evident that the only check upon their ill-doing lies in the certainty of their disagreement as to the particular kind of confusion which they may think it expedient to create. Some will wish to accomplish their common object by one kind of verbal ambiguity, some by another; some by laws clearly enough (to them) unconstitutional, others by contradictory statutes, or statutes secretly repealing wholesome ones already existing. A clear, simple and just code would deprive them of their means of livelihood and compel them to seek some honest employment.

So great are the uncertainties of the law in Tortirra that an eminent judge once confessed to me that it was his conscientious belief that if all cases were decided by the impartial arbitrament of the do-tusis (a process similar to our "throw of the dice") substantial justice would be done far more frequently than under the present system; and there is reason to believe that in many instances cases at law are so decided—but only at the close of tedious and costly trials which have impoverished the litigants and correspondingly enriched the lawyers.

Of the interminable train of shames and brutalities entailed by this pernicious system, I shall mention here only a single one—the sentencing and punishment of an accused person in the midst of the proceedings against him, and while his guilt is not finally and definitively established. It frequently occurs that a man convicted of crime in one of the lower courts is at once hurried off to prison while he has still the right of appeal to a higher tribunal, and while that appeal is pending. After months and sometimes years of punishment his case is reached in the appellate court, his appeal found valid and a new trial granted, resulting in his acquittal. He has been imprisoned for a crime of which he is eventually declared not to have been properly convicted. But he has no redress; he is simply set free to bear through all his after life the stain of dishonor and nourish an ineffectual resentment. Imagine the storm of popular indignation that would be evoked in America by an instance of so foul injustice!

In the great public square of Itsami, the capital of Tortirra, stands a golden statue of Estari-Kumpro, a famous judge of the Civil Court[2]. This great man was celebrated throughout the kingdom for the wisdom and justice of his decisions and the virtues of his private life. So profound were the veneration in which he was held and the awe that his presence inspired, that none of the advocates in his court ever ventured to address him except in formal pleas: all motions, objections, and so forth, were addressed to the clerk and by him disposed of without dissent: the silence of the judge, who never was heard to utter a word, was understood as sanctioning the acts of his subordinate. For thirty years, promptly at sunrise, the

---

[2] Klikat um Delu Ovwi

great hall of justice was thrown open, disclosing the judge seated on a loftly dais beneath a black canopy, partly in shadow, and quite inaccessible. At sunset all proceedings for the day terminated, everyone left the hall and the portal closed. The decisions of this august and learned jurist were always read aloud by the clerk, and a copy supplied to the counsel on each side. They were brief, clear and remarkable, not only for their unimpeachable justice, but for their conformity to the fundamental principles of law. Not one of them was ever set aside, and during the last fifteen years of the great judge's service no litigant ever took an appeal, although none ever ventured before that infallible tribunal unless conscientiously persuaded that his cause was just.

One day it happened during the progress of an important trial that a sharp shock of earthquake occurred, throwing the whole assembly into confusion. When order had been restored a cry of horror and dismay burst from the multitude—the judge's head lay flattened upon the floor, a dozen feet below the bench, and from the neck of the rapidly collapsing body, which had pitched forward upon his desk, poured a thick stream of sawdust! For thirty years that great and good man had been represented by a stuffed manikin. For thirty years he had not entered his own court, nor heard a word of evidence or argument. At the moment of the accident to his simulacrum he was in his library at his home, writing his decision of the case on trial, and was killed by a falling chandelier. It was afterward learned that his clerk, twenty-five years dead, had all the time been personated by a twin brother, who was an idiot from birth and knew no law.

HITHER

Listening to the history of the golden statue in the great square, as related by a Tortirran storyteller, I fell asleep. On waking I found myself lying in a cot-bed amidst unfamiliar surroundings. A bandage was fastened obliquely about my head, covering my left eye, in which was a dull throbbing pain. Seeing an attendant near by I beckoned him to my bedside and asked: "Where am I?"

"Hospital," he replied, tersely but not unkindly. He added: "You have a bad eye." "Yes," I said, "I always had; but I could name more than one Tortirran who has a bad heart."

"What is a Tortirran?" he asked.

FOR THE AHKOOND

In the year 4591 I accepted from his gracious Majesty the Ahkoond of Citrusia a commission to explore the unknown region lying to the eastward of the Ultimate Hills, the range which that learned archæologist, Simeon Tucker, affirms to be identical with the "Rocky Mountains" of the ancients. For this proof of his Majesty's favor I was indebted, doubtless, to a certain distinction that I had been fortunate enough to acquire by explorations in the heart of Darkest Europe. His Majesty kindly offered to raise and equip a large expeditionary force to accompany me, and I was given the widest discretion in the matter of outfit; I could draw upon the royal treasury for any sum that I might require, and upon the royal university for all the scientific apparatus and assistance necessary to my purpose. Declining these encumbrances, I took my electric rifle and a portable waterproof case containing a few simple instruments and writing materials and set out. Among the instruments was, of course, an aerial isochronophone which I set by the one in the Ahkoond's private dining-room at the palace. His Majesty invariably dined alone at 18 o'clock, and sat at table six hours: it was my intention to send him all my reports at the hour of 23, just as dessert would be served, and he would be in a proper frame of mind to appreciate my discoveries and my services to the crown.

At 9 o'clock on the 13th of Meijh I left Sanf Rachisco and after a tedious journey of nearly fifty minutes arrived at Bolosson, the eastern terminus of the magnetic tube, on the summit of the Ultimate Hills. According to Tucker this was anciently a station on the Central Peaceful Railway, and was called "German," in honor of an illustrious dancing master. Prof. Nupper, however, says it was the ancient Nevraska, the capital of Kikago, and geographers generally have accepted that view.

Finding nothing at Bolosson to interest me except a fine view of the volcano Carlema, then in active eruption, I shouldered my electric rifle and with my case of instruments strapped upon my back plunged at once into the wilderness, down the eastern slope. As I descended the character of the vegetation altered. The pines of the higher altitudes gave place to oaks, these to ash, beech and maple. To these succeeded the tamarack and such trees as affect a moist and marshy habitat; and finally, when for four months I had been steadily descending, I found myself in a primeval flora consisting mainly of giant ferns, some of them as much as twenty surindas in diameter. They grew upon the margins of vast stagnant lakes which I was compelled to navigate by means of rude rafts made from their trunks lashed together with vines.

In the fauna of the region that I had traversed I had noted changes corresponding to those in the flora. On the upper slope there was nothing but the mountain sheep, but I passed successively through the habitats of the bear, the deer and the horse. This last mentioned creature, which our naturalists have believed long extinct, and which Dorbley declares our ancestors domesticated, I found in vast numbers on high table lands covered with grass upon which it feeds. The animal answers the current description of the horse very nearly, but all that I saw were destitute of the horns, and none had the characteristic forked tail. This member, on the contrary, is a tassel of straight wiry hair, reaching nearly to the ground—a surprising sight. Lower still I came upon the mastodon, the lion, the tiger, hippopotamus and alligator, all differing very little from those infesting Central Europe, as described in my "Travels in the Forgotten Continent."

In the lake region where I now found myself, the waters abounded with ichthyosauri, and along the margins the iguanodon dragged his obscene bulk in indolent immunity. Great flocks of pterodactyls, their bodies as large as those of oxen and their necks enormously long, clamored and fought in the air, the broad membranes of their wings making a singular musical humming, unlike anything that I had ever heard. Between them and the ichthyosauri there was incessant battle, and I was constantly reminded of the ancient poet's splendid and original comparison of man to

> dragons of the prime
> That tare each other in their slime.

When brought down with my electric rifle and properly roasted, the pterodactyl proved very good eating, particularly the pads of the toes.

In urging my raft along the shore line of one of the stagnant lagoons one day I was surprised to find a broad rock jutting out from the shore, its upper surface some ten coprets above the water. Disembarking, I ascended it, and on examination recognized it as the remnant of an immense mountain which at one time must have been 5,000 coprets in height and doubtless the dominating peak of a long range. From the striations all over it I discovered that it had been worn away to its present trivial size by glacial action. Opening my case of instruments, I took out my petrochronologue and applied it to the worn and scratched surface of the rock. The indicator at once pointed to K 59 xpc ½! At this astonishing result I was nearly overcome by excitement: the last erosions of the ice-masses upon this vestige of a stupendous mountain range which they had worn away, had been made as recently as the year 1945! Hastily applying my nymograph, I found that the name of this particular mountain at the time when it began to be enveloped in the mass of ice moving down upon it from the north, was "Pike's Peak." Other observations with other instruments showed that at that time the country circumjacent to it had been inhabited by a partly civilized race of people known as Galoots, the name of their capital city being Denver.

That evening at the hour of 23 I set up my aerial isochronophone[3] and reported to his gracious Majesty the Ahkoond as follows:

"Sire: I have the honor to report that I have made a startling discovery. The primeval region into which I have penetrated, as I informed you yesterday—the ichthyosaurus belt—was peopled by tribes considerably advanced in some of the arts almost within historic times: in 1920. They were exterminated by a glacial period not exceeding one hundred and twenty-five years in duration. Your Majesty can conceive the magnitude and violence of the natural forces which overwhelmed their country with moving sheets of ice not less that 5,000 coprets in thickness, grinding down every eminence, destroying (of course) all animal and vegetable life and leaving the region a fathomless bog of detritus. Out of this vast sea of mud Nature has had to evolve another creation, beginning de novo, with her lowest forms. It has long been known, your Majesty, that the region east of the Ultimate Hills, betwen them and the Wintry Sea, was once the seat of an ancient civilization, some scraps and shreds of whose history, arts and literature have been wafted to us across the gulf of time; but it was reserved for your gracious Majesty, through me, your humble and unworthy instrument, to ascertain the astonishing fact that these were a pre-glacial people—that between them and us stands, as it were, a wall of impenetrable ice. That all local records of this unfortunate race have perished your Majesty needs not to be told: we can supplement our present imperfect knowledge of them by instrumental observation only."

To this message I received the following extraordinary reply:

"All right—another bottle of—ice goes: push on—this cheese is

---

[3] This satire was published in the San Francisco Examiner many years before the invention of wireless telegraphy; so I retain my own name for the instrument.—A.B.

too—spare no effort to—hand me those nuts—learn all you can—damn you!"

His most gracious Majesty was being served with dessert, and served badly.

I now resolved to go directly north toward the source of the ice-flow and investigate its cause, but examining my barometer found that I was more than 8,000 coprets below the sea-level; the moving ice had not only ground down the face of the country, planing off the eminences and filling the depressions, but its enormous weight had caused the earth's crust to sag, and with the lessening of the weight from evaporation it had not recovered.

I had no desire to continue in this depression, as I should in going north, for I should find nothing but lakes, marshes and ferneries, infested with the same primitive and monstrous forms of life. So I continued my course eastward and soon had the satisfaction to find myself meeting the sluggish current of such streams as I encountered in my way. By vigorous use of the new double-distance telepode, which enables the wearer to step eighty surindas instead of forty, as with the instrument in popular use, I was soon again at a considerable elevation above the sea-level and nearly 200 prastams from "Pike's Peak." A little farther along the water courses began to flow to the eastward. The flora and fauna had again altered in character, and now began to grow sparse; the soil was thin and arid, and in a week I found myself in a region absolutely destitute of organic life and without a vestige of soil. All was barren rock. The surface for hundreds of prastams, as I continued my advance, was nearly level, with a slight dip to the eastward. The rock was singularly striated, the scratches arranged concentrically and in helicoidal curves. This circumstance puzzled me and I resolved to take some more instrumental observations, bitterly regretting my improvidence in not availing myself of the Ahkoond's permission to bring with me such apparatus and assistants as would have given me knowledge vastly more copious and accurate than I could acquire with my simple pocket appliances.

I need not here go into the details of my observations with such instruments as I had, nor into the calculations of which these observations were the basic data. Suffice it that after two months' labor I reported the results to his Majesty in Sanf Rachisco in the words following:

"Sire: It is my high privilege to apprise you of my arrival on the western slope of a mighty depression running through the center of the continent north and south, formerly known as the Mississippi Valley. It was once the seat of a thriving and prosperous population known as the Pukes, but is now a vast expanse of bare rock, from which every particle of soil and everything movable, including people, animals and vegetation, have been lifted by terrific cyclones and scattered afar, falling in other lands and at sea in the form of what was called meteoric dust! I find that these terrible phenomena began to occur about the year 1860, and lasted, with increasing frequency and power, through a century, culminating about the middle of that glacial period which saw the extinction of the Galoots and their neighboring tribes. There was, of course, a close connection between the two malefic phenomena, both, doubtless, being due to the same cause, which I have been unable to trace. A cyclone, I venture to remind your gracious Majesty, is a mighty whirlwind, accompanied by the most startling meteorological phenomena, such as electrical disturbances, floods of falling water, darkness and so forth. It moves with great speed, sucking up everything and reducing it to powder. In many days' journey I have not found a square copret of the country that did not suffer a visitation. If any human being escaped he must speedily have perished from starvation. For some twenty centuries the Pukes have been an extinct race, and their country a desolation in which no living thing can dwell, unless, like me, it is supplied with Dr. Blobob's Condensed Life-pills."

The Ahkoond replied that he was pleased to feel the most poignant grief for the fate of the unfortunate Pukes, and if I should by chance find the ancient king of the country I was to do my best to revive him with the patent resuscitator and present him the assurances of his Majesty's distinguished consideration; but as the politoscope showed that the nation had been a republic I gave myself no trouble in the matter.

My next report was made six months later and was in substance this:

"Sire: I address your Majesty from a point 430 coprets vertically above the site of the famous ancient city of Buffalo, once the capital of a powerful nation called the Smugwumps. I can approach no nearer because of the hardness of the snow, which is very firmly packed. For hundreds of prastams in every direction, and for thousands to the north and west, the land is covered with this substance, which, as your Majesty is doubtless aware, is extremely cold to the touch, but by application of sufficient heat can be turned into water. It falls from the heavens, and is believed by the learned among your Majesty's subjects to have a sidereal origin.

"The Smugwumps were a hardy and intelligent race, but they entertained the vain delusion that they could subdue Nature. Their year was divided into two seasons—summer and winter, the former warm, the latter cold. About the beginning of the nineteenth century according to my archæthermograph, the summers began to grow shorter and hotter, the winters longer and colder. At every point in their country, and every day in the year, when they had not the hottest weather ever known in that place, they had the coldest. When they were not dying by hundreds from sunstroke they were dying by thousands from frost. But these heroic and devoted people struggled on, believing that they were becoming acclimated faster than the climate was becoming insupportable. Those called away on business were even afflicted with nostalgia, and with a fatal infatuation returned to grill or freeze, according to the season of their arrival. Finally there was no summer at all, though the last flash of heat slew several millions and set most of their cities afire, and winter reigned eternal.

"The Smugwumps were now keenly sensible of the perils environing them, and, abandoning their homes, endeavored to reach their kindred, the Californians, on the western side of the continent in what is now your Majesty's ever-blessed realm. But it was too late: the snow growing deeper and deeper day by day, besieged them in their towns and dwellings, and they were unable to escape. The last one of them perished about the year 1943, and may God have mercy on his fool soul!"

To this dispatch the Ahkoond replied that it was the royal opinion that the Smugwumps were served very well right.

Some weeks later I reported thus:

"Sire: The country which your Majesty's munificence is enabling your devoted servant to explore extends southward and southwestward from Smugwumpia many hundreds of prastams, its eastern and southern borders being the Wintry Sea and the Fiery Gulf, respectively. The population in ancient times was composed of Whites and Blacks in about equal numbers and of about equal moral worth—at least that is the record on the dial of my ethnograph when set for the twentieth century and given a southern exposure. The Whites were called Crackers and the Blacks known as Coons.

"I find here none of the barrenness and desolation characterizing the land of the ancient Pukes, and the climate is not so rigorous and thrilling as that of the country of the late Smugwumps. It is, indeed, rather agreeable in point of temperature, and the soil being fertile exceedingly, the whole land is covered with a dense and rank vegetation. I have yet to find a square smig of it that is open ground, or one that is not the lair of some savage beast, the haunt of some venomous reptile, or the roost of some offensive bird. Crackers and Coons alike are long extinct, and these are their successors.

"Nothing could be more forbidding and unwholesome than these interminable jungles, with their horrible wealth of organic life in its most objectionable forms. By repeated observations with the necrohistoriograph I find that the inhabitants of this country, who had always been more or less dead, were wholly extirpated contemporaneously with the disastrous events which swept away the Galoots, the Pukes and the Smugwumps. The agency of their effacement was an endemic disorder known as yellow fever. The ravages of this frightful disease were of frequent recurrence, every point of the country being a center of infection; but in some seasons it was worse than in others. Once in every half century at first, and afterward every year[4] it broke out somewhere and swept over wide areas with such fatal effect that there were not enough of the living to plunder the dead; but at the first frost it would subside. During the ensuing two or three months of immunity the stupid survivors returned to the infected homes from which they had fled and were ready for the next outbreak. Emigration would have saved them all, but although the Californians (over whose happy and prosperous descendants your Majesty has the goodness to reign) invited them again and again to their beautiful land, where sickness and death were hardly known, they would not go, and by the year 1946 the last one of them, may it please your gracious Majesty, was dead and damned."

Having spoken this into the transmitter of the aerial isochronophone at the usual hour of 23 o'clock I applied the receiver to my ear, confidently expecting the customary commendation. Imagine my astonishment and dismay when my master's well-remembered voice was heard in utterance of the most awful imprecations on me and my work, followed by appalling threats against my life!

The Ahkoond had changed his dinner-time to five hours later and I had been speaking into the ears of an empty stomach!

---

[4] At one time it was foolishly believed that the disease had been eradicated by slapping the mosquitoes which were thought to produce it; but a few years later it broke out with greater violence than ever before, although the mosquitoes had left the country.

JOHN SMITH, LIBERATOR

(From a Newspaper of the Far Future)

At the quiet little village of Smithcester, which certain archæologists have professed to "identify" as the ancient London, will be celebrated to-day the thirtieth centennial anniversary of the birth of this remarkable man, the foremost figure of antiquity. The recurrence of what no more than six centuries ago was a popular fête day and even now is seldom permitted to pass without recognition by those to whom liberty means something more precious than opportunity for gain, excites a peculiar emotion. It matters little whether or no tradition has correctly fixed the time and place of Smith's birth. That he was born; that being born he wrought nobly at the work that his hand found to do; that by the mere force of his powerful intellect he established and perfected our present benign form of government, under which civilization has attained its highest and ripest development—these are facts beside which mere questions of chronology and geography are trivial and without significance.

That this extraordinary man originated the Smithocratic form of government is, perhaps, open to intelligent doubt; possibly it had a de facto existence in crude and uncertain shapes as early as the time of Edward XVII,—an existence local, unorganized and intermittent. But that he cleared it of its overlying errors and superstitions, gave it definite form and shaped it into a coherent and practical scheme there is unquestionable evidence in fragments of ancestral literature that have come down to us, disfigured though they are with amazingly contradictory statements regarding his birth, parentage and manner of life before he strode out upon the political stage as the Liberator of Mankind. It is said that Shakspar, a poet whose works had in their day a considerable vogue, though it is difficult to say why, alludes to him as "the noblest Roman of them all," our forefathers of the period being known as Romans or Englishmen, indifferently. In the only authentic fragment of Shakspar extant, however, this passage is not included.

Smith's military power is amply attested in an ancient manuscript of undoubted authenticity which has recently been translated from the Siamese. It is an account of the water battle of Loo, by an eye-witness whose name, unfortunately, has not reached us. It is stated that in this famous engagement Smith overthrew the great Neapolitan general, whom he captured and conveyed in chains to the island of Chickenhurst.

In his "Political History of Europe" the late Professor Mimble has this luminous sentence: "With the single exception of Ecuador there was no European government that the Liberator did not transform into a pure Smithocracy, and although some of them relapsed transiently into the primitive forms, and others grew into extravagant and fanciful systems begotten of the intellectual activity to which he had stirred the whole world, yet so firmly did he establish the principle that in the thirty-second century the civilized world had become, and has remained, virtually Smithocratic."

It may be noted here as a singular coincidence that the year which is believed to have seen the birth of him who founded rational government witnessed the death of him who perfected literature: Martin Farquhar Tupper (after Smith the most noted name in history) starved to death in the streets of London. Like that of Smith his origin is wrapped in obscurity. No fewer than seven British cities claim the honor of his nativity. Meager indeed is our knowledge of this only British bard whose works have endured through thirty centuries. All that is certain is that he was once arrested for deer-stealing; that, although blind, he fought a duel with a person named Salmasius, for which he was thrown into Bedford gaol, whence he escaped to the Tower of London; that the manuscript of his "Proverbial Philosophy" was for many years hidden in a hollow oak tree, where it was found by his grandmother, Ella Wheeler Tupper, who fled with it to America and published many brilliant passages from it over her own name. Had Smith and Tupper been contemporaries the iron deeds of the former would doubtless have been recorded in the golden pages of the latter, to the incalculable enrichment of Roman history.

Strangely unimpressible indeed must be the mind which, looking backward through the mists of the centuries upon the primitive race from which we are believed to have sprung, can repress a feeling of sympathetic interest. The names of John Smith and Martin Farquhar Tupper, blazoned upon the page of that dim past and surrounded by the lesser names of Shakspar, the first Neapolitan, Oliver Cornwell, that Mynheer Baloon who was known as the Flying Dutchman, Julia Cæsar, commonly known as the Serpent of the Nile—all these are richly suggestive. They call to mind the odd custom of wearing "clothes"; the incredible error of Copernicus and other wide and wild guesses of ancient "science"; the lost arts of telegramy, steam locomotion, printing, and the tempering of iron. They set us thinking of the zealous idolatry that led men on pious pilgrimages to the accessible regions about the north pole and into the then savage interior of Africa in search of the fountain of youth. They conjure up visions of bloodthirsty

"Emperors," tyrannical "Kings," vampire "Presidents," and robber "Parliaments"—grotesque and horrible shapes in terrible contrast with the serene and benign figures and features of our modern Smithocracy.

Let us to-day rejoice and give thanks to Bungoot that the old order of things has passed forever away. Let us praise Him that our lot has been cast in more wholesome days than those in which Smith wrought and Tupper sang. And yet let us not forget whatever there was of good, if any, in the pre-Smithian period, when men cherished quaint superstitions and rode on the backs of beasts—when they settled questions of right and expediency by counting noses—when cows were enslaved and women free—when science had not dawned to chase away the shadows of imagination and the fear of immortality—and when the cabalistic letters "A.D.," which from habit we still affix to numerals designating the date, had perhaps a known signification. It is indeed well to live in this golden age, under the benign sway of that supreme and culminating product of Smithocracy, our gracious sovereign, his Majesty John CLXXVIII.

BITS OF AUTOBIOGRAPHY

ON A MOUNTAIN

They say that the lumberman has looked upon the Cheat Mountain country and seen that it is good, and I hear that some wealthy gentlemen have been there and made a game preserve. There must be lumber and, I suppose, sport, but some things one could wish were ordered otherwise. Looking back upon it through the haze of near half a century, I see that region as a veritable realm of enchantment; the Alleghanies as the Delectable Mountains. I note again their dim, blue billows, ridge after ridge interminable, beyond purple valleys full of sleep, "in which it seemed always afternoon." Miles and miles away, where the lift of earth meets the stoop of sky, I discern an imperfection in the tint, a faint graying of the blue above the main range—the smoke of an enemy's camp.

It was in the autumn of that "most immemorial year," the 1861st of our Lord, and of our Heroic Age the first, that a small brigade of raw troops—troops were all raw in those days—had been pushed in across the Ohio border and after various vicissitudes of fortune and mismanagement found itself, greatly to its own surprise, at Cheat Mountain Pass, holding a road that ran from Nowhere to the southeast. Some of us had served through the summer in the "three-months' regiments," which responded to the President's first call for troops. We were regarded by the others with profound respect as "old soldiers." (Our ages, if equalized, would, I fancy, have given about twenty years to each man.) We gave ourselves, this aristocracy of service, no end of military airs; some of us even going to the extreme of keeping our jackets buttoned and our hair combed. We had been in action, too; had shot off a Confederate leg at Philippi, "the first battle of the war," and had lost as many as a dozen men at Laurel Hill and Carrick's Ford, whither the enemy had fled in trying, Heaven knows why, to get away from us. We now "brought to the task" of subduing the Rebellion a patriotism which never for a moment doubted that a rebel was a fiend accursed of God and the angels—one for whose extirpation by force and arms each youth of us considered himself specially "raised up."

It was a strange country. Nine in ten of us had never seen a mountain, nor a hill as high as a church spire, until we had crossed the Ohio River. In power upon the emotions nothing, I think, is comparable to a first sight of mountains. To a member of a plains-tribe, born and reared on the flats of Ohio or Indiana, a mountain region was a perpetual miracle. Space seemed to have taken on a new dimension; areas to have not only length and breadth, but thickness.

Modern literature is full of evidence that our great grandfathers looked upon mountains with aversion and horror. The poets of even the seventeenth century never tire of damning them in good, set terms. If they had had the unhappiness to read the opening lines of "The Pleasures of Hope," they would assuredly have thought Master Campbell had gone funny and should be shut up lest he do himself an injury.

The flatlanders who invaded the Cheat Mountain country had been suckled in another creed, and to them western Virginia—there was, as yet, no West Virginia—was an enchanted land. How we reveled in its savage beauties! With what pure delight we inhaled its fragrances of spruce and pine! How we stared with something like awe at its clumps of laurel!—real laurel, as we understood the matter, whose foliage had been once accounted excellent for the heads of illustrious Romans and such—mayhap to reduce the swelling. We carved its roots into fingerrings and pipes. We gathered spruce-gum and sent it to our sweethearts in letters. We ascended every hill within our picket-lines and called it a "peak."

And, by the way, during those halcyon days (the halcyon was there, too, chattering above every creek, as he is all over the world) we fought another battle. It has not got into history, but it had a real objective existence although by a felicitous afterthought called by us who were defeated a "reconnaissance in force." Its short and simple annals are that we marched a long way and lay down before a fortified camp of the enemy at the farther edge of a valley. Our commander had the forethought to see that we lay well out of range of the small-arms of the period. A disadvantage of this arrangement was that the enemy was out of reach of us as well, for our rifles were no better than his. Unfortunately—one might almost say unfairly—he had a few pieces of artillery very well protected, and with those he mauled us to the eminent satisfaction of his mind and heart. So we parted from him in anger and returned to our own place, leaving our dead—not many.

Among them was a chap belonging to my company, named Abbott; it is not odd that I recollect it, for there was something unusual in the manner of Abbott's taking off. He was lying flat upon his stomach and was killed by being struck in the side by a nearly spent cannon-shot that came rolling in among us. The shot remained in him until removed. It was a solid round-shot, evidently cast in some private foundry, whose proprietor, setting the laws of thrift above those of ballistics, had put his "imprint" upon it: it bore, in slightly sunken letters, the name "Abbott." That is what I was told—I was not present.

It was after this, when the nights had acquired a trick of biting and the morning sun appeared to shiver with cold, that we moved up to the summit of Cheat Mountain to guard the pass through which nobody wanted to go. Here we slew the forest and built us giant habitations (astride the road from Nowhere to the southeast) commodious to lodge an army and fitly loopholed for discomfiture of the adversary. The long logs that it was our pride to cut and carry! The accuracy with which we laid them one upon another, hewn to the line and bullet-proof! The Cyclopean doors that we hung, with sliding bolts fit to be "the mast of some great admiral"! And when we had "made the pile complete" some marplot of the Regular Army came that way and chatted a few moments with our commander, and we made an earthwork away off on one side of the road (leaving the other side to take care of itself) and camped outside it in tents! But the Regular Army fellow had not the heart to suggest the demolition of our Towers of Babel, and the foundations remain to this day to attest the genius of the American volunteer soldiery.

We were the original game-preservers of the Cheat Mountain region, for although we hunted in season and out of season over as wide an area as we dared to cover we took less game, probably, than would have been taken by a certain single hunter of disloyal views whom we scared away. There were bear galore and deer in quantity, and many a winter day, in snow up to his knees, did the writer of this pass in tracking bruin to his den, where, I am bound to say, I commonly left him. I agreed with my lamented friend, the late Robert Weeks, poet:

> Pursuit may be, it seems to me,
> Perfect without possession.

There can be no doubt that the wealthy sportsmen who have made a preserve of the Cheat Mountain region will find plenty of game if it has not died since 1861. We left it there.

Yet hunting and idling were not the whole of life's programme up there on that wild ridge with its shaggy pelt of spruce and firs, and in the riparian lowlands that it parted. We had a bit of war now and again. There was an occasional "affair of outposts"; sometimes a hazardous scout into the enemy's country, ordered, I fear, more to keep up the appearance of doing something than with a hope of accomplishing a military result. But one day it was bruited about that a movement in force was to be made on the enemy's position miles away, at the summit of the main ridge of the Alleghanies—the camp whose faint blue smoke we had watched for weary days. The movement was made, as was the fashion in those 'prentice days of warfare, in two columns, which were to pounce upon the foeman from opposite sides at the same moment. Led over unknown roads by untrusty guides, encountering obstacles not foreseen—miles apart and without communication, the two columns invariably failed to execute the movement with requisite secrecy and precision. The enemy, in enjoyment of that inestimable military advantage known in civilian speech as being "surrounded," always beat the attacking columns one at a time or, turning red-handed from the wreck of the first, frightened the other away.

All one bright wintry day we marched down from our eyrie; all one bright wintry night we climbed the great wooded ridge opposite. How romantic it all was; the sunset valleys full of visible sleep; the glades suffused and interpenetrated with moonlight; the long valley of the Greenbrier stretching away to we knew not what silent cities; the river itself unseen under its "astral body" of mist! Then there was the "spice of danger."

Once we heard shots in front; then there was a long wait. As we trudged on we passed something—some things—lying by the wayside. During another wait we examined them, curiously lifting the blankets from their yellow-clay faces. How repulsive they looked with their blood-smears, their blank, staring eyes, their teeth uncovered by contraction of the lips! The frost had begun already to whiten their deranged clothing. We were as patriotic as ever, but we did not wish to be that way. For an hour afterward the injunction of silence in the ranks was needless.

Repassing the spot the next day, a beaten, dispirited and exhausted force, feeble from fatigue and savage from defeat, some of us had life enough left, such as it was, to observe that these bodies had altered their position. They appeared also to have thrown off some of their clothing, which lay near by, in disorder. Their expression, too, had an added blankness—they had no faces.

As soon as the head of our straggling column had reached the spot a desultory firing had begun. One might have thought the living paid honors to the dead. No; the firing was a military execution; the condemned, a herd of galloping swine. They had eaten our fallen, but—touching magnanimity!—we did not eat theirs.

The shooting of several kinds was very good in the Cheat Mountain country, even in 1861.

WHAT I SAW OF SHILOH

I

This is a simple story of a battle; such a tale as may be told by a soldier who is no writer to a reader who is no soldier.

The morning of Sunday, the sixth day of April, 1862, was bright and warm. Reveille had been sounded rather late, for the troops, wearied with long marching, were to have a day of rest. The men were idling about the embers of their bivouac fires; some preparing breakfast, others looking carelessly to the condition of their arms and accoutrements, against the inevitable inspection; still others were chatting with indolent dogmatism on that never-failing theme, the end and object of the campaign. Sentinels paced up and down the confused front with a lounging freedom of mien and stride that would not have been tolerated at another time. A few of them limped unsoldierly in deference to blistered feet. At a little distance in rear of the stacked arms were a few tents out of which frowsy-headed officers occasionally peered, languidly calling to their servants to fetch a basin of water, dust a coat or polish a scabbard. Trim young mounted orderlies, bearing dispatches obviously unimportant, urged their lazy nags by devious ways amongst the men, enduring with unconcern their good-humored raillery, the penalty of superior station. Little negroes of not very clearly defined status and function lolled on their stomachs, kicking their long, bare heels in the sunshine, or slumbered peacefully, unaware of the practical waggery prepared by white hands for their undoing.

Presently the flag hanging limp and lifeless at headquarters was seen to lift itself spiritedly from the staff. At the same instant was heard a dull, distant sound like the heavy breathing of some great animal below the horizon. The flag had lifted its head to listen. There was a momentary lull in the hum of the human swarm; then, as the flag drooped the hush passed away. But there were some hundreds more men on their feet than before; some thousands of hearts beating with a quicker pulse.

Again the flag made a warning sign, and again the breeze bore to our ears the long, deep sighing of iron lungs. The division, as if it had received the sharp word of command, sprang to its feet, and stood in groups at "attention." Even the little blacks got up. I have since seen similar effects produced by earthquakes; I am not sure but the ground was trembling then. The mess-cooks, wise in their generation, lifted the steaming camp-kettles off the fire and stood by to cast out. The mounted orderlies had somehow disappeared.

Officers came ducking from beneath their tents and gathered in groups. Headquarters had become a swarming hive.

The sound of the great guns now came in regular throbbings—the strong, full pulse of the fever of battle. The flag flapped excitedly, shaking out its blazonry of stars and stripes with a sort of fierce delight. Toward the knot of officers in its shadow dashed from somewhere—he seemed to have burst out of the ground in a cloud of dust—a mounted aide-de-camp, and on the instant rose the sharp, clear notes of a bugle, caught up and repeated, and passed on by other bugles, until the level reaches of brown fields, the line of woods trending away to far hills, and the unseen valleys beyond were "telling of the sound," the farther, fainter strains half drowned in ringing cheers as the men ran to range themselves behind the stacks of arms. For this call was not the wearisome "general" before which the tents go down; it was the exhilarating "assembly," which goes to the heart as wine and stirs the blood like the kisses of a beautiful woman. Who that has heard it calling to him above the grumble of great guns can forget the wild intoxication of its music?

II

The Confederate forces in Kentucky and Tennessee had suffered a series of reverses, culminating in the loss of Nashville. The blow was severe: immense quantities of war material had fallen to the victor, together with all the important strategic points. General Johnston withdrew Beauregard's army to Corinth, in northern Mississippi, where he hoped so to recruit and equip it as to enable it to assume the offensive and retake the lost territory.

The town of Corinth was a wretched place—the capital of a swamp. It is a two days' march west of the Tennessee River, which here and for a hundred and fifty miles farther, to where it falls into the Ohio at Paducah, runs nearly north. It is navigable to this point—that is to say, to Pittsburg Landing, where Corinth got to it by a road worn through a thickly wooded country seamed with ravines and bayous, rising nobody knows where and running into the river under sylvan arches heavily draped with Spanish moss. In some places they were obstructed by fallen trees. The Corinth road was at certain seasons a branch of the Tennessee River. Its mouth was Pittsburg Landing. Here in 1862 were some fields and a house or two; now there are a national cemetery and other improvements.

It was at Pittsburg Landing that Grant established his army, with a river in his rear and two toy steamboats as a means of communication with the east side, whither General Buell with thirty thousand men was moving from Nashville to join him. The question has been asked, Why did General Grant occupy the enemy's side of the river in the face of a superior force before the arrival of Buell? Buell had a long way to come; perhaps Grant was weary of waiting. Certainly Johnston was, for in the gray of the morning of April 6th, when Buell's leading division was en bivouac near the little town of Savannah, eight or ten miles below, the Confederate forces, having moved out of Corinth two days before, fell upon Grant's advance brigades and destroyed them. Grant was at Savannah, but hastened to the Landing in time to find his camps in the hands of the enemy and the remnants of his beaten army cooped up with an impassable river at their backs for moral support. I have related how the news of this affair came to us at Savannah. It came on the wind—a messenger that does not bear copious details.

III

On the side of the Tennessee River, over against Pittsburg Landing, are some low bare hills, partly inclosed by a forest. In the dusk of the evening of April 6 this open space, as seen from the other side of the stream—whence, indeed, it was anxiously watched by thousands of eyes, to many of which it grew dark long before the sun went down—would have appeared to have been ruled in long, dark lines, with new lines being constantly drawn across. These lines were the regiments of Buell's leading division, which having moved up from Savannah through a country presenting nothing but interminable swamps and pathless "bottom lands," with rank overgrowths of jungle, was arriving at the scene of action breathless, footsore and faint with hunger. It had been a terrible race; some regiments had lost a third of their number from fatigue, the men dropping from the ranks as if shot, and left to recover or die at their leisure. Nor was the scene to which they had been invited likely to inspire the moral confidence that medicines physical fatigue. True, the air was full of thunder and the earth was trembling beneath their feet; and if there is truth in the theory of the conversion of force, these men were storing up energy from every shock that burst its waves upon their bodies. Perhaps this theory may better than another explain the tremendous endurance of men in battle. But the eyes reported only matter for despair.

Before us ran the turbulent river, vexed with plunging shells and obscured in spots by blue sheets of low-lying smoke. The two little steamers were doing their duty well. They came over to us empty and went back crowded, sitting very low in the water, apparently on the point of capsizing. The farther edge of the water could not be seen; the boats came out of the obscurity, took on their passengers and vanished in the darkness. But on the heights above, the battle was burning brightly enough; a thousand lights kindled and expired in every second of time. There were broad flushings in the sky, against which the branches of the trees showed black. Sudden flames burst out here and there, singly and in dozens. Fleeting streaks of fire crossed over to us by way of welcome. These expired in blinding flashes and fierce little rolls of smoke, attended with the peculiar metallic ring of bursting shells, and followed by the musical humming of the fragments as they struck into the ground on every side, making us wince, but doing little harm. The air was full of noises. To the right and the left the musketry rattled smartly and petulantly; directly in front it sighed and growled. To the experienced ear this meant that the death-line was an arc of which the river was the chord. There were deep, shaking explosions and smart shocks; the whisper of stray bullets and the hurtle of conical shells; the rush of round shot. There were faint, desultory cheers, such as announce a momentary or partial triumph. Occasionally, against the glare behind the trees, could be seen moving black figures, singularly distinct but apparently no longer than a thumb. They seemed to me ludicrously like the figures of demons in old allegorical prints of hell. To destroy these and all their belongings the enemy needed but another hour of daylight; the steamers in that case would have been doing him fine service by bringing more fish to his net. Those of us who had the good fortune to arrive late could then have eaten our teeth in impotent rage. Nay, to make his victory sure it did not need that the sun should pause in the heavens; one of the many random shots falling into the river would have done the business had chance directed it into the engine-room of a steamer. You can perhaps fancy the anxiety with which we watched them leaping down.

But we had two other allies besides the night. Just where the enemy had pushed his right flank to the river was the mouth of a wide bayou, and here two gunboats had taken station. They too were of the toy sort, plated perhaps with railway metals, perhaps with boiler-iron. They staggered under a heavy gun or two each. The bayou made an opening in the high bank of the river. The bank was a parapet, behind which the gunboats crouched, firing up the bayou as through an embrasure. The enemy was at this disadvantage: he could not get at the gunboats, and he could advance only by exposing his flank to their ponderous missiles, one of which would have broken a half-mile of his bones and made nothing of it. Very annoying this must have been—these twenty gunners beating back an army because a sluggish creek had been pleased to fall into a river at one point rather than another. Such is the part that accident may play in the game of war.

As a spectacle this was rather fine. We could just discern the black bodies of these boats, looking very much like turtles. But when they let off their big guns there was a conflagration. The river shuddered in its banks, and hurried on, bloody, wounded, terrified! Objects a mile away sprang toward our eyes as a snake strikes at the face of its victim. The report stung us to the brain, but we blessed it audibly. Then we could hear the great shell tearing away through the air until the sound died out in the distance; then, a surprisingly long time afterward, a dull, distant explosion and a sudden silence of small-arms told their own tale.

IV

There was, I remember, no elephant on the boat that passed us across that evening, nor, I think, any hippopotamus. These would have been out of place. We had, however, a woman. Whether the baby was somewhere on board I did not learn. She was a fine creature, this woman; somebody's wife. Her mission, as she understood it, was to inspire the failing heart with courage; and when she selected mine I felt less flattered by her preference than astonished by her penetration. How did she learn? She stood on the upper deck with the red blaze of battle bathing her beautiful face, the twinkle of a thousand rifles mirrored in her eyes; and displaying a small ivory-handled pistol, she told me in a sentence punctuated by the thunder of great guns that if it came to the worst she would do her duty like a man! I am proud to remember that I took off my hat to this little fool.

V

Along the sheltered strip of beach between the river bank and the water was a confused mass of humanity—several thousands of men. They were mostly unarmed; many were wounded; some dead. All the camp-following tribes were there; all the cowards; a few officers. Not one of them knew where his regiment was, nor if he had a regiment. Many had not. These men were defeated, beaten, cowed. They were deaf to duty and dead to shame. A more demented crew never drifted to the rear of broken battalions. They would have stood in their tracks and been shot down to a man by a provost-marshal's guard, but they could not have been urged up that bank. An army's bravest men are its cowards. The death which they would not meet at the hands of the enemy they will meet at the hands of their officers, with never a flinching.

Whenever a steamboat would land, this abominable mob had to be kept off her with bayonets; when she pulled away, they sprang on her and were pushed by scores into the water, where they were suffered to drown one another in their own way. The men disembarking insulted them, shoved them, struck them. In return they expressed their unholy delight in the certainty of our destruction by the enemy.

By the time my regiment had reached the plateau night had put an end to the struggle. A sputter of rifles would break out now and then, followed perhaps by a spiritless hurrah. Occasionally a shell from a far-away battery would come pitching down somewhere near, with a whir crescendo, or flit above our heads with a whisper like that made by the wings of a night bird, to smother itself in the river. But there was no more fighting. The gunboats, however, blazed away at set intervals all night long, just to make the enemy uncomfortable and break him of his rest.

For us there was no rest. Foot by foot we moved through the dusky fields, we knew not whither. There were men all about us, but no camp-fires; to have made a blaze would have been madness. The men were of strange regiments; they mentioned the names of unknown generals. They gathered in groups by the wayside, asking eagerly our numbers. They recounted the depressing incidents of the day. A thoughtful officer shut their mouths with a sharp word as he passed; a wise one coming after encouraged them to repeat their doleful tale all along the line.

Hidden in hollows and behind clumps of rank brambles were large tents, dimly lighted with candles, but looking comfortable. The kind of comfort they supplied was indicated by pairs of men entering and reappearing, bearing litters; by low moans from within and by long rows of dead with covered faces outside. These tents were constantly receiving the wounded, yet were never full; they were continually ejecting the dead, yet were never empty. It was as if the helpless had been carried in and murdered, that they might not hamper those whose business it was to fall to-morrow.

The night was now black-dark; as is usual after a battle, it had begun to rain. Still we moved; we were being put into position by somebody. Inch by inch we crept along, treading on one another's heels by way of keeping together. Commands were passed along the line in whispers; more commonly none were given. When the men had pressed so closely together that they could advance no farther they stood stock-still, sheltering the locks of their rifles with their ponchos. In this position many fell asleep. When those in front suddenly stepped away those in the rear, roused by the tramping, hastened after with such zeal that the line was soon choked again. Evidently the head of the division was being piloted at a snail's pace by some one who did not feel sure of his ground. Very often we struck our feet against the dead; more frequently against those who still had spirit enough to resent it with a moan. These were lifted carefully to one side and abandoned. Some had sense enough to ask in their weak way for water. Absurd! Their clothes were soaken, their hair dank; their white faces, dimly discernible, were clammy and cold. Besides, none of us had any water. There was plenty coming, though, for before midnight a thunderstorm broke upon us with great violence. The rain, which had for hours been a dull drizzle, fell with a copiousness that stifled us; we moved in running water up to our ankles. Happily, we were in a forest of great trees heavily "decorated" with Spanish moss, or with an enemy standing to his guns the disclosures of the lightning might have been inconvenient. As it was, the incessant blaze enabled us to consult our watches and encouraged us by displaying our numbers; our black, sinuous line, creeping like a giant serpent beneath the trees, was apparently interminable. I am almost ashamed to say how sweet I found the companionship of those coarse men.

So the long night wore away, and as the glimmer of morning crept in through the forest we found ourselves in a more open country. But where? Not a sign of battle was here. The trees were neither splintered nor scarred, the underbrush was unmown, the ground had no footprints but our own. It was as if we had broken into glades sacred to eternal silence. I should not have been surprised to see sleek leopards come fawning about our feet, and milk-white deer confront us with human eyes.

A few inaudible commands from an invisible leader had placed us in order of battle. But where was the enemy? Where, too, were the riddled regiments that we had come to save? Had our other divisions arrived during the night and passed the river to assist us? or were we to oppose our paltry five thousand breasts to an army flushed with victory? What protected our right? Who lay upon our left? Was there really anything in our front?

There came, borne to us on the raw morning air, the long, weird note of a bugle. It was directly before us. It rose with a low, clear, deliberate warble, and seemed to float in the gray sky like the note of a lark. The bugle calls of the Federal and the Confederate armies were the same: it was the "assembly"! As it died away I observed that the atmosphere had suffered a change; despite the equilibrium established by the storm, it was electric. Wings were growing on blistered feet. Bruised muscles and jolted bones, shoulders pounded by the cruel knapsack, eyelids leaden from lack of sleep—all were pervaded by the subtle fluid, all were unconscious of their clay. The men thrust forward their heads, expanded their eyes and clenched their teeth. They breathed hard, as if throttled by tugging at the leash. If you had laid your hand in the beard or hair of one of these men it would have crackled and shot sparks.

VI

I suppose the country lying between Corinth and Pittsburg Landing could boast a few inhabitants other than alligators. What manner of people they were it is impossible to say, inasmuch as the fighting dispersed, or possibly exterminated them; perhaps in merely classing them as non-saurian I shall describe them with sufficient particularity and at the same time avert from myself the natural suspicion attaching to a writer who points out to persons who do not know him the peculiarities of persons whom he does not know. One thing, however, I hope I may without offense affirm of these swamp-dwellers—they were pious. To what deity their veneration was given—whether, like the Egyptians, they worshiped the crocodile, or, like other Americans, adored themselves, I do not presume to guess. But whoever, or whatever, may have been the divinity whose ends they shaped, unto Him, or It, they had builded a temple. This humble edifice, centrally situated in the heart of a solitude, and conveniently accessible to the supersylvan crow, had been christened Shiloh Chapel, whence the name of the battle. The fact of a Christian church—assuming it to have been a Christian church—giving name to a wholesale cutting of Christian throats by Christian hands need not be dwelt on here; the frequency of its recurrence in the history of our species has somewhat abated the moral interest that would otherwise attach to it.

VII

Owing to the darkness, the storm and the absence of a road, it had been impossible to move the artillery from the open ground about the Landing. The privation was much greater in a moral than in a material sense. The infantry soldier feels a confidence in this cumbrous arm quite unwarranted by its actual achievements in thinning out the opposition. There is something that inspires confidence in the way a gun dashes up to the front, shoving fifty or a hundred men to one side as if it said, "Permit me!" Then it squares its shoulders, calmly dislocates a joint in its back, sends away its twenty-four legs and settles down with a quiet rattle which says as plainly as possible, "I've come to stay." There is a superb scorn in its grimly defiant attitude, with its nose in the air; it appears not so much to threaten the enemy as deride him.

Our batteries were probably toiling after us somewhere; we could only hope the enemy might delay his attack until they should arrive. "He may delay his defense if he like," said a sententious young officer to whom I had imparted this natural wish. He had read the signs aright; the words were hardly spoken when a group of staff officers about the brigade commander shot away in divergent lines as if scattered by a whirlwind, and galloping each to the commander of a regiment gave the word. There was a momentary confusion of tongues, a thin line of skirmishers detached itself from the compact front and pushed forward, followed by its diminutive reserves of half a company each—one of which platoons it was my fortune to command. When the straggling line of skirmishers had swept four or five hundred yards ahead, "See," said one of my comrades, "she moves!" She did indeed, and in fine style, her front as straight as a string, her reserve regiments in columns doubled on the center, following in true subordination; no braying of brass to apprise the enemy, no fifing and drumming to amuse him; no ostentation of gaudy flags; no nonsense. This was a matter of business.

In a few moments we had passed out of the singular oasis that had so marvelously escaped the desolation of battle, and now the evidences of the previous day's struggle were present in profusion. The ground was tolerably level here, the forest less dense, mostly clear of undergrowth, and occasionally opening out into small natural meadows. Here and there were small pools—mere discs of rainwater with a tinge of blood. Riven and torn with cannon-shot, the trunks of the trees protruded bunches of splinters like hands, the fingers above the wound interlacing with those below. Large branches had been lopped, and hung their green heads to the ground, or swung critically in their netting of vines, as in a hammock. Many had been cut clean off and their masses of foliage seriously impeded the progress of the troops. The bark of these trees, from the root upward to a height of ten or twenty feet, was so thickly pierced with bullets and grape that one could not have laid a hand on it without covering several punctures. None had escaped. How the human body survives a storm like this must be explained by the fact that it is exposed to it but a few moments at a time, whereas these grand old trees had had no one to take their places, from the rising to the going down of the sun. Angular bits of iron, concavo-convex, sticking in the sides of muddy depressions, showed where shells had exploded in their furrows. Knapsacks, canteens, haversacks distended with soaken and swollen biscuits, gaping to disgorge, blankets beaten into the soil by the rain, rifles with bent barrels or splintered stocks, waist-belts, hats and the omnipresent sardine-box—all the wretched debris of the battle still littered the spongy earth as far as one could see, in every direction. Dead horses were everywhere; a few disabled caissons, or limbers, reclining on one elbow, as it were; ammunition wagons standing disconsolate behind four or six sprawling mules. Men? There were men enough; all dead, apparently, except one, who lay near where I had halted my platoon to await the slower movement of the line—a Federal sergeant, variously hurt, who had been a fine giant in his time. He lay face upward, taking in his breath in convulsive, rattling snorts, and blowing it out in sputters of froth which crawled creamily down his cheeks, piling itself alongside his neck and ears. A bullet had clipped a groove in his skull, above the temple; from this the brain protruded in bosses, dropping off in flakes and strings. I had not previously known one could get on, even in this unsatisfactory fashion, with so little brain. One of my men, whom I knew for a womanish fellow, asked if he should put his bayonet through him. Inexpressibly shocked by the cold-blooded proposal, I told him I thought not; it was unusual, and too many were looking.

VIII

It was plain that the enemy had retreated to Corinth. The arrival of our fresh troops and their successful passage of the river had disheartened him. Three or four of his gray cavalry videttes moving amongst the trees on the crest of a hill in our front, and galloping out of sight at the crack of our skirmishers' rifles, confirmed us in the belief; an army face to face with its enemy does not employ cavalry to watch its front. True, they might be a general and his staff. Crowning this rise we found a level field, a quarter of a mile in width; beyond it a gentle acclivity, covered with an undergrowth of young oaks, impervious to sight. We pushed on into the open, but the division halted at the edge. Having orders to conform to its movements, we halted too; but that did not suit; we received an intimation to proceed. I had performed this sort of service before, and in the exercise of my discretion deployed my platoon, pushing it forward at a run, with trailed arms, to strengthen the skirmish line, which I overtook some thirty or forty yards from the wood. Then—I can't describe it—the forest seemed all at once to flame up and disappear with a crash like that of a great wave upon the beach—a crash that expired in hot hissings, and the sickening "spat" of lead against flesh. A dozen of my brave fellows tumbled over like ten-pins. Some struggled to their feet, only to go down again, and yet again. Those who stood fired into the smoking brush and doggedly retired. We had expected to find, at most, a line of skirmishers similar to our own; it was with a view to overcoming them by a sudden coup at the moment of collision that I had thrown forward my little reserve. What we had found was a line of battle, coolly holding its fire till it could count our teeth. There was no more to be done but get back across the open ground, every superficial yard of which was throwing up its little jet of mud provoked by an impinging bullet. We got back, most of us, and I shall never forget the ludicrous incident of a young officer who had taken part in the affair walking up to his colonel, who had been a calm and apparently impartial spectator, and gravely reporting: "The enemy is in force just beyond this field, sir."

IX

In subordination to the design of this narrative, as defined by its title, the incidents related necessarily group themselves about my own personality as a center; and, as this center, during the few terrible hours of the engagement, maintained a variably constant relation to the open field already mentioned, it is important that the reader should bear in mind the topographical and tactical features of the local situation. The hither side of the field was occupied by the front of my brigade—a length of two regiments in line, with proper intervals for field batteries. During the entire fight the enemy held the slight wooded acclivity beyond. The debatable ground to the right and left of the open was broken and thickly wooded for miles, in some places quite inaccessible to artillery and at very few points offering opportunities for its successful employment. As a consequence of this the two sides of the field were soon studded thickly with confronting guns, which flamed away at one another with amazing zeal and rather startling effect. Of course, an infantry attack delivered from either side was not to be thought of when the covered flanks offered inducements so unquestionably superior; and I believe the riddled bodies of my poor skirmishers were the only ones left on this "neutral ground" that day. But there was a very pretty line of dead continually growing in our rear, and doubtless the enemy had at his back a similar encouragement.

The configuration of the ground offered us no protection. By lying flat on our faces between the guns we were screened from view by a straggling row of brambles, which marked the course of an obsolete fence; but the enemy's grape was sharper than his eyes, and it was poor consolation to know that his gunners could not see what they were doing, so long as they did it. The shock of our own pieces nearly deafened us, but in the brief intervals we could hear the battle roaring and stammering in the dark reaches of the forest to the right and left, where our other divisions were dashing themselves again and again into the smoking jungle. What would we not have given to join them in their brave, hopeless task! But to lie inglorious beneath showers of shrapnel darting divergent from the unassailable sky—meekly to be blown out of life by level gusts of grape—to clench our teeth and shrink helpless before big shot pushing noisily through the consenting air—this was horrible! "Lie down, there!" a captain would shout, and then get up himself to see that his order was obeyed. "Captain, take cover, sir!" the lieutenant-colonel would shriek, pacing up and down in the most exposed position that he could find.

O those cursed guns!—not the enemy's, but our own. Had it not been for them, we might have died like men. They must be supported, forsooth, the feeble, boasting bullies! It was impossible to conceive that these pieces were doing the enemy as excellent a mischief as his were doing us; they seemed to raise their "cloud by day" solely to direct aright the streaming procession of Confederate missiles. They no longer inspired confidence, but begot apprehension; and it was with grim satisfaction that I saw the carriage of one and another smashed into matchwood by a whooping shot and bundled out of the line.

X

The dense forests wholly or partly in which were fought so many battles of the Civil War, lay upon the earth in each autumn a thick deposit of dead leaves and stems, the decay of which forms a soil of surprising depth and richness. In dry weather the upper stratum is as inflammable as tinder. A fire once kindled in it will spread with a slow, persistent advance as far as local conditions permit, leaving a bed of light ashes beneath which the less combustible accretions of previous years will smolder until extinguished by rains. In many of the engagements of the war the fallen leaves took fire and roasted the fallen men. At Shiloh, during the first day's fighting, wide tracts of woodland were burned over in this way and scores of wounded who might have recovered perished in slow torture. I remember a deep ravine a little to the left and rear of the field I have described, in which, by some mad freak of heroic incompetence, a part of an Illinois regiment had been surrounded, and refusing to surrender was destroyed, as it very well deserved. My regiment having at last been relieved at the guns and moved over to the heights above this ravine for no obvious purpose, I obtained leave to go down into the valley of death and gratify a reprehensible curiosity.

Forbidding enough it was in every way. The fire had swept every superficial foot of it; and at every step I sank into ashes to the ankle. It had contained a thick undergrowth of young saplings, every one of which had been severed by a bullet, the foliage of the prostrate tops being afterward burnt and the stumps charred. Death had put his sickle into this thicket and fire had gleaned the field. Along a line which was not that of extreme depression, but was at every point significantly equidistant from the heights on either hand, lay the bodies, half buried in ashes; some in the unlovely looseness of attitude denoting sudden death by the bullet, but by far the greater number in postures of agony that told of the tormenting flame. Their clothing was half burnt away—their hair and beard entirely; the rain had come too late to save their nails. Some were swollen to double girth; others shriveled to manikins. According to degree of exposure, their faces were bloated and black or yellow and shrunken. The contraction of muscles which had given them claws for hands had cursed each countenance with a hideous grin. Faugh! I cannot catalogue the charms of these gallant gentlemen who had got what they enlisted for.

XI

It was now three o'clock in the afternoon, and raining. For fifteen hours we had been wet to the skin. Chilled, sleepy, hungry and disappointed—profoundly disgusted with the inglorious part to which they had been condemned—the men of my regiment did everything doggedly. The spirit had gone quite out of them. Blue sheets of powder smoke, drifting amongst the trees, settling against the hillsides and beaten into nothingness by the falling rain, filled the air with their peculiar pungent odor, but it no longer stimulated. For miles on either hand could be heard the hoarse murmur of the battle, breaking out near by with frightful distinctness, or sinking to a murmur in the distance; and the one sound aroused no more attention than the other.

We had been placed again in rear of those guns, but even they and their iron antagonists seemed to have tired of their feud, pounding away at one another with amiable infrequency. The right of the regiment extended a little beyond the field. On the prolongation of the line in that direction were some regiments of another division, with one in reserve. A third of a mile back lay the remnant of somebody's brigade looking to its wounds. The line of forest bounding this end of the field stretched as straight as a wall from the right of my regiment to Heaven knows what regiment of the enemy. There suddenly appeared, marching down along this wall, not more than two hundred yards in our front, a dozen files of gray-clad men with rifles on the right shoulder. At an interval of fifty yards they were followed by perhaps half as many more; and in fair supporting distance of these stalked with confident mien a single man! There seemed to me something indescribably ludicrous in the advance of this handful of men upon an army, albeit with their left flank protected by a forest. It does not so impress me now. They were the exposed flanks of three lines of infantry, each half a mile in length. In a moment our gunners had grappled with the nearest pieces, swung them half round, and were pouring streams of canister into the invaded wood. The infantry rose in masses, springing into line. Our threatened regiments stood like a wall, their loaded rifles at "ready," their bayonets hanging quietly in the scabbards. The right wing of my own regiment was thrown slightly backward to threaten the flank of the assault. The battered brigade away to the rear pulled itself together.

Then the storm burst. A great gray cloud seemed to spring out of the forest into the faces of the waiting battalions. It was received with a crash that made the very trees turn up their leaves. For one instant the assailants paused above their dead, then struggled forward, their bayonets glittering in the eyes that shone behind the smoke. One moment, and those unmoved men in blue would be impaled. What were they about? Why did they not fix bayonets? Were they stunned by their own volley? Their inaction was maddening! Another tremendous crash!—the rear rank had fired! Humanity, thank Heaven! is not made for this, and the shattered gray mass drew back a score of paces, opening a feeble fire. Lead had scored its old-time victory over steel; the heroic had broken its great heart against the commonplace. There are those who say that it is sometimes otherwise.

All this had taken but a minute of time, and now the second Confederate line swept down and poured in its fire. The line of blue staggered and gave way; in those two terrific volleys it seemed to have quite poured out its spirit. To this deadly work our reserve regiment now came up with a run. It was surprising to see it spitting fire with never a sound, for such was the infernal din that the ear could take in no more. This fearful scene was enacted within fifty paces of our toes, but we were rooted to the ground as if we had grown there. But now our commanding officer rode from behind us to the front, waved his hand with the courteous gesture that says apres vous, and with a barely audible cheer we sprang into the fight. Again the smoking front of gray receded, and again, as the enemy's third line emerged from its leafy covert, it pushed forward across the piles of dead and wounded to threaten with protruded steel. Never was seen so striking a proof of the paramount importance of numbers. Within an area of three hundred yards by fifty there struggled for front places no fewer than six regiments; and the accession of each, after the first collision, had it not been immediately counterpoised, would have turned the scale.

As matters stood, we were now very evenly matched, and how long we might have held out God only knows. But all at once something appeared to have gone wrong with the enemy's left; our men had somewhere pierced his line. A moment later his whole front gave way, and springing forward with fixed bayonets we pushed him in utter confusion back to his original line. Here, among the tents from which Grant's people had been expelled the day before, our broken and disordered regiments inextricably intermingled, and drunken with the wine of triumph, dashed confidently against a pair of trim battalions, provoking a tempest of hissing lead that made us stagger under its very weight. The sharp onset of another against our flank sent us whirling back with fire at our heels and fresh foes in merciless pursuit—who in their turn were broken upon the front of the invalided brigade previously mentioned, which had moved up from the rear to assist in this lively work.

As we rallied to reform behind our beloved guns and noted the ridiculous brevity of our line—as we sank from sheer fatigue, and tried to moderate the terrific thumping of our hearts—as we caught our breath to ask who had seen such-and-such a comrade, and laughed hysterically at the reply—there swept past us and over us into the open field a long regiment with fixed bayonets and rifles on the right shoulder. Another followed, and another; two—three—four! Heavens! where do all these men come from, and why did they not come before? How grandly and confidently they go sweeping on like long blue waves of ocean chasing one another to the cruel rocks! Involuntarily we draw in our weary feet beneath us as we sit, ready to spring up and interpose our breasts when these gallant lines shall come back to us across the terrible field, and sift brokenly through among the trees with spouting fires at their backs. We still our breathing to catch the full grandeur of the volleys that are to tear them to shreds. Minute after minute passes and the sound does not come. Then for the first time we note that the silence of the whole region is not comparative, but absolute. Have we become stone deaf? See; here comes a stretcher-bearer, and there a surgeon! Good heavens! a chaplain!

The battle was indeed at an end.

XII

And this was, O so long ago! How they come back to me—dimly and brokenly, but with what a magic spell—those years of youth when I was soldiering! Again I hear the far warble of blown bugles. Again I see the tall, blue smoke of camp-fires ascending from the dim valleys of Wonderland. There steals upon my sense the ghost of an odor from pines that canopy the ambuscade. I feel upon my cheek the morning mist that shrouds the hostile camp unaware of its doom, and my blood stirs at the ringing rifle-shot of the solitary sentinel. Unfamiliar landscapes, glittering with sunshine or sullen with rain, come to me demanding recognition, pass, vanish and give place to others. Here in the night stretches a wide and blasted field studded with half-extinct fires burning redly with I know not what presage of evil. Again I shudder as I note its desolation and its awful silence. Where was it? To what monstrous inharmony of death was it the visible prelude?

O days when all the world was beautiful and strange; when unfamiliar constellations burned in the Southern midnights, and the mocking-bird poured out his heart in the moon-gilded magnolia; when there was something new under a new sun; will your fine, far memories ever cease to lay contrasting pictures athwart the harsher features of this later world, accentuating the ugliness of the longer and tamer life? Is it not strange that the phantoms of a blood-stained period have so airy a grace and look with so tender eyes?—that I recall with difficulty the danger and death and horrors of the time, and without effort all that was gracious and picturesque? Ah, Youth, there is no such wizard as thou! Give me but one touch of thine artist hand upon the dull canvas of the Present; gild for but one moment the drear and somber scenes of to-day, and I will willingly surrender an other life than the one that I should have thrown away at Shiloh.

A LITTLE OF CHICKAMAUGA

The history of that awful struggle is well known—I have not the intention to record it here, but only to relate some part of what I saw of it; my purpose not instruction, but entertainment.

I was an officer of the staff of a Federal brigade. Chickamauga was not my first battle by many, for although hardly more than a boy in years, I had served at the front from the beginning of the trouble, and had seen enough of war to give me a fair understanding of it. We knew well enough that there was to be a fight: the fact that we did not want one would have told us that, for Bragg always retired when we wanted to fight and fought when we most desired peace. We had manoeuvred him out of Chattanooga, but had not manoeuvred our entire army into it, and he fell back so sullenly that those of us who followed, keeping him actually in sight, were a good deal more concerned about effecting a junction with the rest of our army than to push the pursuit. By the time that Rosecrans had got his three scattered corps together we were a long way from Chattanooga, with our line of communication with it so exposed that Bragg turned to seize it. Chickamauga was a fight for possession of a road.

Back along this road raced Crittenden's corps, with those of Thomas and McCook, which had not before traversed it. The whole army was moving by its left.

There was sharp fighting all along and all day, for the forest was so dense that the hostile lines came almost into contact before fighting was possible. One instance was particularly horrible. After some hours of close engagement my brigade, with foul pieces and exhausted cartridge boxes, was relieved and withdrawn to the road to protect several batteries of artillery—probably two dozen pieces—which commanded an open field in the rear of our line. Before our weary and virtually disarmed men had actually reached the guns the line in front gave way, fell back behind the guns and went on, the Lord knows whither. A moment later the field was gray with Confederates in pursuit. Then the guns opened fire with grape and canister and for perhaps five minutes—it seemed an hour—nothing could be heard but the infernal din of their discharge and nothing seen through the smoke but a great ascension of dust from the smitten soil. When all was over, and the dust cloud had lifted, the spectacle was too dreadful to describe. The Confederates were still there—all of them, it seemed—some almost under the muzzles of the guns. But not a man of all these brave fellows was on his feet, and so thickly were all covered with dust that they looked as if they had been reclothed in yellow.

"We bury our dead," said a gunner, grimly, though doubtless all were afterward dug out, for some were partly alive.

To a "day of danger" succeeded a "night of waking." The enemy, everywhere held back from the road, continued to stretch his line northward in the hope to overlap us and put himself between us and Chattanooga. We neither saw nor heard his movement, but any man with half a head would have known that he was making it, and we met it by a parallel movement to our left. By morning we had edged along a good way and thrown up rude intrenchments at a little distance from the road, on the threatened side. The day was not very far advanced when we were attacked furiously all along the line, beginning at the left. When repulsed, the enemy came again and again—his persistence was dispiriting. He seemed to be using against us the law of probabilities: of so many efforts one would eventually succeed.

One did, and it was my luck to see it win. I had been sent by my chief, General Hazen, to order up some artillery ammunition and rode away to the right and rear in search of it. Finding an ordnance train I obtained from the officer in charge a few wagons loaded with what I wanted, but he seemed in doubt as to our occupancy of the region across which I proposed to guide them. Although assured that I had just traversed it, and that it lay immediately behind Wood's division, he insisted on riding to the top of the ridge behind which his train lay and overlooking the ground. We did so, when to my astonishment I saw the entire country in front swarming with Confederates; the very earth seemed to be moving toward us! They came on in thousands, and so rapidly that we had barely time to turn tail and gallop down the hill and away, leaving them in possession of the train, many of the wagons being upset by frantic efforts to put them about. By what miracle that officer had sensed the situation I did not learn, for we parted company then and there and I never again saw him.

By a misunderstanding Wood's division had been withdrawn from our line of battle just as the enemy was making an assault. Through the gap of half a mile the Confederates charged without opposition, cutting our army clean in two. The right divisions were broken up and with General Rosecrans in their midst fled how they could across the country, eventually bringing up in Chattanooga, whence Rosecrans telegraphed to Washington the destruction of the rest of his army. The rest of his army was standing its ground.

A good deal of nonsense used to be talked about the heroism of General Garfield, who, caught in the rout of the right, nevertheless went back and joined the undefeated left under General Thomas. There was no great heroism in it; that is what every man should have done, including the commander of the army. We could hear Thomas's guns going—those of us who had ears for them—and all that was needful was to make a sufficiently wide detour and then move toward the sound. I did so myself, and have never felt that it ought to make me President. Moreover, on my way I met General Negley, and my duties as topographical engineer having given me some knowledge of the lay of the land offered to pilot him back to glory or the grave. I am sorry to say my good offices were rejected a little uncivilly, which I charitably attributed to the general's obvious absence of mind. His mind, I think, was in Nashville, behind a breastwork.

Unable to find my brigade, I reported to General Thomas, who directed me to remain with him. He had assumed command of all the forces still intact and was pretty closely beset. The battle was fierce and continuous, the enemy extending his lines farther and farther around our right, toward our line of retreat. We could not meet the extension otherwise than by "refusing" our right flank and letting him inclose us; which but for gallant Gordon Granger he would inevitably have done.

This was the way of it. Looking across the fields in our rear (rather longingly) I had the happy distinction of a discoverer. What I saw was the shimmer of sunlight on metal: lines of troops were coming in behind us! The distance was too great, the atmosphere too hazy to distinguish the color of their uniform, even with a glass. Reporting my momentous "find" I was directed by the general to go and see who they were. Galloping toward them until near enough to see that they were of our kidney I hastened back with the glad tidings and was sent again, to guide them to the general's position.

It was General Granger with two strong brigades of the reserve, moving soldier-like toward the sound of heavy firing. Meeting him and his staff I directed him to Thomas, and unable to think of anything better to do decided to go visiting. I knew I had a brother in that gang—an officer of an Ohio battery. I soon found him near the head of a column, and as we moved forward we had a comfortable chat amongst such of the enemy's bullets as had inconsiderately been fired too high. The incident was a trifle marred by one of them unhorsing another officer of the battery, whom we propped against a tree and left. A few moments later Granger's force was put in on the right and the fighting was terrific!

By accident I now found Hazen's brigade—or what remained of it—which had made a half-mile march to add itself to the unrouted at the memorable Snodgrass Hill. Hazen's first remark to me was an inquiry about that artillery ammunition that he had sent me for.

It was needed badly enough, as were other kinds: for the last hour or two of that interminable day Granger's were the only men that had enough ammunition to make a five minutes' fight. Had the Confederates made one more general attack we should have had to meet them with the bayonet alone. I don't know why they did not; probably they were short of ammunition. I know, though, that while the sun was taking its own time to set we lived through the agony of at least one death each, waiting for them to come on.

At last it grew too dark to fight. Then away to our left and rear some of Bragg's people set up "the rebel yell." It was taken up successively and passed round to our front, along our right and in behind us again, until it seemed almost to have got to the point whence it started. It was the ugliest sound that any mortal ever heard—even a mortal exhausted and unnerved by two days of hard fighting, without sleep, without rest, without food and without hope. There was, however, a space somewhere at the back of us across which that horrible yell did not prolong itself; and through that we finally retired in profound silence and dejection, unmolested.

To those of us who have survived the attacks of both Bragg and Time, and who keep in memory the dear dead comrades whom we left upon that fateful field, the place means much. May it mean something less to the younger men whose tents are now pitched where, with bended heads and clasped hands, God's great angels stood invisible among the heroes in blue and the heroes in gray, sleeping their last sleep in the woods of Chickamauga.

1898

THE CRIME AT PICKETT'S MILL

There is a class of events which by their very nature, and despite any intrinsic interest that they may possess, are foredoomed to oblivion. They are merged in the general story of those greater events of which they were a part, as the thunder of a billow breaking on a distant beach is unnoted in the continuous roar. To how many having knowledge of the battles of our Civil War does the name Pickett's Mill suggest acts of heroism and devotion performed in scenes of awful carnage to accomplish the impossible? Buried in the official reports of the victors there are indeed imperfect accounts of the engagement: the vanquished have not thought it expedient to relate it. It is ignored by General Sherman in his memoirs, yet Sherman ordered it. General Howard wrote an account of the campaign of which it was an incident, and dismissed it in a single sentence; yet General Howard planned it, and it was fought as an isolated and independent action under his eye. Whether it was so trifling an affair as to justify this inattention let the reader judge.

The fight occurred on the 27th of May, 1864, while the armies of Generals Sherman and Johnston confronted each other near Dallas, Georgia, during the memorable "Atlanta campaign." For three weeks we had been pushing the Confederates southward, partly by manoeuvring, partly by fighting, out of Dalton, out of Resaca, through Adairsville, Kingston and Cassville. Each army offered battle everywhere, but would accept it only on its own terms. At Dallas Johnston made another stand and Sherman, facing the hostile line, began his customary manoeuvring for an advantage. General Wood's division of Howard's corps occupied a position opposite the Confederate right. Johnston finding himself on the 26th overlapped by Schofield, still farther to Wood's left, retired his right (Polk) across a creek, whither we followed him into the woods with a deal of desultory bickering, and at nightfall had established the new lines at nearly a right angle with the old—Schofield reaching well around and threatening the Confederate rear.

The civilian reader must not suppose when he reads accounts of military operations in which relative positions of the forces are defined, as in the foregoing passages, that these were matters of general knowledge to those engaged. Such statements are commonly made, even by those high in command, in the light of later disclosures, such as the enemy's official reports. It is seldom, indeed, that a subordinate officer knows anything about the disposition of the enemy's forces—except that it is unaimable—or precisely whom he is fighting. As to the rank and file, they can know nothing more of the matter than the arms they carry. They hardly know what troops are upon their own right or left the length of a regiment away. If it is a cloudy day they are ignorant even of the points of the compass. It may be said, generally, that a soldier's knowledge of what is going on about him is coterminous with his official relation to it and his personal connection with it; what is going on in front of him he does not know at all until he learns it afterward.

At nine o'clock on the morning of the 27th Wood's division was withdrawn and replaced by Stanley's. Supported by Johnson's division, it moved at ten o'clock to the left, in the rear of Schofield, a distance of four miles through a forest, and at two o'clock in the afternoon had reached a position where General Howard believed himself free to move in behind the enemy's forces and attack them in the rear, or at least, striking them in the flank, crush his way along their line in the direction of its length, throw them into confusion and prepare an easy victory for a supporting attack in front. In selecting General Howard for this bold adventure General Sherman was doubtless not unmindful of Chancellorsville, where Stonewall Jackson had executed a similar manoeuvre for Howard's instruction. Experience is a normal school: it teaches how to teach.

There are some differences to be noted. At Chancellorsville it was Jackson who attacked; at Pickett's Mill, Howard. At Chancellorsville it was Howard who was assailed; at Pickett's Mill, Hood. The significance of the first distinction is doubled by that of the second.

The attack, it was understood, was to be made in column of brigades, Hazen's brigade of Wood's division leading. That such was at least Hazen's understanding I learned from his own lips during the movement, as I was an officer of his staff. But after a march of less than a mile an hour and a further delay of three hours at the end of it to acquaint the enemy of our intention to surprise him, our single shrunken brigade of fifteen hundred men was sent forward without support to double up the army of General Johnston. "We will put in Hazen and see what success he has." In these words of General Wood to General Howard we were first apprised of the true nature of the distinction about to be conferred upon us.

General W.B. Hazen, a born fighter, an educated soldier, after the war Chief Signal Officer of the Army and now long dead, was the best hated man that I ever knew, and his very memory is a terror to every unworthy soul in the service. His was a stormy life: he was in trouble all round. Grant, Sherman, Sheridan and a countless multitude of the less eminent luckless had the misfortune, at one time and another, to incur his disfavor, and he tried to punish them all. He was always—after the war—the central figure of a court-martial or a Congressional inquiry, was accused of everything, from stealing to cowardice, was banished to obscure posts, "jumped on" by the press, traduced in public and in private, and always emerged triumphant. While Signal Officer, he went up against the Secretary of War and put him to the controversial sword. He convicted Sheridan of falsehood, Sherman of barbarism, Grant of inefficiency. He was aggressive, arrogant, tyrannical, honorable, truthful, courageous—skillful soldier, a faithful friend and one of the most exasperating of men Duty was his religion, and like the Moslem he proselyted with the sword. His missionary efforts were directed chiefly against the spiritual darkness of his superiors in rank, though he would turn aside from pursuit of his erring commander to set a chicken-thieving orderly astride a wooden horse, with a heavy stone attached to each foot. "Hazen," said a brother brigadier, "is a synonym of insubordination." For my commander and my friend, my master in the art of war, now unable to answer for himself, let this fact answer: when he heard Wood say they would put him in and see what success he would have in defeating an army—when he saw Howard assent—he uttered never a word, rode to the head of his feeble brigade and patiently awaited the command to go. Only by a look which I knew how to read did he betray his sense of the criminal blunder.

The enemy had now had seven hours in which to learn of the movement and prepare to meet it. General Johnston says:

"The Federal troops extended their intrenched line [we did not intrench] so rapidly to their left that it was found necessary to transfer Cleburne's division to Hardee's corps to our right, where it was formed on the prolongation of Polk's line."

General Hood, commanding the enemy's right corps, says:

"On the morning of the 27th the enemy were known to be rapidly extending their left, attempting to turn my right as they extended. Cleburne was deployed to meet them, and at half-past five P.M. a very stubborn attack was made on this division, extending to the right, where Major-General Wheeler with his cavalry division was engaging them. The assault was continued with great determination upon both Cleburne and Wheeler."

That, then, was the situation: a weak brigade of fifteen hundred men, with masses of idle troops behind in the character of audience, waiting for the word to march a quarter-mile up hill through almost impassable tangles of underwood, along and across precipitous ravines, and attack breastworks constructed at leisure and manned with two divisions of troops as good as themselves. True, we did not know all this, but if any man on that ground besides Wood and Howard expected a "walkover" his must have been a singularly hopeful disposition. As topographical engineer it had been my duty to make a hasty examination of the ground in front. In doing so I had pushed far enough forward through the forest to hear distinctly the murmur of the enemy awaiting us, and this had been duly reported; but from our lines nothing could be heard but the wind among the trees and the songs of birds. Some one said it was a pity to frighten them, but there would necessarily be more or less noise. We laughed at that: men awaiting death on the battlefield laugh easily, though not infectiously.

The brigade was formed in four battalions, two in front and two in rear. This gave us a front of about two hundred yards. The right front battalion was commanded by Colonel R.L. Kimberly of the 41st Ohio, the left by Colonel O.H. Payne of the 124th Ohio, the rear battalions by Colonel J.C. Foy, 23d Kentucky, and Colonel W.W. Berry, 5th Kentucky—all brave and skillful officers, tested by experience on many fields. The whole command (known as the Second Brigade, Third Division, Fourth Corps) consisted of no fewer than nine regiments, reduced by long service to an average of less than two hundred men each. With full ranks and only the necessary details for special duty we should have had some eight thousand rifles in line.

We moved forward. In less than one minute the trim battalions had become simply a swarm of men struggling through the undergrowth of the forest, pushing and crowding. The front was irregularly serrated, the strongest and bravest in advance, the others following in fan-like formations, variable and inconstant, ever defining themselves anew. For the first two hundred yards our course lay along the left bank of a small creek in a deep ravine, our left battalions sweeping along its steep slope. Then we came to the fork of the ravine. A part of us crossed below, the rest above, passing over both branches, the regiments inextricably intermingled, rendering all military formation impossible. The color-bearers kept well to the front with their flags, closely furled, aslant backward over their shoulders. Displayed, they would have been torn to rags by the boughs of the trees. Horses were all sent to the rear; the general and staff and all the field officers toiled along on foot as best they could. "We shall halt and form when we get out of this," said an aide-de-camp.

Suddenly there were a ringing rattle of musketry, the familiar hissing of bullets, and before us the interspaces of the forest were all blue with smoke. Hoarse, fierce yells broke out of a thousand throats. The forward fringe of brave and hardy assailants was arrested in its mutable extensions; the edge of our swarm grew dense and clearly defined as the foremost halted, and the rest pressed forward to align themselves beside them, all firing. The uproar was deafening; the air was sibilant with streams and sheets of missiles. In the steady, unvarying roar of small-arms the frequent shock of the cannon was rather felt than heard, but the gusts of grape which they blew into that populous wood were audible enough, screaming among the trees and cracking against their stems and branches. We had, of course, no artillery to reply.

Our brave color-bearers were now all in the forefront of battle in the open, for the enemy had cleared a space in front of his breastworks. They held the colors erect, shook out their glories, waved them forward and back to keep them spread, for there was no wind. From where I stood, at the right of the line—we had "halted and formed," indeed—I could see six of our flags at one time. Occasionally one would go down, only to be instantly lifted by other hands.

I must here quote again from General Johnston's account of this engagement, for nothing could more truly indicate the resolute nature of the attack than the Confederate belief that it was made by the whole Fourth Corps, instead of one weak brigade:

"The Fourth Corps came on in deep order and assailed the Texans with great vigor, receiving their close and accurate fire with the fortitude always exhibited by General Sherman's troops in the actions of this campaign.... The Federal troops approached within a few yards of the Confederates, but at last were forced to give way by their storm of well-directed bullets, and fell back to the shelter of a hollow near and behind them. They left hundreds of corpses within twenty paces of the Confederate line. When the United States troops paused in their advance within fifteen paces of the Texan front rank one of their color-bearers planted his colors eight or ten feet in front of his regiment, and was instantly shot dead. A soldier sprang forward to his place and fell also as he grasped the color-staff. A second and third followed successively, and each received death as speedily as his predecessors. A fourth, however, seized and bore back the object of soldierly devotion."

Such incidents have occurred in battle from time to time since men began to venerate the symbols of their cause, but they are not commonly related by the enemy. If General Johnston had known that his veteran divisions were throwing their successive lines against fewer than fifteen hundred men his glowing tribute to his enemy's valor could hardly have been more generously expressed. I can attest the truth of his soldierly praise: I saw the occurrence that he relates and regret that I am unable to recall even the name of the regiment whose colors were so gallantly saved.

Early in my military experience I used to ask myself how it was that brave troops could retreat while still their courage was high. As long as a man is not disabled he can go forward; can it be anything but fear that makes him stop and finally retire? Are there signs by which he can infallibly know the struggle to be hopeless? In this engagement, as in others, my doubts were answered as to the fact; the explanation is still obscure. In many instances which have come under my observation, when hostile lines of infantry engage at close range and the assailants afterward retire, there was a "dead-line" beyond which no man advanced but to fall. Not a soul of them ever reached the enemy's front to be bayoneted or captured. It was a matter of the difference of three or four paces—too small a distance to affect the accuracy of aim. In these affairs no aim is taken at individual antagonists; the soldier delivers his fire at the thickest mass in his front. The fire is, of course, as deadly at twenty paces as at fifteen; at fifteen as at ten. Nevertheless, there is the "dead-line," with its well-defined edge of corpses—those of the bravest. Where both lines are fighting without cover—as in a charge met by a counter-charge—each has its "dead-line," and between the two is a clear space—neutral ground, devoid of dead, for the living cannot reach it to fall there.

I observed this phenomenon at Pickett's Mill. Standing at the right of the line I had an unobstructed view of the narrow, open space across which the two lines fought. It was dim with smoke, but not greatly obscured: the smoke rose and spread in sheets among the branches of the trees. Most of our men fought kneeling as they fired, many of them behind trees, stones and whatever cover they could get, but there were considerable groups that stood. Occasionally one of these groups, which had endured the storm of missiles for moments without perceptible reduction, would push forward, moved by a common despair, and wholly detach itself from the line. In a second every man of the group would be down. There had been no visible movement of the enemy, no audible change in the awful, even roar of the firing—yet all were down. Frequently the dim figure of an individual soldier would be seen to spring away from his comrades, advancing alone toward that fateful interspace, with leveled bayonet. He got no farther than the farthest of his predecessors. Of the "hundreds of corpses within twenty paces of the Confederate line," I venture to say that a third were within fifteen paces, and not one within ten.

It is the perception—perhaps unconscious—of this inexplicable phenomenon that causes the still unharmed, still vigorous and still courageous soldier to retire without having come into actual contact with his foe. He sees, or feels, that he cannot. His bayonet is a useless weapon for slaughter; its purpose is a moral one. Its mandate exhausted, he sheathes it and trusts to the bullet. That failing, he retreats. He has done all that he could do with such appliances as he has.

No command to fall back was given, none could have been heard. Man by man, the survivors withdrew at will, sifting through the trees into the cover of the ravines, among the wounded who could drag themselves back; among the skulkers whom nothing could have dragged forward. The left of our short line had fought at the corner of a cornfield, the fence along the right side of which was parallel to the direction of our retreat. As the disorganized groups fell back along this fence on the wooded side, they were attacked by a flanking force of the enemy moving through the field in a direction nearly parallel with what had been our front. This force, I infer from General Johnston's account, consisted of the brigade of General Lowry, or two Arkansas regiments under Colonel Baucum. I had been sent by General Hazen to that point and arrived in time to witness this formidable movement. But already our retreating men, in obedience to their officers, their courage and their instinct of self-preservation, had formed along the fence and opened fire. The apparently slight advantage of the imperfect cover and the open range worked its customary miracle: the assault, a singularly spiritless one, considering the advantages it promised and that it was made by an organized and victorious force against a broken and retreating one, was checked. The assailants actually retired, and if they afterward renewed the movement they encountered none but our dead and wounded.

The battle, as a battle, was at an end, but there was still some slaughtering that it was possible to incur before nightfall; and as the wreck of our brigade drifted back through the forest we met the brigade (Gibson's) which, had the attack been made in column, as it should have been, would have been but five minutes behind our heels, with another five minutes behind its own. As it was, just forty-five minutes had elapsed, during which the enemy had destroyed us and was now ready to perform the same kindly office for our successors. Neither Gibson nor the brigade which was sent to his "relief" as tardily as he to ours accomplished, or could have hoped to accomplish, anything whatever. I did not note their movements, having other duties, but Hazen in his "Narrative of Military Service" says:

"I witnessed the attack of the two brigades following my own, and none of these (troops) advanced nearer than one hundred yards of the enemy's works. They went in at a run, and as organizations were broken in less than a minute."

Nevertheless their losses were considerable, including several hundred prisoners taken from a sheltered place whence they did not care to rise and run. The entire loss was about fourteen hundred men, of whom nearly one-half fell killed and wounded in Hazen's brigade in less than thirty minutes of actual fighting.

General Johnston says:

"The Federal dead lying near our line were counted by many persons, officers and soldiers. According to these counts there were seven hundred of them."

This is obviously erroneous, though I have not the means at hand to ascertain the true number. I remember that we were all astonished at the uncommonly large proportion of dead to wounded—a consequence of the uncommonly close range at which most of the fighting was done.

The action took its name from a water-power mill near by. This was on a branch of a stream having, I am sorry to say, the prosaic name of Pumpkin Vine Creek. I have my own reasons for suggesting that the name of that water-course be altered to Sunday-School Run.

FOUR DAYS IN DIXIE

During a part of the month of October, 1864, the Federal and Confederate armies of Sherman and Hood respectively, having performed a surprising and resultless series of marches and countermarches since the fall of Atlanta, confronted each other along the separating line of the Coosa River in the vicinity of Gaylesville, Alabama. Here for several days they remained at rest—at least most of the infantry and artillery did; what the cavalry was doing nobody but itself ever knew or greatly cared. It was an interregnum of expectancy between two régimes of activity.

I was on the staff of Colonel McConnell, who commanded an infantry brigade in the absence of its regular commander. McConnell was a good man, but he did not keep a very tight rein upon the half dozen restless and reckless young fellows who (for his sins) constituted his "military family." In most matters we followed the trend of our desires, which commonly ran in the direction of adventure—it did not greatly matter what kind. In pursuance of this policy of escapades, one bright Sunday morning Lieutenant Cobb, an aide-de-camp, and I mounted and set out to "seek our fortunes," as the story books have it. Striking into a road of which we knew nothing except that it led toward the river, we followed it for a mile or such a matter, when we found our advance interrupted by a considerable creek, which we must ford or go back. We consulted a moment and then rode at it as hard as we could, possibly in the belief that a high momentum would act as it does in the instance of a skater passing over thin ice. Cobb was fortunate enough to get across comparatively dry, but his hapless companion was utterly submerged. The disaster was all the greater from my having on a resplendent new uniform, of which I had been pardonably vain. Ah, what a gorgeous new uniform it never was again!

A half-hour devoted to wringing my clothing and dry-charging my revolver, and we were away. A brisk canter of a half-hour under the arches of the trees brought us to the river, where it was our ill luck to find a boat and three soldiers of our brigade. These men had been for several hours concealed in the brush patiently watching the opposite bank in the amiable hope of getting a shot at some unwary Confederate, but had seen none. For a great distance up and down the stream on the other side, and for at least a mile back from it, extended cornfields. Beyond the cornfields, on slightly higher ground, was a thin forest, with breaks here and there in its continuity, denoting plantations, probably. No houses were in sight, and no camps. We knew that it was the enemy's ground, but whether his forces were disposed along the slightly higher country bordering the bottom lands, or at strategic points miles back, as ours were, we knew no more than the least curious private in our army. In any case the river line would naturally be picketed or patrolled. But the charm of the unknown was upon us: the mysterious exerted its old-time fascination, beckoning to us from that silent shore so peaceful and dreamy in the beauty of the quiet Sunday morning. The temptation was strong and we fell. The soldiers were as eager for the hazard as we, and readily volunteered for the madmen's enterprise. Concealing our horses in a cane-brake, we unmoored the boat and rowed across unmolested.

Arrived at a kind of "landing" on the other side, our first care was so to secure the boat under the bank as to favor a hasty re-embarking in case we should be so unfortunate as to incur the natural consequence of our act; then, following an old road through the ranks of standing corn, we moved in force upon the Confederate position, five strong, with an armament of three Springfield rifles and two Colt's revolvers. We had not the further advantage of music and banners. One thing favored the expedition, giving it an apparent assurance of success: it was well officered—an officer to each man and a half.

After marching about a mile we came into a neck of woods and crossed an intersecting road which showed no wheel-tracks, but was rich in hoof-prints. We observed them and kept right on about our business, whatever that may have been. A few hundred yards farther brought us to a plantation bordering our road upon the right. The fields, as was the Southern fashion at that period of the war, were uncultivated and overgrown with brambles. A large white house stood at some little distance from the road; we saw women and children and a few negroes there. On our left ran the thin forest,

pervious to cavalry. Directly ahead an ascent in the r[...] crest beyond which we could see nothing.

On this crest suddenly appeared two horsemen i[...] outlined against the sky—men and animals looking g[...] same instant a jingling and tramping were audible [...] turning in that direction I saw a score of mounte[...] forward at a trot. In the meantime the giants o[...] multiplied surprisingly. Our invasion of the C[...] apparently failed.

There was lively work in the next few seconds[...] thick and fast—and uncommonly loud; none, I thi[...] Cobb was on the extreme left of our advance, I o[...] two paces apart. He instantly dived into the woo[...] and I climbed across the fence somehow and str[...] field—actuated, doubtless, by an intelligent fo[...] horseback could not immediately follow. Passi[...] now swarming like a hive of bees, we made for a [...] hundred yards away, where I concealed mys[...] others continuing—as a defeated commander [...] back. In my cover, where I lay panting like a [...] deal of shouting and hard riding and an occ[...] some one calling dogs, and the thought of b[...] fine suggestiveness to the other fancies appro[...]

Finding myself unpursued after the lap[...] hour, but was probably a few minutes, I ca[...] where, still concealed, I could obtain a view [...] only enemy in sight was a group of horseme[...] mile away. Toward this group a woman w[...] the eyes of everybody about the house. I th[...] my hiding-place and was going to "give [...] hands and knees I crept as rapidly as poss[...] brambles directly back toward the point [...] met the enemy and failed to make him o[...] into a patch of briars within ten feet [...] undiscovered during the remainder of th[...] of disparaging remarks upon Yankee[...] declarations of intention conditional o[...] the Opposition passed and repassed [...] discuss the morning's events. In this [...] privates had been headed off and cau[...] destination would naturally be Ander[...] of them God knows. Their captors pa[...] canvass of the swamp for me.

When night had fallen I [...]

more vigilant sentinel, posted in the heart of a thicket, who fired at me without challenge. To a soldier an unexpected shot ringing out at dead of night is fraught with an awful significance. In my circumstances—cut off from my comrades, groping about an unknown country, surrounded by invisible perils which such a signal would call into eager activity—the flash and shock of that firearm were unspeakably dreadful! In any case I should and ought to have fled, and did so; but how much or little of conscious prudence there was in the prompting I do not care to discover by analysis of memory. I went back into the corn, found the river, followed it back a long way and mounted into the fork of a low tree. There I perched until the dawn, a most uncomfortable bird.

In the gray light of the morning I discovered that I was opposite an island of considerable length, separated from the mainland by a narrow and shallow channel, which I promptly waded. The island was low and flat, covered with an almost impenetrable cane-brake interlaced with vines. Working my way through these to the other side, I obtained another look at God's country—Shermany, so to speak. There were no visible inhabitants. The forest and the water met. This did not deter me. For the chill of the water I had no further care, and laying off my boots and outer clothing I prepared to swim. A strange thing now occurred—more accurately, a familiar thing occurred at a strange moment. A black cloud seemed to pass before my eyes—the water, the trees, the sky, all vanished in a profound darkness. I heard the roaring of a great cataract, felt the earth sinking from beneath my feet. Then I heard and felt no more.

At the battle of Kennesaw Mountain in the previous June I had been badly wounded in the head, and for three months was incapacitated for service. In truth, I had done no actual duty since, being then, as for many years afterward, subject to fits of fainting, sometimes without assignable immediate cause, but mostly when suffering from exposure, excitement or excessive fatigue. This combination of them all had broken me down—most opportunely, it would seem.

When I regained my consciousness the sun was high. I was still giddy and half blind. To have taken to the water would have been madness; I must have a raft. Exploring my island, I found a pen of slender logs: an old structure without roof or rafters, built for what purpose I do not know. Several of these logs I managed with patient toil to detach and convey to the water, where I floated them, lashing them together with vines. Just before sunset my raft was complete and freighted with my outer clothing, boots and pistol. Having shipped the last article, I returned into the brake, seeking something from which to improvise a paddle. While peering about I heard a sharp metallic click—the cocking of a rifle! I was a prisoner.

The history of this great disaster to the Union arms is brief and simple. A Confederate "home guard," hearing something going on upon the island, rode across, concealed his horse and still-hunted me. And, reader, when you are "held up" in the same way may it be by as fine a fellow. He not only spared my life, but even overlooked a feeble and ungrateful after-attempt upon his own (the particulars of which I shall not relate), merely exacting my word of honor that I would not again try to escape while in his custody. Escape! I could not have escaped a new-born babe.

At my captor's house that evening there was a reception, attended by the élite of the whole vicinity. A Yankee officer in full fig—minus only the boots, which could not be got on to his swollen feet—was something worth seeing, and those who came to scoff remained to stare. What most interested them, I think, was my eating—an entertainment that was prolonged to a late hour. They were a trifle disappointed by the absence of horns, hoof and tail, but bore their chagrin with good-natured fortitude. Among my visitors was a charming young woman from the plantation where we had met the foe the day before—the same lady whom I had suspected of an intention to reveal my hiding-place. She had had no such design; she had run over to the group of horsemen to learn if her father had been hurt—by whom, I should like to know. No restraint was put upon me; my captor even left me with the women and children and went off for instructions as to what disposition he should make of me. Altogether the reception was "a pronounced success," though it is to be regretted that the guest of the evening had the incivility to fall dead asleep in the midst of the festivities, and was put to bed by sympathetic and, he has reason to believe, fair hands.

The next morning I was started off to the rear in custody of two mounted men, heavily armed. They had another prisoner, picked up in some raid beyond the river. He was a most offensive brute—a foreigner of some mongrel sort, with just sufficient command of our tongue to show that he could not control his own. We traveled all day, meeting occasional small bodies of cavalrymen, by whom, with one exception—a Texan officer—was civilly treated. My guards said, however, that if we should chance to meet Jeff Gatewood he would probably take me from them and hang me to the nearest tree; and once or twice, hearing horsemen approach, they directed me to stand aside, concealed in the brush, one of them remaining near by to keep an eye on me, the other going forward with my fellow-prisoner, for whose neck they seemed to have less tenderness, and whom I heartily wished well hanged.

Jeff Gatewood was a "guerrilla" chief of local notoriety, who was a greater terror to his friends than to his other foes. My guards related almost incredible tales of his cruelties and infamies. By their account it was into his camp that I had blundered on Sunday night.

We put up for the night at a farmhouse, having gone not more than fifteen miles, owing to the condition of my feet. Here we got a bite of supper and were permitted to lie before the fire. My fellow-prisoner took off his boots and was soon sound asleep. I took off nothing and, despite exhaustion, remained equally sound awake. One of the guards also removed his footgear and outer clothing, placed his weapons under his neck and slept the sleep of innocence; the other sat in the chimney corner on watch. The house was a double log cabin, with an open space between the two parts, roofed over—a common type of habitation in that region. The room we were in had its entrance in this open space, the fireplace opposite, at the end. Beside the door was a bed, occupied by the old man of the house and his wife. It was partly curtained off from the room.

In an hour or two the chap on watch began to yawn, then to nod. Pretty soon he stretched himself on the floor, facing us, pistol in hand. For a while he supported himself on his elbow, then laid his head on his arm, blinking like an owl. I performed an occasional snore, watching him narrowly between my eyelashes from the shadow of my arm. The inevitable occurred—he slept audibly.

A half-hour later I rose quietly to my feet, particularly careful not to disturb the blackguard at my side, and moved as silently as possible to the door. Despite my care the latch clicked. The old lady sat bolt upright in bed and stared at me. She was too late. I sprang through the door and struck out for the nearest point of woods, in a direction previously selected, vaulting fences like an accomplished gymnast and followed by a multitude of dogs. It is said that the State of Alabama has more dogs than school-children, and that they cost more for their keep. The estimate of cost is probably too high.

Looking backward as I ran, I saw and heard the place in a turmoil and uproar; and to my joy the old man, evidently oblivious to the facts of the situation, was lifting up his voice and calling his dogs. They were good dogs: they went back; otherwise the malicious old rascal would have had my skeleton. Again the traditional bloodhound did not materialize. Other pursuit there was no reason to fear; my foreign gentleman would occupy the attention of one of the soldiers, and in the darkness of the forest I could easily elude the other, or, if need be, get him at a disadvantage. In point of fact there was no pursuit.

I now took my course by the north star (which I can never sufficiently bless), avoiding all roads and open places about houses, laboriously boring my way through forests, driving myself like a wedge into brush and bramble, swimming every stream I came to (some of them more than once, probably), and pulling myself out of the water by boughs and briars—whatever could be grasped. Let any one try to go a little way across even the most familiar country on a moonless night, and he will have an experience to remember. By dawn I had probably not made three miles. My clothing and skin were alike in rags.

During the day I was compelled to make wide detours to avoid even the fields, unless they were of corn; but in other respects the going was distinctly better. A light breakfast of raw sweet potatoes and persimmons cheered the inner man; a good part of the outer was decorating the several thorns, boughs and sharp rocks along my sylvan wake.

Late in the afternoon I found the river, at what point it was impossible to say. After a half-hour's rest, concluding with a fervent prayer that I might go to the bottom, I swam across. Creeping up the bank and holding my course still northward through a dense undergrowth, I suddenly reeled into a dusty highway and saw a more heavenly vision than ever the eyes of a dying saint were blessed withal—two patriots in blue carrying a stolen pig slung upon a pole!

Late that evening Colonel McConnell and his staff were chatting by a camp-fire in front of his headquarters. They were in a pleasant humor: some one had just finished a funny story about a man cut in two by a cannon-shot. Suddenly something staggered in among them from the outer darkness and fell into the fire. Somebody dragged it out by what seemed to be a leg. They turned the animal on its back and examined it—they were no cowards.

"What is it, Cobb?" said the chief, who had not taken the trouble to rise.

"I don't know, Colonel, but thank God it is dead!"

It was not.

WHAT OCCURRED AT FRANKLIN

For several days, in snow and rain, General Schofield's little army had crouched in its hastily constructed defenses at Columbia, Tennessee. It had retreated in hot haste from Pulaski, thirty miles to the south, arriving just in time to foil Hood, who, marching from Florence, Alabama, by another road, with a force of more than double our strength, had hoped to intercept us. Had he succeeded, he would indubitably have bagged the whole bunch of us. As it was, he simply took position in front of us and gave us plenty of employment, but did not attack; he knew a trick worth two of that.

Duck River was directly in our rear; I suppose both our flanks rested on it. The town was between them. One night—that of November 27, 1864—we pulled up stakes and crossed to the north bank to continue our retreat to Nashville, where Thomas and safety lay—such safety as is known in war. It was high time too, for before noon of the next day Forrest's cavalry forded the river a few miles above us and began pushing back our own horse toward Spring Hill, ten miles in our rear, on our only road. Why our infantry was not immediately put in motion toward the threatened point, so vital to our safety, General Schofield could have told better than I. Howbeit, we lay there inactive all day.

The next morning—a bright and beautiful one—the brigade of Colonel P. Sidney Post was thrown out, up the river four or five miles, to see what it could see. What it saw was Hood's head-of-column coming over on a pontoon bridge, and a right pretty spectacle it would have been to one whom it did not concern. It concerned us rather keenly.

As a member of Colonel Post's staff, I was naturally favored with a good view of the performance. We formed in line of battle at a distance of perhaps a half-mile from the bridge-head, but that unending column of gray and steel gave us no more attention than if we had been a crowd of farmer-folk. Why should it? It had only to face to the left to be itself a line of battle. Meantime it had more urgent business on hand than brushing away a small brigade whose only offense was curiosity; it was making for Spring Hill with all its legs and wheels. Hour after hour we watched that unceasing flow of infantry and artillery toward the rear of our army. It was an unnerving spectacle, yet we never for a moment doubted that, acting on the intelligence supplied by our succession of couriers, our entire force was moving rapidly to the point of contact. The battle of Spring Hill was obviously decreed. Obviously, too, our brigade of observation would be among the last to have a hand in it. The thought annoyed us, made us restless and resentful. Our mounted men rode forward and back behind the line, nervous and distressed; the men in the ranks sought relief in frequent changes of posture, in shifting their weight from one leg to the other, in needless inspection of their weapons and in that unfailing resource of the discontented soldier, audible damning of those in the saddles of authority. But never for more than a moment at a time did any one remove his eyes from that fascinating and portentous pageant.

Toward evening we were recalled, to learn that of our five divisions of infantry, with their batteries, numbering twenty-three thousand men, only one—Stanley's, four thousand weak—had been sent to Spring Hill to meet that formidable movement of Hood's three veteran corps! Why Stanley was not immediately effaced is still a matter of controversy. Hood, who was early on the ground, declared that he gave the needful orders and tried vainly to enforce them; Cheatham, in command of his leading corps, that he did not. Doubtless the dispute is still being carried on between these chieftains from their beds of asphodel and moly in Elysium. So much is certain: Stanley drove away Forrest and successfully held the junction of the roads against Cleburne's division, the only infantry that attacked him.

That night the entire Confederate army lay within a half mile of our road, while we all sneaked by, infantry, artillery, and trains. The enemy's camp-fires shone redly—miles of them—seemingly only a stone's throw from our hurrying column. His men were plainly visible about them, cooking their suppers—a sight so incredible that many of our own, thinking them friends, strayed over to them and did not return. At intervals of a few hundred yards we passed dim figures on horseback by the roadside, enjoining silence. Needless precaution; we could not have spoken if we had tried, for our hearts were in our throats. But fools are God's peculiar care, arid one of his protective methods is the stupidity of other fools. By daybreak our last man and last wagon had passed the fateful spot unchallenged, and our first were entering Franklin, ten miles away. Despite spirited cavalry attacks on trains and rear-guard, all were in Franklin by noon and such of the men as could be kept awake were throwing up a slight line of defense, inclosing the town.

Franklin lies—or at that time did lie; I know not what exploration might now disclose—on the south bank of a small river, the Harpeth by name. For two miles southward was a nearly flat, open plain, extending to a range of low hills through which passed the turnpike by which we had come. From some bluffs on the precipitous north bank of the river was a commanding overlook of all this open ground, which, although more than a mile away, seemed almost at one's feet. On this elevated ground the wagon-train had been parked and General Schofield had stationed himself—the former for security, the latter for outlook. Both were guarded by General Wood's infantry division, of which my brigade was a part. "We are in beautiful luck," said a member of the division staff. With some prevision of what was to come and a lively recollection of the nervous strain of helpless observation, I did not think it luck. In the activity of battle one does not feel one's hair going gray with vicissitudes of emotion.

For some reason to the writer unknown General Schofield had brought along with him General D.S. Stanley, who commanded two of his divisions—ours and another, which was not "in luck." In the ensuing battle, when this excellent officer could stand the strain no longer, he bolted across the bridge like a shot and found relief in the hell below, where he was promptly tumbled out of the saddle by a bullet.

Our line, with its reserve brigades, was about a mile and a half long, both flanks on the river, above and below the town—a mere bridge-head. It did not look a very formidable obstacle to the march of an army of more than forty thousand men. In a more tranquil temper than his failure at Spring Hill had put him into Hood would probably have passed around our left and turned us out with ease—which would justly have entitled him to the Humane Society's great gold medal. Apparently that was not his day for saving life.

About the middle of the afternoon our field-glasses picked up the Confederate head-of-column emerging from the range of hills previously mentioned, where it is cut by the Columbia road. But—ominous circumstance!—it did not come on. It turned to its left, at a right angle, moving along the base of the hills, parallel to our line. Other heads-of-column came through other gaps and over the crests farther along, impudently deploying on the level ground with a spectacular display of flags and glitter of arms. I do not remember that they were molested, even by the guns of General Wagner, who had been foolishly posted with two small brigades across the turnpike, a half-mile in our front, where he was needless for apprisal and powerless for resistance. My recollection is that our fellows down there in their shallow trenches noted these portentous dispositions without the least manifestation of incivility. As a matter of fact, many of them were permitted by their compassionate officers to sleep. And truly it was good weather for that: sleep was in the very atmosphere. The sun burned crimson in a gray-blue sky through a delicate Indian-summer haze, as beautiful as a day-dream in paradise. If one had been given to moralizing one might have found material a-plenty for homilies in the contrast between that peaceful autumn afternoon and the bloody business that it had in hand. If any good chaplain failed to "improve the occasion" let us hope that he lived to lament in sack-cloth-of-gold and ashes-of-roses his intellectual unthrift.

The putting of that army into battle shape—its change from columns into lines—could not have occupied more than an hour or two, yet it seemed an eternity. Its leisurely evolutions were irritating, but at last it moved forward with atoning rapidity and the fight was on. First, the storm struck Wagner's isolated brigades, which, vanishing in fire and smoke, instantly reappeared as a confused mass of fugitives inextricably intermingled with their pursuers. They had not stayed the advance a moment, and as might have been foreseen were now a peril to the main line, which could protect itself only by the slaughter of its friends. To the right and left, however, our guns got into play, and simultaneously a furious infantry fire broke out along the entire front, the paralyzed center excepted. But nothing could stay those gallant rebels from a hand-to-hand encounter with bayonet and butt, and it was accorded to them with hearty good-will.

Meantime Wagner's conquerors were pouring across the breastwork like water over a dam. The guns that had spared the fugitives had now no time to fire; their infantry supports gave way and for a space of more than two hundred yards in the very center of our line the assailants, mad with exultation, had everything their own way. From the right and the left their gray masses converged into the gap, pushed through, and then, spreading, turned our men out of the works so hardly held against the attack in their front. From our viewpoint on the bluff we could mark the constant widening of the gap, the steady encroachment of that blazing and smoking mass against its disordered opposition.

"It is all up with us," said Captain Dawson, of Wood's staff; "I am going to have a quiet smoke."

I do not doubt that he supposed himself to have borne the heat and burden of the strife. In the midst of his preparations for a smoke he paused and looked again—a new tumult of musketry had broken loose. Colonel Emerson Opdycke had rushed his reserve brigade into the mêlée and was bitterly disputing the Confederate advantage. Other fresh regiments joined in the counterchargé, commanderless groups of retreating men returned to their work, and there ensued a hand-to-hand contest of incredible fury. Two long, irregular, mutable, and tumultuous blurs of color were consuming each other's edge along the line of contact. Such devil's work does not last long, and we had the great joy to see it ending, not as it began, but "more nearly to the heart's desire." Slowly the mobile blur moved away from the town, and presently the gray half of it dissolved into its elemental units, all in slow recession. The retaken guns in the embrasures pushed up towering clouds of white smoke; to east and to west along the reoccupied parapet ran a line of misty red till the spitfire crest was without a break from flank to flank. Probably there was some Yankee cheering, as doubtless there had been the "rebel yell," but my memory recalls neither. There are many battles in a war, and many incidents in a battle: one does not recollect everything. Possibly I have not a retentive ear.

While this lively work had been doing in the center, there had been no lack of diligence elsewhere, and now all were as busy as bees. I have read of many "successive attacks"—"charge after charge"—but I think the only assaults after the first were those of the second Confederate lines and possibly some of the reserves; certainly there were no visible abatement and renewal of effort anywhere except where the men who had been pushed out of the works backward tried to reenter. And all the time there was fighting.

After resetting their line the victors could not clear their front, for the baffled assailants would not desist. All over the open country in their rear, clear back to the base of the hills, drifted the wreck of battle, the wounded that were able to walk; and through the receding throng pushed forward, here and there, horsemen with orders and footmen whom we knew to be bearing ammunition. There were no wagons, no caissons: the enemy was not using, and could not use, his artillery. Along the line of fire we could see, dimly in the smoke, mounted officers, singly and in small groups, attempting to force their horses across the slight parapet, but all went down. Of this devoted band was the gallant General Adams, whose body was found upon the slope, and whose animal's forefeet were actually inside the crest. General Cleburne lay a few paces farther out, and five or six other general officers sprawled elsewhere. It was a great day for Confederates in the line of promotion.

For many minutes at a time broad spaces of battle were veiled in smoke. Of what might be occurring there conjecture gave a terrifying report. In a visible peril observation is a kind of defense; against the unseen we lift a trembling hand. Always from these regions of obscurity we expected the worst, but always the lifted cloud revealed an unaltered situation.

The assailants began to give way. There was no general retreat; at many points the fight continued, with lessening ferocity and lengthening range, well into the night. It became an affair of twinkling musketry and broad flares of artillery; then it sank to silence in the dark.

Under orders to continue his retreat, Schofield could now do so unmolested: Hood had suffered so terrible a loss in life and morale that he was in no condition for effective pursuit. As at Spring Hill, daybreak found us on the road with all our impedimenta except some of our wounded, and that night we encamped under the protecting guns of Thomas, at Nashville. Our gallant enemy audaciously followed, and fortified himself within rifle-reach, where he remained for two weeks without firing a gun and was then destroyed.

'WAY DOWN IN ALABAM'

At the break-up of the great Rebellion I found myself at Selma, Alabama, still in the service of the United States, and although my duties were now purely civil my treatment was not uniformly so, and I am not surprised that it was not. I was a minor official in the Treasury Department, engaged in performance of duties exceedingly disagreeable not only to the people of the vicinity, but to myself as well. They consisted in the collection and custody of "captured and abandoned property." The Treasury had covered pretty nearly the entire area of "the States lately in rebellion" with a hierarchy of officials, consisting, as nearly as memory serves, of one supervising agent and a multitude of special agents. Each special agent held dominion over a collection district and was allowed an "agency aide" to assist him in his purposeful activity, besides such clerks, laborers and so forth as he could persuade himself to need. My humble position was that of agency aide. When the special agent was present for duty I was his chief executive officer; in his absence I represented him (with greater or less fidelity to the original and to my conscience) and was invested with his powers. In the Selma agency the property that we were expected to seize and defend as best we might was mostly plantations (whose owners had disappeared; some were dead, others in hiding) and cotton. The country was full of cotton which had been sold to the Confederate Government, but not removed from the plantations to take its chance of export through the blockade. It had been decided that it now belonged to the United States. It was worth about five hundred dollars a bale—say one dollar a pound. The world agreed that that was a pretty good price for cotton.

Naturally the original owners, having received nothing for their product but Confederate money which the result of the war had made worthless, manifested an unamiable reluctance to give it up, for if they could market it for themselves it would more than recoup them for all their losses in the war. They had therefore exercised a considerable ingenuity in effacing all record of its transfer to the Confederate Government, obliterating the marks on the bales, and hiding these away in swamps and other inconspicuous places, fortifying their claims to private ownership with appalling affidavits and "covering their tracks" in an infinite variety of ways generally.

In effecting their purpose they encountered many difficulties. Cotton in bales is not very portable property; it requires for movement and concealment a good deal of coöperation by persons having no interest in keeping the secret and easily accessible to the blandishments of those interested in tracing it. The negroes, by whom the work was necessarily done, were zealous to pay for emancipation by fidelity to the new régime, and many poor devils among them forfeited their lives by services performed with more loyalty than discretion. Railways—even those having a more than nominal equipment of rails and rolling stock—were unavailable for secret conveyance of the cotton. Navigating the Alabama and Tombigbee rivers were a few small steamboats, the half-dozen pilots familiar with these streams exacting one hundred dollars a day for their services; but our agents, backed by military authority, were at all the principal shipping points and no boat could leave without their consent. The port of Mobile was in our hands and the lower waters were patrolled by gunboats. Cotton might, indeed, be dumped down a "slide" by night at some private landing and fall upon the deck of a steamer idling innocently below. It might even arrive at Mobile, but secretly to transfer it to a deep-water vessel and get it out of the country—that was a dream.

On the movement of private cotton we put no restrictions; and such were the freight rates that it was possible to purchase a steamboat at Mobile, go up the river in ballast, bring down a cargo of cotton and make a handsome profit, after deducting the cost of the boat and all expenses of the venture, including the wage of the pilot. With no great knowledge of "business" I venture to think that in Alabama in the latter part of the year of grace 1865 commercial conditions were hardly normal.

Nor were social conditions what I trust they have now become. There was no law in the country except of the unsatisfactory sort known as "martial," and that was effective only within areas covered by the guns of isolated forts and the physical activities of their small garrisons. True, there were the immemorial laws of self-preservation and retaliation, both of which were liberally interpreted. The latter was faithfully administered, mostly against straggling Federal soldiers and too zealous government officials. When my chief had been ordered to Selma he had arrived just in time to act as sole mourner at the funeral of his predecessor—who had had the bad luck to interpret his instructions in a sense that was disagreeable to a gentleman whose interests were affected by the interpretation. Early one pleasant morning shortly afterward two United States marshals were observed by the roadside in a suburb of the town. They looked comfortable enough there in the sunshine, but each

>had that across his throat
>Which you had hardly cared to see.

When dispatched on business of a delicate nature men in the service of the agency had a significant trick of disappearing—they were of "the unreturning brave." Really the mortality among the unacclimated in the Selma district at that time was excessive. When my chief and I parted at dinner time (our palates were not in harmony) we commonly shook hands and tried to say something memorable that was worthy to serve as "last words." We had been in the army together and had many a time gone into battle without having taken that precaution in the interest of history.

Of course the better class of the people were not accountable for this state of affairs, and I do not remember that I greatly blamed the others. The country was full of the "elements of combustion." The people were impoverished and smarting with a sense of defeat. Organized resistance was no longer possible, but many men trained to the use of arms did not consider themselves included in the surrender and conscientiously believed it both right and expedient to prolong the struggle by private enterprise. Many, no doubt, made the easy and natural transition from soldiering to assassination by insensible degrees, unconscious of the moral difference, such as it is. Selma was little better than a ruin; in the concluding period of the war General Wilson's cavalry had raided it and nearly destroyed it, and the work begun by the battery had been completed by the torch. The conflagration was generally attributed to the negroes, who certainly augmented it, for a number of those suspected of the crime were flung into the flames by the maddened populace. None the less were the Yankee invaders held responsible.

Every Northern man represented some form or phase of an authority which these luckless people horribly hated, and to which they submitted only because, and in so far as, they had to. Fancy such a community, utterly without the restraints of law and with no means of ascertaining public opinion—for newspapers were not—denied even the moral advantage of the pulpit! Considering what human nature has the misfortune to be, it is wonderful that there was so little of violence and crime.

As the carcass invites the vulture, this prostrate land drew adventurers from all points of the compass. Many, I am sorry to say, were in the service of the United States Government. Truth to tell, the special agents of the Treasury were themselves, as a body, not altogether spotless. I could name some of them, and some of their assistants, who made large fortunes by their opportunities. The special agents were allowed one-fourth of the value of the confiscated cotton for expenses of collection—none too much, considering the arduous and perilous character of the service; but the plan opened up such possibilities of fraud as have seldom been accorded by any system of conducting the public business, and never without disastrous results to official morality. Against bribery no provision could have provided an adequate safeguard; the magnitude of the interests involved was too great, the administration of the trust too loose and irresponsible. The system as it was, hastily devised in the storm and stress of a closing war, broke down in the end, and it is doubtful if the Government might not more profitably have let the "captured and abandoned property" alone.

As an instance of the temptations to which we were exposed, and of our tactical dispositions in resistance, I venture to relate a single experience of my own. During an absence of my chief I got upon the trail of a lot of cotton—seven hundred bales, as nearly as I now recollect—which had been hidden with so exceptional ingenuity that I was unable to trace it. One day there came to my office two well-dressed and mannerly fellows who suffered me to infer that they knew all about this cotton and controlled it. When our conference on the subject ended it was past dinner time and they civilly invited me to dine with them, which, in hope of eliciting information over the wine, I did. I knew well enough that they indulged a similar selfish hope, so I had no scruples about using their hospitality to their disadvantage if I could. The subject, however, was not mentioned at table, and we were all singularly abstemious in the matter of champagne—so much so that as we rose from a rather long session at the board we disclosed our sense of the ludicrousness of the situation by laughing outright. Nevertheless, neither party would accept defeat, and for the next few weeks the war of hospitality was fast and furious. We dined together nearly every day, sometimes at my expense, sometimes at theirs. We drove, rode, walked, played at billiards and made many a night of it; but youth and temperance (in drink) pulled me through without serious inroads on my health. We had early come to an understanding and a deadlock. Failing to get the slenderest clew to the location of the cotton I offered them one-fourth if they would surrender it or disclose its hiding-place; they offered me one-fourth if I would sign a permit for its shipment as private property.

All things have an end, and this amusing contest finally closed. Over the remains of a farewell dinner, unusually luxurious, as befitted the occasion, we parted with expressions of mutual esteem—not, I hope, altogether insincere, and the ultimate fate of the cotton is to me unknown. Up to the date of my departure from the agency not a bale of it had either come into possession of the Government or found an outlet. I am sometimes disloyal enough to indulge myself in the hope that they baffled my successors as skilfully as they did me. One cannot help feeling a certain tenderness for men who know and value a good dinner.

Another corrupt proposal that I had the good fortune to be afraid to entertain came, as it were, from within. There was a daredevil fellow whom, as I know him to be dead, I feel justified in naming Jack Harris. He was engaged in all manner of speculative ventures on his own account, but the special agent had so frequently employed him in "enterprises of great pith and moment" that he was in a certain sense and to a certain extent one of us. He seemed to me at the time unique, but shortly afterward I had learned to classify him as a type of the Californian adventurer with whose peculiarities of manner, speech and disposition most of us are to-day familiar enough. He never spoke of his past, having doubtless good reasons for reticence, but any one learned in Western slang—a knowledge then denied me—would have catalogued him with infallible accuracy. He was a rather large, strong fellow, swarthy, black-bearded, black-eyed, black-hearted and entertaining, no end; ignorant with an ignorance whose frankness redeemed it from offensiveness, vulgar with a vulgarity that expressed itself in such metaphors and similes as would have made its peace with the most implacable refinement. He drank hard, gambled high, swore like a parrot, scoffed at everything, was openly and proudly a rascal, did not know the meaning of fear, borrowed money abundantly, and squandered it with royal disregard. Desiring one day to go to Mobile, but reluctant to leave Montgomery and its pleasures—unwilling to quit certainty for hope—he persuaded the captain of a loaded steamboat to wait four days for him at an expense of $400 a day; and lest time should hang too heavy on the obliging skipper's hands, Jack permitted him to share the orgies gratis. But that is not my story.

One day Jack came to me with a rather more sinful proposal than he had heretofore done me the honor to submit. He knew of about a thousand bales of cotton, some of it private property, some of it confiscable, stored at various points on the banks of the Alabama. He had a steamboat in readiness, "with a gallant, gallant crew," and he proposed to drop quietly down to the various landings by night, seize the cotton, load it on his boat and make off down the river. What he wanted from me, and was willing to pay for, was only my official signature to some blank shipping permits; or if I would accompany the expedition and share its fortunes no papers would be necessary. In declining this truly generous offer I felt that I owed it to Jack to give him a reason that he was capable of understanding, so I explained to him the arrangements at Mobile, which would prevent him from transferring his cargo to a ship and getting the necessary papers permitting her to sail. He was astonished and, I think, pained by my simplicity. Did I think him a fool? He did not purpose—not he—to tranship at all: the perfected plan was to dispense with all hampering formality by slipping through Mobile Bay in the black of the night and navigating his laden river craft across the Gulf to Havana! The rascal was in dead earnest, and that natural timidity of disposition which compelled me to withhold my coöperation greatly lowered me in his esteem, I fear.

It was in Cuba, by the way, that Jack came to grief some years later. He was one of the crew of the filibustering vessel Virginius, and was captured and shot along with the others. Something in his demeanor as he knelt in the line to receive the fatal fusillade prompted a priest to inquire his religion. "I am an atheist, by God!" said Jack, and with this quiet profession of faith that gentle spirit winged its way to other tropics.

Having expounded with some particularity the precarious tenure by which I held my office and my life in those "thrilling regions" where my duties lay, I ought to explain by what unhappy chance I am still able to afflict the reader. There lived in Selma a certain once wealthy and still influential citizen, whose two sons, of about my own age, had served as officers in the Confederate Army. I will designate them simply as Charles and Frank. They were types of a class now, I fear, almost extinct. Born and bred in luxury and knowing nothing of the seamy side of life—except, indeed, what they had learned in the war—well educated, brave, generous, sensitive to points of honor, and of engaging manners, these brothers were by all respected, by many loved and by some feared. For they had quick fingers upon the pistol-trigger withal, and would rather fight a duel than eat—nay, drink. Nor were they over-particular about the combat taking the form of a duel—almost any form was good enough. I made their acquaintance by chance and cultivated it for the pleasure it gave me. It was long afterward that I gave a thought to its advantages; but from the time that I became generally known as their friend my safety was assured through all that region; an army with banners could not have given me the same immunity from danger, obstruction or even insult in the performance of my disagreeable duties. What glorious fellows they were, to be sure—these my late antagonists of the dark days when, God forgive us, we were trying to cut one another's throat. To this day I feel a sense of regret when I think of my instrumentality, however small, in depriving the world of many such men in the criminal insanity that we call battle.

Life in Selma became worth living even as the chance of living it augmented. With my new friends and a friend of theirs, whose name—the more shame to me—I cannot now recall, but should not write here if I could, I passed most of my leisure hours. At the houses of themselves and their friends I did most of my dining; and, heaven be praised! there was no necessity for moderation in wine. In their society I committed my sins, and together beneath that noble orb unknown to colder skies, the Southern moon, we atoned for them by acts of devotion performed with song and lute beneath the shrine window of many a local divinity.

One night we had an adventure. We were out late—so late that it was night only astronomically. The streets were "deserted and drear," and, of course, unlighted—the late Confederacy had no gas and no oil. Nevertheless, we saw that we were followed. A man keeping at a fixed distance behind turned as we turned, paused as we paused, and pursued as we moved on. We stopped, went back and remonstrated; asked his intentions in, I dare say, no gentle words. He gave us no reply, but as we left him he followed. Again we stopped, and I felt my pistol plucked out of my pocket. Frank had unceremoniously possessed himself of it and was advancing on the enemy. I do not remember if I had any wish to interpose a protest—anyhow there was no time. Frank fired and the man fell. In a moment all the chamber-windows in the street were thrown open with a head visible (and audible) in each. We told Frank to go home, which to our surprise he did; the rest of us, assisted by somebody's private policeman—who afterward apprised us that we were in arrest—carried the man to a hotel. It was found that his leg was broken above the knee, and the next day it was amputated. We paid his surgeon and his hotel bill, and when he had sufficiently recovered sent him to an address which he gave us in Mobile; but not a word could anybody get out of him as to who he had the misfortune to be, or why he had persisted, against the light, in following a quartet of stray revelers.

On the morning of the shooting, when everything possible had been done for the comfort of the victim, we three accomplices were released on our own recognizance by an old gentleman of severe aspect, who had resumed his function of justice of the peace where he had laid it down during the war. I did not then know that he had no more legal authority than I had myself, and I was somewhat disturbed in mind as I reflected on the possibilities of the situation. The opportunity to get rid of an offensive Federal official must of course be very tempting, and after all the shooting was a trifle hasty and not altogether justifiable.

On the day appointed for our preliminary examination, all of us except Frank were released and put on the witness-stand. We gave a true and congruent history of the affair. The holdover justice listened to it all very patiently and then, with commendable brevity and directness of action, fined Frank five dollars and costs for disorderly conduct. There was no appeal.

There were queer characters in Alabama in those days, as you shall see. Once upon a time the special agent and I started down the Tombigbee River with a steamboat load of government cotton—some six hundred bales. At one of the military stations we took on a guard of a dozen or fifteen soldiers under command of a non-commissioned officer. One evening, just before dusk, as we were rounding a bend where the current set strongly against the left bank of the stream and the channel lay close to that shore, we were suddenly saluted with a volley of bullets and buckshot from that direction. The din of the firing, the rattle and crash of the missiles splintering the woodwork and the jingle of broken glass made a very rude arousing from the tranquil indolence of a warm afternoon on the sluggish Tombigbee. The left bank, which at this point was a trifle higher than the hurricane deck of a steamer, was now swarming with men who, almost near enough to jump aboard, looked unreasonably large and active as they sprang about from cover to cover, pouring in their fire. At the first volley the pilot had deserted his wheel, as well he might, and the boat, drifting in to the bank under the boughs of a tree, was helpless. Her jackstaff and yawl were carried away, her guards broken in, and her deck-load of cotton was tumbling into the stream a dozen bales at once. The captain was nowhere to be seen, the engineer had evidently abandoned his post and the special agent had gone to hunt up the soldiers. I happened to be on the hurricane deck, armed with a revolver, which I fired as rapidly as I could, listening all the time for the fire of the soldiers—and listening in vain. It transpired later that they had not a cartridge among them; and of all helpless mortals a soldier without a cartridge is the most imbecile. But all this time the continuous rattle of the enemy's guns and the petulant pop of my own pocket firearm were punctuated, as it were, by pretty regularly recurring loud explosions, as of a small cannon. They came from somewhere forward—I supposed from the opposition, as I knew we had no artillery on board.

The failure of our military guard made the situation somewhat grave. For two of us, at least, capture meant hanging out of hand. I had never been hanged in all my life and was not enamored of the prospect. Fortunately for us the bandits had selected their point of attack without military foresight. Immediately below them a bayou, impassable to them, let into the river. The moment we had drifted below it we were safe from boarding and capture. The captain was found in hiding and an empty pistol at his ear persuaded him to resume command of his vessel; the engineer and pilot were encouraged to go back to their posts and after some remarkably long minutes, during which we were under an increasingly long-range fire, we got under way. A few cotton bales piled about the pilot-house made us tolerably safe from that sort of thing in the future and then we took account of our damages. Nobody had been killed and only a few were wounded. This gratifying result was attributable to the fact that, being unarmed, nearly everybody had dived below at the first fire and taken cover among the cotton bales. While issuing a multitude of needless commands from the front of the hurricane-deck I looked below, and there, stretched out at full length on his stomach, lay a long, ungainly person, clad in faded butternut, bare-headed, his long, lank hair falling down each side of his neck, his coat-tails similarly parted, and his enormous feet spreading their soles to the blue sky. He had an old-fashioned horse-pistol, some two feet long, which he was in the act of sighting across his left palm for a parting shot at the now distant assailants. A more ludicrous figure I never saw; I laughed outright; but when his weapon went off it was matter for gratitude to be above it instead of before it. It was the "cannon" whose note I had marked all through the unequal fray.

The fellow was a returned Confederate whom we had taken on at one of the upper landings as our only passenger; we were dead-heading him to Mobile. He was undoubtedly in hearty sympathy with the enemy, and I at first suspected him of collusion, but circumstances not necessary to detail here rendered this impossible. Moreover, I had distinctly seen one of the "guerrillas" fall and remain down after my own weapon was empty, and no man else on board except the passenger had fired a shot or had a shot to fire.

When everything had been made snug again, and we were gliding along under the stars, without apprehension; when I had counted fifty-odd bullet holes through the pilot-house (which had not received the attention that by its prominence and importance it was justly entitled to) and everybody was variously boasting his prowess, I approached my butternut comrade-in-arms and thanked him for his kindly aid. "But," said I, "how the devil does it happen that you fight that crowd?"

"Wal, Cap," he drawled, as he rubbed the powder grime from his antique artillery, "I allowed it was mouty clever in you-all to take me on, seein' I hadn't ary cent, so I thought I'd jist kinder work my passage."

WORKING FOR AN EMPRESS

In the spring of 1874 I was living in the pretty English town of Leamington, a place that will be remembered by most Americans who have visited the grave of Shakespeare at Stratford-on-Avon, or by personal inspection of the ruins of Kenilworth Castle have verified their knowledge of English history derived from Scott's incomparable romance. I was at that time connected with several London newspapers, among them the Figaro, a small weekly publication, semi-humorous, semi-theatrical, with a remarkable aptitude for managing the political affairs of France in the interest of the Imperialists. This last peculiarity it owed to the personal sympathies of its editor and proprietor, Mr. James Mortimer, a gentleman who for some twenty years before the overthrow of the Empire had lived in Paris. Mr. Mortimer had been a personal friend of the Emperor and Empress, and on the flight of the latter to England had rendered her important service; and after the release of the Emperor from captivity among the Germans Mr. Mortimer was a frequent visitor to the imperial exiles at Chiselhurst.

One day at Leamington my London mail brought a letter from Mr. Mortimer, informing me that he intended to publish a new satirical journal, which he wished me to write. I was to do all the writing, he the editing; and it would not be necessary for me to come up to London; I could send manuscript by mail. The new journal was not to appear at stated periods, but "occasionally." Would I submit to him a list of suitable titles for it, from which he could make a selection?

With some surprise at what seemed to me the singularly whimsical and unbusiness-like features of the enterprise I wrote him earnestly advising him either to abandon it or materially to modify his plan. I represented to him that such a journal, so conducted, could not in my judgment succeed; but he was obdurate and after a good deal of correspondence I consented to do all the writing if he was willing to do all the losing money. I submitted a number of names which I thought suitable for the paper, but all were rejected, and he finally wrote that he had decided to call the new journal The Lantern. This decision elicited from me another energetic protest. The title was not original, but obviously borrowed from M. Rochefort's famous journal, La Lanterne. True, that publication was dead, and its audacious editor deported to New Caledonia with his Communistic following; but the name could hardly be agreeable to Mr. Mortimer's Imperialist friends, particularly the Empress—the Emperor was then dead. To my surprise Mr. Mortimer not only adhered to his resolution but suggested the propriety of my taking M. Rochefort's late lamented journal as a model for our own. This I flatly declined to do and carried my point; I was delighted to promise, however, that the new paper should resemble the old in one particular: it should be irritatingly disrespectful of existing institutions and exalted personages.

On the 18th of May, 1874, there was published at the corner of St. Bride Street and Shoe Lane, E.C., London, the first number of "The Lantern—Appearing Occasionally. Illuminated by Faustin. Price, sixpence." It was a twelve-page paper with four pages of superb illustrations in six colors. I winced when I contemplated its artistic and mechanical excellence, for I knew at what a price that quality had been obtained. A gold mine would be required to maintain that journal, and that journal could by no means ever be itself a gold mine. A copy lies before me as I write and noting it critically I cannot help thinking that the illuminated title-page of this pioneer in the field of chromatic journalism is the finest thing of the kind that ever came from a press.

Of the literary contents I am less qualified for judgment, inasmuch as I wrote every line in the paper. It may perhaps be said without immodesty that the new "candidate for popular favor" was not distinguished by servile flattery of the British character and meek subservience to the British Government, as might perhaps be inferred from the following extract from an article on General Sir Garnet Wolseley, who had just received the thanks of his Sovereign and a munificent reward from Parliament for his successful plundering expedition through Ashantee:

"We feel a comfortable sense of satisfaction in the thought that The Lantern will never fail to shed the light of its loyal approval upon any unworthy act by which our country shall secure an adequate and permanent advantage. When the great heart of England is stirred by quick cupidity to profitable crime, far be it from us to lift our palms in deprecation. In the wrangle for existence nations, equally with individuals, work by diverse means to a common end—the spoiling of the weak; and when by whatever of outrage we have pushed a feeble competitor to the wall, in Heaven's name let us pin him fast and relieve his pockets of the material good to which, in bestowing it upon him, the bountiful Lord has invited our thieving hand. But these Ashantee women were not worth garroting. Their fal-lals, precious to them, are worthless to us; the entire loot fetched only £11,000—of which sum the man who brought home the trinkets took a little more than four halves. We submit that with practiced agents in every corner of the world and a watchful government at home this great commercial nation might dispose of its honor to better advantage."

With the candor of repentance it may now be confessed that, however unscrupulous it may be abroad, a government which tolerates this kind of criticism cannot rightly be charged with tyranny at home.

By way (as I supposed) of gratitude to M. Rochefort for the use of the title of his defunct journal it had been suggested by Mr. Mortimer that he be given a little wholesome admonition here and there in the paper and I had cheerfully complied. M. Rochefort had escaped from New Caledonia some months before. A disagreeable cartoon was devised for his discomfort and he received a number of such delicate attentions as that following, which in the issue of July 15th greeted him on his arrival in England along with his distinguished compatriot, M. Pascal Grousset:

"M. Rochefort is a gentleman who has lost his standing. There have been greater falls than his. Kings before now have become servitors, honest men bandits, thieves communists. Insignificant in his fortunes as in his abilities, M. Rochefort, who was never very high, is not now very low—he has avoided the falsehood of extremes: never quite a count, he is now but half a convict. Having missed the eminence that would have given him calumniation, he is also denied the obscurity that would bring misconstruction. He is not even a miserable; he is a person. It is curious to note how persistently this man has perverted his gifts. With talents that might have corrupted panegyric, he preferred to refine detraction; fitted to disgrace the salon, he has elected to adorn the cell; the qualities that would have endeared him to a blackguard he has wasted upon Pascal Grousset.

"As we write, it is reported that this person is in England. It is further affirmed that it is his intention to proceed to Belgium or Switzerland to fight certain journalists who have not had the courtesy to suppress the truth about him, though he never told it of them. We presume, however, this rumor is false; M. Rochefort must retain enough of the knowledge he acquired when he was esteemed a gentleman to be aware that a meeting between him and a journalist is now impossible. This is the more to be regretted, because M. Paul de Cassagnac would have much pleasure in taking M. Rochefort's life and we in lamenting his fall.

"M. Rochefort, we believe, is already suffering from an unhealed wound. It is his mouth."

There was a good deal of such "scurril jesting" in the paper, especially in a department called "Prattle." There were verses on all manner of subjects—mostly the nobility and their works and ways, from the viewpoint of disapproval—and epigrams, generally ill-humorous, like the following, headed "Novum Organum":

"In Bacon see the culminating prime
Of British intellect and British crime.
He died, and Nature, settling his affairs,
Parted his powers among us, his heirs:
To each a pinch of common-sense, for seed,
And, to develop it, a pinch of greed.
Each frugal heir, to make the gift suffice,
Buries the talent to manure the vice."

When the first issue of The Lantern appeared I wrote to Mr. Mortimer, again urging him to modify his plans and alter the character of the journal. He replied that it suited him as it was and he would let me know when to prepare "copy" for the second number. That eventually appeared on July 15th. I never was instructed to prepare any more copy, and there has been, I believe, no further issue of that interesting sheet as yet.

Taking a retrospective view of this singular venture in journalism, one day, the explanation of the whole matter came to my understanding in the light of a revelation, and was confirmed later by Mr. Mortimer.

In the days when Napoleon III was at the zenith of his glory and power there was a thorn in his side. It was the pen of M. Henri Rochefort, le Comte de Luçay, journalist and communard. Despite fines, "suppressions," and imprisonments, this gifted writer and unscrupulous blackguard had, as every one knows, made incessant war upon the Empire and all its personnel. The bitter and unfair attacks of his paper, La Lanterne, made life at the Tuilleries exceedingly uncomfortable. His rancor against the Empress was something horrible, and went to the length of denying the legitimacy of the Prince Imperial. His existence was a menace and a terror to the illustrious lady, even when she was in exile at Chiselhurst and he in confinement on the distant island of New Caledonia. When the news of his escape from that penal colony arrived at Chiselhurst the widowed Empress was in despair; and when, on his way to England, he announced his intention of reviving La Lanterne in London (of course he dared not cross the borders of France) she was utterly prostrated by the fear of his pitiless animosity. But what could she do? Not prevent the revival of his dreadful newspaper, certainly, but—well, she could send for Mr. Mortimer. That ingenious gentleman was not long at a loss for an expedient that would accomplish what was possible. He shut Rochefort out of London by forestalling him. At the very time when Mortimer was asking me to suggest a suitable name for the new satirical journal he had already registered at Stationers' Hall—that is to say, copyrighted—the title of The Lantern, a precaution which M. Rochefort's French friends had neglected to take, although they had expended thousands of pounds in a plant for their venture. Mr. Mortimer cruelly permitted them to go on with their costly preparations, and the first intimation they had that the field was occupied came from the newsdealers selling The Lantern. After some futile attempts at relief and redress, M. Rochefort took himself off and set up his paper in Belgium.

The expenses of The Lantern—including a generous douceur to myself—were all defrayed by the Empress. She was the sole owner of it and, I was gratified to learn, took so lively an interest in her venture that a special French edition was printed for her private reading. I was told that she especially enjoyed the articles on M. le Comte de Luçay, though I dare say some of the delicate subtleties of their literary style were lost in translation.

Being in London later in the year, I received through Mortimer an invitation to visit the poor lady, en famille, at Chiselhurst; but as the iron rules of imperial etiquette, even in exile, required that the hospitable request be made in the form of a "command," my republican independence took alarm and I had the incivility to disobey; and I still think it a sufficient distinction to be probably the only American journalist who was ever employed by an Empress in so congenial a pursuit as the pursuit of another journalist.

ACROSS THE PLAINS

That noted pioneer, General John Bidwell, of California, once made a longish step up the western slope of our American Parnassus by an account of his journey "across the plains" seven years before the lamented Mr. Marshall had found the least and worst of all possible reasons for making the "trek." General Bidwell had not the distinction to be a great writer, but in order to command admiration and respect in that province of the Republic of Letters which lies in the Sacramento Valley above the mouth of the Yuba the gift of writing greatly is a needless endowment. Nevertheless I read his narrative with an interest which on analysis turns out to be a by-product of personal experience: among my youthful indiscretions was a journey over much of the same ground, which I took in much the same way—as did many thousands before and after.

It was a far cry from 1841 to 1866, yet the country between the Missouri River and the Sierra Nevada had not greatly improved: civilization had halted at the river, awaiting transportation. A railroad had set out from Omaha westward, and another at Sacramento was solemnly considering the impossible suggestion of going eastward to meet it. There were lunatics in those days, as there are in these. I left the one road a few miles out of the Nebraskan village and met the other at Dutch Flat, in California.

Waste no compassion on the loneliness of my journey: a thriving colony of Mormons had planted itself in the valley of Salt Lake and there were "forts" at a few points along the way, where ambitious young army officers passed the best years of their lives guarding live stock and teaching the mysteries of Hardee's tactics to that alien patriot, the American regular. There was a dusty wagon road, bordered with bones—not always those of animals—with an occasional mound, sometimes dignified with a warped and rotting head-board bearing an illegible inscription. (One inscription not entirely illegible is said to have concluded with this touching tribute to the worth of the departed: "He was a good egg." Another was: "He done his damnedest") In other particulars the "Great American Desert" of our fathers was very like what it was when General Bidwell's party traversed it with that hereditary instinct, that delicacy of spiritual nose which served the Western man of that day in place of a map and guide-book. Westward the course of empire had taken its way, but excepting these poor vestiges it had for some fifteen hundred miles left no trace of its march. The Indian of the plains had as yet seen little to unsettle his assurance of everlasting dominion. Of the slender lines of metal creeping slowly toward him from East and West he knew little; and had he known more, how could he have foreseen their momentous effect upon his "ancient solitary reign"?

I remember very well, as so many must, some of the marked features of the route that General Bidwell mentions. One of the most imposing of these is Court House Rock, near the North Platte. Surely no object of such dignity ever had a more belittling name— given it in good faith no doubt by some untraveled wight whose county court-house was the most "reverend pile" of which he had any conception. It should have been called the Titan's Castle. What a gracious memory I have of the pomp and splendor of its aspect, with the crimson glories of the setting sun fringing its outlines, illuminating its western walls like the glow of Mammon's fires for the witches' revel in the Hartz, and flung like banners from its crest!

I suppose Court House Rock is familiar enough and commonplace enough to the dwellers in that land (riparian tribes once infesting the low lands of Ohio and Indiana and the flats of Iowa), but to me, tipsy with youth, full-fed on Mayne Reid's romances, and now first entering the enchanted region that he so charmingly lied about, it was a revelation and a dream. I wish that anything in the heavens, on the earth, or in the waters under the earth would give me now such an emotion as I experienced in the shadow of that "great rock in a weary land."

I was not a pilgrim, but an engineer attaché to an expedition through Dakota and Montana, to inspect some new military posts. The expedition consisted, where the Indians preserved the peace, of the late General W.B. Hazen, myself, a cook and a teamster; elsewhere we had an escort of cavalry. My duty, as I was given to understand it, was to amuse the general and other large game, make myself as comfortable as possible without too much discomfort to others, and when in an unknown country survey and map our route for the benefit of those who might come after. The posts which the general was to inspect had recently been established along a military road, one end of which was at the North Platte and the other—there was no other end; up about Fort C.F. Smith at the foot of the Big-Horn Mountains the road became a buffalo trail and was lost in the weeds. But it was a useful road, for by leaving it before going too far one could reach a place near the headwaters of the Yellowstone, where the National Park is now.

By a master stroke of military humor we were ordered to return (to Washington) via Salt Lake City, San Francisco and Panama. I obeyed until I got as far as San Francisco, where, finding myself appointed to a second lieutenancy in the Regular Army, ingratitude, more strong than traitors' arms, quite vanquished me: I resigned, parted from Hazen more in sorrow than in anger and remained in California.

I have thought since that this may have been a youthful error: the Government probably meant no harm, and if I had served long enough I might have become a captain. In time, if I lived, I should naturally have become the senior captain of the Army; and then if there were another war and any of the field officers did me the favor to paunch a bullet I should become the junior major, certain of another step upward as soon as a number of my superiors equal to the whole number of majors should be killed, resign or die of old age—enchanting prospect! But I am getting a long way off the trail.

It was near Fort C.F. Smith that we found our first buffaloes, and abundant they were. We had to guard our camp at night with fire and sword to keep them from biting us as they grazed. Actually one of them half-scalped a teamster as he lay dreaming of home with his long fair hair commingled with the toothsome grass. His utterances as the well-meaning beast lifted him from the ground and tried to shake the earth from his roots were neither wise nor sweet, but they made a profound impression on the herd, which, arching its multitude of tails, absented itself to pastures new like an army with banners.

At Fort C.F. Smith we parted with our impedimenta, and with an escort of about two dozen cavalrymen and a few pack animals struck out on horseback through an unexplored country northwest for old Fort Benton, on the upper Missouri. The journey was not without its perils. Our only guide was my compass; we knew nothing of the natural obstacles that we must encounter; the Indians were on the warpath, and our course led us through the very heart of their country. Luckily for us they were gathering their clans into one great army for a descent upon the posts that we had left behind; a little later some three thousand of them moved upon Fort Phil Kearney, lured a force of ninety men and officers outside and slaughtered them to the last man. This was one of the posts that we had inspected, and the officers killed had hospitably entertained us.

In that lively and interesting book, "Indian Fights and Fighters," Dr. Cyrus Townsend Brady says of this "outpost of civilization":

"The most careful watchfulness was necessary at all hours of the day and night. The wood trains to fetch logs to the sawmills were heavily guarded. There was fighting all the time. Casualties among the men were by no means rare. At first it was difficult to keep men within the limits of the camp; but stragglers who failed to return, and some who had been cut off, scalped and left for dead, but who had crawled back to die, convinced every one of the wisdom of the commanding officer's repeated orders and cautions. To chronicle the constant succession of petty skirmishes would be wearisome; yet they often resulted in torture and loss of life on the part of the soldiers, although the Indians in most instances suffered the more severely."

In a footnote the author relates this characteristic instance of the Government's inability to understand: "Just when the alarms were most frequent a messenger came to the headquarters, announcing that a train en route from Fort Laramie, with special messengers from that post, was corraled by Indians, and demanded immediate help. An entire company of infantry in wagons, with a mountain howitzer and several rounds of grapeshot, was hastened to their relief. It proved to be a train with mail from the Laramie Commission, announcing the confirmation of a 'satisfactory treaty of peace with all the Indians of the Northwest,' and assuring the district commander of the fact. The messenger was brought in in safety, and peace lasted until his message was delivered. So much was gained—that the messenger did not lose his scalp."

Through this interesting environment our expeditionary force of four men had moved to the relief of the beleaguered post, but finding it impossible to "raise the siege" had—with a score of troopers—pushed on to Fort C.F. Smith, and thence into the Unknown.

The first part of this new journey was well enough; there were game and water. Where we swam the Yellowstone we had an abundance of both, for the entire river valley, two or three miles wide, was dotted with elk. There were hundreds. As we advanced they became scarce; buffalo became scarce; bear, deer, rabbits, sage-hens, even prairie dogs gave out, and we were near starving. Water gave out too, and starvation was a welcome state: our hunger was so much less disagreeable than our thirst that it was a real treat.

However, we got to Benton, Heaven knows how and why, but we were a sorry-looking lot, though our scalps were intact. If in all that region there is a mountain that I have not climbed, a river that I have not swum, an alkali pool that I have not thrust my muzzle into, or an Indian that I have not shuddered to think about, I am ready to go back in a Pullman sleeper and do my duty.

From Fort Benton we came down through Helena and Virginia City, Montana—then new mining camps—to Salt Lake, thence westward to California. Our last bivouac was on the old camp of the Donner party, where, in the flickering lights and dancing shadows made by our camp-fire, I first heard the story of that awful winter, and in the fragrance of the meat upon the coals fancied I could detect something significantly uncanny. The meat which the Donner party had cooked at that spot was not quite like ours. Pardon: I mean it was not like that which we cooked.

THE MIRAGE

Since the overland railways have long been carrying many thousands of persons across the elevated plateaus of the continent the mirage in many of its customary aspects has become pretty well known to great numbers of persons all over the Union, and the tales of early observers who came "der blains agross" are received with a less frigid inhospitality than they formerly were by incredulous pioneers who had come "der Horn aroundt," as the illustrious Hans Breitmann phrases it; but in its rarer and more marvelous manifestations, the mirage is still a rock upon which many a reputation for veracity is wrecked remediless. With an ambition intrepidly to brave this disaster, and possibly share it with the hundreds of devoted souls whose disregard of the injunction never to tell an incredible truth has branded them as hardy and impenitent liars, I purpose to note here a few of the more remarkable illusions by which my own sense of sight has been befooled by the freaks of the enchanter.

It is apart from my purpose to explain the mirage scientifically, and not altogether in my power. Every schoolboy can do so, I suppose, to the satisfaction of his teacher if the teacher has not himself seen the phenomenon, or has seen it only in the broken, feeble and evanescent phases familiar to the overland passenger; but for my part I am unable to understand how the simple causes affirmed in the text-books sufficiently account for the infinite variety and complexity of some of the effects said to be produced by them. But of this the reader shall judge for himself.

One summer morning in the upper North Platte country I rose from my blankets, performed the pious acts of sun-worship by yawning toward the east, kicked together the parted embers of my camp-fire, and bethought me of water for my ablutions. We had gone into bivouac late in the night on the open plain, and without any clear notion of where we were. There were a half-dozen of us, our chief on a tour of inspection of the new military posts in Wyoming. I accompanied the expedition as surveyor. Having an aspiration for water I naturally looked about to see what might be the prospect of obtaining it, and to my surprise and delight saw a long line of willows, apparently some three hundred yards away. Willows implied water, and snatching up a camp-kettle I started forward without taking the trouble to put on my coat and hat. For the first mile or two I preserved a certain cheerful hopefulness; but when the sun had risen farther toward the meridian and began to affect my bare head most uncomfortably, and the picketed horses at the camp were hull down on the horizon in the rear, and the willows in front increased their pace out of all proportion to mine, I began to grow discouraged and sat down on a stone to wish myself back. Perceiving that the willows also had halted for breath I determined to make a dash at them, leaving the camp-kettle behind to make its way back to camp as best it could. I was now traveling "flying light," and had no doubt of my ability to overtake the enemy, which had, however, disappeared over the crest of a low sandhill. Ascending this I was treated to a surprise. Right ahead of me lay a barren waste of sand extending to the right and left as far as I could see. Its width in the direction that I was going I judged to be about twenty miles. On its farther border the cactus plain began again, sloping gradually upward to the horizon, along which was a fringe of cedar trees—the willows of my vision! In that country a cedar will not grow within thirty miles of water if it knows it.

On my return journey I coldly ignored the appeals of the camp-kettle, and when I met the rescuing party which had been for some hours trailing me made no allusion to the real purpose of my excursion. When the chief asked if I purposed to enter a plea of temporary insanity I replied that I would reserve my defense for the present; and in fact I never did disclose it until now.

I had afterward the satisfaction of seeing the chief, an experienced plainsman, consume a full hour, rifle in hand, working round to the leeward of a dead coyote in the sure and certain hope of bagging a sleeping buffalo. Mirage or no mirage, you must not too implicitly trust your eyes in the fantastic atmosphere of the high plains.

I remember that one forenoon I looked forward to the base of the Big Horn Mountains and selected a most engaging nook for the night's camp. My good opinion of it was confirmed when we reached it three days later. The deception in this instance was due to nothing but the marvelous lucidity of the atmosphere and the absence of objects of known dimensions, and these sources of error are sometimes sufficient of themselves to produce the most incredible illusions. When they are in alliance with the mirage the combination's pranks are bewildering.

One of the most grotesque and least comfortable of my experiences with the magicians of the air occurred near the forks of the Platte. There had been a tremendous thunder-storm, lasting all night. In the morning my party set forward over the soaken prairie under a cloudless sky intensely blue. I was riding in advance, absorbed in thought, when I was suddenly roused to a sense of material things by exclamations of astonishment and apprehension from the men behind. Looking forward, I beheld a truly terrifying spectacle. Immediately in front, at a distance, apparently, of not more than a quarter-mile, was a long line of the most formidable looking monsters that the imagination ever conceived. They were taller than trees. In them the elements of nature seemed so fantastically and discordantly confused and blended, compounded, too, with architectural and mechanical details, that they partook of the triple character of animals, houses and machines. Legs they had, that an army of elephants could have marched among; bodies that ships might have sailed beneath; heads about which eagles might have delighted to soar, and ears—they were singularly well gifted with ears. But wheels also they were endowed with, and vast sides of blank wall; the wheels as large as the ring of a circus, the walls white and high as cliffs of chalk along an English coast. Among them, on them, beneath, in and a part of them, were figures and fragments of figures of gigantic men. All were inextricably interblended and superposed—a man's head and shoulders blazoned on the side of an animal; a wheel with legs for spokes rolling along the creature's back; a vast section of wall, having no contact with the earth, but (with a tail hanging from its rear, like a note of admiration) moving along the line, obscuring here an anatomical horror and disclosing there a mechanical nightmare. In short, this appalling procession, which was crossing our road with astonishing rapidity, seemed made up of unassigned and unassorted units, out of which some imaginative god might be about to create a world of giants, ready supplied with some of the appliances of a high civilization. Yet the whole apparition had so shadowy and spectral a look that the terror it inspired was itself vague and indefinite, like the terror of a dream. It affected our horses as well as ourselves; they extended their necks and threw forward their ears. For some moments we sat in our saddles surveying the hideous and extravagant spectacle without a word, and our tongues were loosened only when it began rapidly to diminish and recede, and at last was resolved into a train of mules and wagons, barely visible on the horizon. They were miles away and outlined against the blue sky.

I then remembered what my astonishment had not permitted me closely to note—that this pageant had appeared to move along parallel to the foot of a slope extending upward and backward to an immense height, intersected with rivers and presenting all the features of a prairie landscape. The mirage had in effect contracted the entire space between us and the train to a pistol-shot in breadth, and had made a background for its horrible picture by lifting into view Heaven knows how great an extent of country below our horizon. Does refraction account for all this? To this day I cannot without vexation remember the childish astonishment that prevented me from observing the really interesting features of the spectacle and kept my eyes fixed with a foolish distension on a lot of distorted mules, teamsters and wagons.

One of the commonest and best known tricks of the mirage is that of overlaying a dry landscape with ponds and lakes, and by a truly interesting and appropriate coincidence one or more travelers perishing of thirst seem always to be present, properly to appreciate the humor of the deception; but when a gentleman whose narrative suggested this article averred that he had seen these illusory lakes navigated by phantom boats filled with visionary persons he was, I daresay, thought to be drawing the long bow, even by many miragists in good standing. For aught I know he may have been. I can only attest the entirely credible character of the statement.

Away up at the headwaters of the Missouri, near the British possessions, I found myself one afternoon rather unexpectedly on the shore of an ocean. At less than a gunshot from where I stood was as plainly defined a seabeach as one could wish to see. The eye could follow it in either direction, with all its bays, inlets and promontories, to the horizon. The sea was studded with islands, and these with tall trees of many kinds, both islands and trees being reflected in the water with absolute fidelity. On many of the islands were houses, showing white beneath the trees, and on one which lay farthest out seaward was a considerable city, with towers, domes and clusters of steeples. There were ships in the offing whose sails glistened in the sunlight and, closer in, several boats of novel but graceful design, crowded with human figures, moved smoothly among the lesser islands, impelled by some power invisible from my point of view, each boat attended by its inverted reflection "crowding up beneath the keel." It must be admitted that the voyagers were habited after a somewhat uncommon fashion— almost unearthly, I may say—and were so grouped that at my distance I could not clearly distinguish their individual limbs and attitudes. Their features were, of course, entirely invisible. None the less, they were plainly human beings—what other creatures would be boating? Of the other features of the scene—the coast, islands, trees, houses, city and ships hull-down in the offing—I distinctly affirm an absolute identity of visible aspect with those to which we are accustomed in the realm of reality; imagination had simply nothing to do with the matter. True, I had not recently had the advantage of seeing any such objects, except trees, and these had been mighty poor specimens, but, like Macduff, I "could not but remember such things were," nor had I forgotten how they looked.

Of course I was not for an instant deceived by all this: I knew that under it all lay a particularly forbidding and inhospitable expanse of sagebrush and cactus, peopled with nothing more nearly akin to me than prairie dogs, ground owls and jackass rabbits—that with these exceptions the desert was as desolate as the environment of Ozymandias' "vast and trunkless legs of stone." But as a show it was surely the most enchanting that human eyes had ever looked on, and after more years than I care to count it remains one of memory's most precious possessions. The one thing which always somewhat impairs the illusion in such instances—the absence of the horizon water-line—did not greatly abate the vraisemblance in this, for the large island in the distance nearly closed the view seaward, and the ships occupied most of the remaining space. I had but to fancy a slight haze on the farther water, and all was right and regular. For more than a half-hour this charming picture remained intact; then ugly patches of plain began to show through, the islands with their palms and temples slowly dissolved, the boats foundered with every soul on board, the sea drifted over the headlands in a most unwaterlike way, and inside the hour since,

> like stout Cortez, when with eagle eyes
> He stared at the Pacific, and all his men
> Looked at each other with a wild surmise,
> Silent upon a peak in Darien,

I had discovered this unknown sea all this insubstantial pageant had faded like the baseless fabric of the vision that it was and left not a rack behind.

In some of its minor manifestations the mirage is sometimes seen on the western coast of our continent, in the bay of San Francisco, for example, causing no small surprise to the untraveled and unread observer, and no small pain to the spirits of purer fire who are fated to be caught within earshot and hear him pronounce it a "mirridge." I have seen Goat Island without visible means of support and Red Rock suspended in mid-air like the coffin of the Prophet. Looking up toward Mare Island one most ungracious morning when a barbarous norther had purged the air of every stain and the human soul of every virtue, I saw San Pablo Bay margined with cliffs whose altitude must have exceeded considerably that from whose dizzy verge old eyeless Gloster, falling in a heap at his own feet, supposed himself to have sailed like a stone.

One more instance and "I've done, i' faith." Gliding along down the Hudson River one hot summer afternoon in a steamboat, I went out on the afterguard for a breath of fresh air, but there was none to be had. The surface of the river was like oil and the steamer's hull slipped through it with surprisingly little disturbance. Her tremor was for once hardly perceptible; the beating of her paddles was subdued to an almost inaudible rhythm. The air seemed what we call "hollow" and had apparently hardly enough tenuity to convey sounds. Everywhere on the surface of the glassy stream were visible undulations of heat, and the light steam of evaporation lay along the sluggish water and hung like a veil between the eye and the bank. Seated in an armchair and overcome by the heat and the droning of some prosy passengers near by, I fell asleep. When I awoke the guards were crowded with passengers in a high state of excitement, pointing and craning shoreward. Looking in the same direction I saw, through the haze, the sharp outlines of a city in gray silhouette. Roofs, spires, pinnacles, chimneys, angles of wall—all were there, cleanly cut out against the air.

"What is it?" I cried, springing to my feet.

"That, sir," replied a passenger stolidly, "is Poughkeepsie."

It was.

A SOLE SURVIVOR

Among the arts and sciences, the art of Sole Surviving is one of the most interesting, as (to the artist) it is by far the most important. It is not altogether an art, perhaps, for success in it is largely due to accident. One may study how solely to survive, yet, having an imperfect natural aptitude, may fail of proficiency and be early cut off. To the contrary, one little skilled in its methods, and not even well grounded in its fundamental principles, may, by taking the trouble to have been born with a suitable constitution, attain to a considerable eminence in the art. Without undue immodesty, I think I may fairly claim some distinction in it myself, although I have not regularly acquired it as one acquires knowledge and skill in writing, painting and playing the flute. O yes, I am a notable Sole

Survivor, and some of my work in that way attracts great attention, mostly my own.

You would naturally expect, then, to find in me one who has experienced all manner of disaster at sea and the several kinds of calamity incident to a life on dry land. It would seem a just inference from my Sole Survivorship that I am familiar with railroad wrecks, inundations (though these are hardly dry-land phenomena), pestilences, earthquakes, conflagrations and other forms of what the reporters delight to call "a holocaust." This is not entirely true; I have never been shipwrecked, never assisted as "unfortunate sufferer" at a fire or railway collision, and know of the ravages of epidemics only by hearsay. The most destructive temblor of which I have had a personal experience decreased the population of San Francisco by fewer, probably, than ten thousand persons, of whom not more than a dozen were killed; the others moved out of town. It is true that I once followed the perilous trade of a soldier, but my eminence in Sole Surviving is of a later growth and not specially the product of the sword.

Opening the portfolio of memory, I draw out picture after picture—"figure-pieces"—groups of forms and faces whereof mine only now remains, somewhat the worse for wear.

Here are three young men lolling at ease on a grassy bank. One, a handsome, dark-eyed chap, with a forehead like that of a Grecian god, raises his body on his elbow, looks straight away to the horizon, where some black trees hold captive certain vestiges of sunset as if they had torn away the plumage of a flight of flamingoes, and says: "Fellows, I mean to be rich. I shall see every country worth seeing. I shall taste every pleasure worth having. When old, I shall become a hermit."

Said another slender youth, fair-haired: "I shall become President and execute a coup d'etat making myself an absolute monarch. I shall then issue a decree requiring that all hermits be put to death."

The third said nothing. Was he restrained by some prescient sense of the perishable nature of the material upon which he was expected to inscribe the record of his hopes? However it may have been, he flicked his shoe with a hazel switch and kept his own counsel. For twenty years he has been the Sole Survivor of the group.

The scene changes. Six men are on horseback on a hill—a general and his staff. Below, in the gray fog of a winter morning, an army, which has left its intrenchments, is moving upon those of the enemy—creeping silently into position. In an hour the whole wide valley for miles to left and right will be all aroar with musketry stricken to seeming silence now and again by thunder claps of big guns. In the meantime the risen sun has burned a way through the fog, splendoring a part of the beleaguered city.

"Look at that, General," says an aide; "it is like enchantment."

"Go and enchant Colonel Post," said the general, without taking his field-glass from his eyes, "and tell him to pitch in as soon as he hears Smith's guns."

All laughed. But to-day I laugh alone. I am the Sole Survivor.

It would be easy to fill many pages with instances of Sole Survival, from my own experience. I could mention extinct groups composed wholly (myself excepted) of the opposing sex, all of whom, with the same exception, have long ceased their opposition, their warfare accomplished, their pretty noses blue and chill under the daisies. They were good girls, too, mostly, Heaven rest them! There were Maud and Lizzie and Nanette (ah, Nanette, indeed; she is the deadest of the whole bright band) and Emeline and—but really this is not discreet; one should not survive and tell.

The flame of a camp-fire stands up tall and straight toward the black sky. We feed it constantly with sage brush. A circling wall of darkness closes us in; but turn your back to the fire and walk a little away and you shall see the serrated summit-line of snow-capped mountains, ghastly cold in the moonlight. They are in all directions; everywhere they efface the great gold stars near the horizon, leaving the little green ones of the mid-heaven trembling viciously, as bleak as steel. At irregular intervals we hear the distant howling of a wolf—now on this side and again on that. We check our talk to listen; we cast quick glances toward our weapons, our saddles, our picketed horses: the wolves may be of the variety known as Sioux, and there are but four of us.

"What would you do, Jim," said Hazen, "if we were surrounded by Indians?"

Jim Beckwourth was our guide—a life-long frontiersman, an old man "beated and chopped with tanned antiquity." He had at one time been a chief of the Crows.

"I'd spit on that fire," said Jim Beckwourth.

The old man has gone, I hope, where there is no fire to be quenched. And Hazen, and the chap with whom I shared my blanket that winter night on the plains—both gone. One might suppose that I would feel something of the natural exultation of a Sole Survivor; but as Byron found that

> our thoughts take wildest flight
> Even at the moment when they should array
> Themselves in pensive order,

so I find that they sometimes array themselves in pensive order, even at the moment when they ought to be most hilarious.

Of reminiscences there is no end. I have a vast store of them laid up, wherewith to wile away the tedious years of my anecdotage—whenever it shall please Heaven to make me old. Some years that I passed in London as a working journalist are particularly rich in them. Ah! "we were a gallant company" in those days.

I am told that the English are heavy thinkers and dull talkers. My recollection is different; speaking from that, I should say they are no end clever with their tongues. Certainly I have not elsewhere heard such brilliant talk as among the artists and writers of London. Of course they were a picked lot; some of them had attained to some eminence in the world of intellect; others have achieved it since. But they were not all English by many. London draws the best brains of Ireland and Scotland, and there is always a small American contingent, mostly correspondents of the big New York journals.

The typical London journalist is a gentleman. He is usually a graduate of one or the other of the great universities. He is well paid and holds his position, whatever it may be, by a less precarious tenure than his American congener. He rather moves than "dabbles" in literature, and not uncommonly takes a hand at some of the many forms of art. On the whole, he is a good fellow, too, with a skeptical mind, a cynical tongue, and a warm heart. I found these men agreeable, hospitable, intelligent, amusing. We worked too hard, dined too well, frequented too many clubs, and went to bed too late in the forenoon. We were overmuch addicted to shedding the blood of the grape. In short, we diligently, conscientiously, and with a perverse satisfaction burned the candle of life at both ends and in the middle.

This was many a year ago. To-day a list of these men's names with a cross against that of each one whom I know to be dead would look like a Roman Catholic cemetery. I could dine all the survivors at the table on which I write, and I should like to do so. But the dead ones, I must say, were the best diners.

But about Sole Surviving. There was a London publisher named John Camden Hotten. Among American writers he had a pretty dark reputation as a "pirate." They accused him of republishing their books without their assent, which, in absence of international copyright, he had a legal, and it seems to me (a "sufferer") a moral right to do. Through sympathy with their foreign confrères British writers also held him in high disesteem.

I knew Hotten very well, and one day I stood by what purported to be his body, which afterward I assisted to bury in the cemetery at

Highgate. I am sure that it was his body, for I was uncommonly careful in the matter of identification, for a very good reason, which you shall know.

Aside from his "piracy," Hotten had a wide renown as "a hard man to deal with." For several months before his death he had owed me one hundred pounds sterling, and he could not possibly have been more reluctant to part with anything but a larger sum. Even to this day in reviewing the intelligent methods—ranging from delicate finesse to frank effrontery—by which that good man kept me out of mine own I am prostrated with admiration and consumed with envy. Finally by a lucky chance I got him at a disadvantage and seeing my power he sent his manager—a fellow named Chatto, who as a member of the firm of Chatto & Windus afterward succeeded to his business and methods—to negotiate. I was the most implacable creditor in the United Kingdom, and after two mortal hours of me in my most acidulated mood Chatto pulled out a check for the full amount, ready signed by Hotten in anticipation of defeat. Before handing it to me Chatto said: "This check is dated next Saturday. Of course you will not present it until then."

To this I cheerfully consented.

"And now," said Chatto, rising to go, "as everything is satisfactory I hope you will go out to Hotten's house and have a friendly talk. It is his wish."

On Saturday morning I went. In pursuance, doubtless, of his design when he antedated that check he had died of a pork pie promptly on the stroke of twelve o'clock the night before—which invalidated the check! I have met American publishers who thought they knew something about the business of drinking champagne out of writers' skulls. If this narrative—which, upon my soul, is every word true—teaches them humility by showing that genuine commercial sagacity is not bounded by geographical lines it will have served its purpose.

Having assured myself that Mr. Hotten was really no more, I drove furiously bank-ward, hoping that the sad tidings had not preceded me—and they had not.

Alas! on the route was a certain tap-room greatly frequented by authors, artists, newspaper men and "gentlemen of wit and pleasure about town."

Sitting about the customary table were a half-dozen or more choice spirits—George Augustus Sala, Henry Sampson, Tom Hood the younger, Captain Mayne Reid, and others less known to fame. I am sorry to say my somber news affected these sinners in a way that was shocking. Their levity was a thing to shudder at. As Sir Boyle Roche might have said, it grated harshly upon an ear that had a dubious check in its pocket. Having uttered their hilarious minds by word of mouth all they knew how, these hardy and impenitent offenders set about writing "appropriate epitaphs." Thank Heaven, all but one of these have escaped my memory, one that I wrote myself. At the close of the rites, several hours later, I resumed my movement against the bank. Too late—the old, old story of the hare and the tortoise was told again. The "heavy news" had overtaken and passed me as I loitered by the wayside.

All attended the funeral—Sala, Sampson, Hood, Reid, and the undistinguished others, including this present Sole Survivor of the group. As each cast his handful of earth upon the coffin I am very sure that, like Lord Brougham on a somewhat similar occasion, we all felt more than we cared to express. On the death of a political antagonist whom he had not treated with much consideration his lordship was asked, rather rudely, "Have you no regrets now that he is gone?"

After a moment of thoughtful silence he replied, with gravity, "Yes; I favor his return."

One night in the summer of 1880 I was driving in a light wagon through the wildest part of the Black Hills in South Dakota. I had left Deadwood and was well on my way to Rockerville with thirty thousand dollars on my person, belonging to a mining company of which I was the general manager. Naturally, I had taken the precaution to telegraph my secretary at Rockerville to meet me at Rapid City, then a small town, on another route; the telegram was intended to mislead the "gentlemen of the road" whom I knew to be watching my movements, and who might possibly have a confederate in the telegraph office. Beside me on the seat of the wagon sat Boone May.

Permit me to explain the situation. Several months before, it had been the custom to send a "treasure-coach" twice a week from Deadwood to Sidney, Nebraska. Also, it had been the custom to have this coach captured and plundered by "road agents." So intolerable had this practice become—even iron-clad coaches loopholed for rifles proving a vain device—that the mine owners had adopted the more practicable plan of importing from California a half-dozen of the most famous "shotgun messengers" of Wells, Fargo & Co.—fearless and trusty fellows with an instinct for killing, a readiness of resource that was an intuition, and a sense of direction that put a shot where it would do the most good more accurately than the most careful aim. Their feats of marksmanship were so incredible that seeing was scarcely believing.

In a few weeks these chaps had put the road agents out of business and out of life, for they attacked them wherever found. One sunny Sunday morning two of them strolling down a street of Deadwood recognized five or six of the rascals, ran back to their hotel for their rifles, and returning killed them all!

Boone May was one of these avengers. When I employed him, as a messenger, he was under indictment for murder. He had trailed a "road agent" across, the Bad Lands for hundreds of miles, brought him back to within a few miles of Deadwood and picketed him out for the night. The desperate man, tied as he was, had attempted to escape, and May found it expedient to shoot and bury him. The grave by the roadside is perhaps still pointed out to the curious. May gave himself up, was formally charged with murder, released on his own recognizance, and I had to give him leave of absence to go to court and be acquitted. Some of the New York directors of my company having been good enough to signify their disapproval of my action in employing "such a man," I could do no less than make some recognition of their dissent, and thenceforth he was borne upon the pay-rolls as "Boone May, Murderer." Now let me get back to my story.

I knew the road fairly well, for I had previously traveled it by night, on horseback, my pockets bulging with currency and my free hand holding a cocked revolver the entire distance of fifty miles. To make the journey by wagon with a companion was luxury. Still, the drizzle of rain was uncomfortable. May sat hunched up beside me, a rubber poncho over his shoulders and a Winchester rifle in its leathern case between his knees. I thought him a trifle off his guard, but said nothing. The road, barely visible, was rocky, the wagon rattled, and alongside ran a roaring stream. Suddenly we heard through it all the clinking of a horse's shoes directly behind, and simultaneously the short, sharp words of authority: "Throw up your hands!"

With an involuntary jerk at the reins I brought my team to its haunches and reached for my revolver. Quite needless: with the quickest movement that I had ever seen in anything but a cat— almost before the words were out of the horseman's mouth—May had thrown himself backward across the back of the seat, face upward, and the muzzle of his rifle was within a yard of the fellow's breast! What further occurred among the three of us there in the gloom of the forest has, I fancy, never been accurately related.

Boone May is long dead of yellow fever in Brazil, and I am the Sole Survivor.

There was a famous prima donna with whom it was my good fortune to cross the Atlantic to New York. In truth I was charged by a friend of both with the agreeable duty of caring for her safety and comfort. Madame was gracious, clever, altogether charming, and before the voyage was two days old a half-dozen of the men aboard, whom she had permitted me to present, were heels over head in love with her, as I was myself.

Our competition for her favor did not make us enemies; on the contrary we were drawn together into something like an offensive and defensive alliance by a common sorrow—the successful rivalry of a singularly handsome Italian who sat next her at table. So assiduous was he in his attentions that my office as the lady's guide, philosopher and friend was nearly a sinecure, and as to the others, they had hardly one chance a day to prove their devotion: that enterprising son of Italy dominated the entire situation. By some diabolical prevision he anticipated Madame's every need and wish—placed her reclining-chair in the most sheltered spots on deck, smothered her in layer upon layer of wraps, and conducted himself, generally, in the most inconsiderate way. Worse still, Madame accepted his good offices with a shameless grace "which said as plain as whisper in the ear" that there was a perfect understanding between them. What made it harder to bear was the fellow's faulty civility to the rest of us; he seemed hardly aware of our existence.

Our indignation was not loud, but deep. Every day in the smoking-room we contrived the most ingenious and monstrous, plans for his undoing in this world and the next; the least cruel being a project to lure him to the upper deck on a dark night and send him unshriven to his account by way of the lee rail; but as none of us knew enough Italian to tell him the needful falsehood that scheme of justice came to nothing, as did all the others. At the wharf in New York we parted from Madame more in sorrow than in anger, and from her conquering cavalier with polite manifestations of the contempt we did not feel.

That evening I called on her at her hotel, facing Union Square. Soon after my arrival there was an audible commotion out in front: the populace, headed by a brass band and incited, doubtless, by pure love of art, had arrived to do honor to the great singer. There was music—a serenade—followed by shoutings of the lady's name. She seemed a trifle nervous, but I led her to the balcony, where she made a very pretty little speech, piquant with her most charming accent. When the tumult and shouting had died we re-entered her apartment to resume our conversation. Would it please monsieur to have a glass, of wine? It would. She left the room for a moment; then came the wine and glasses on a tray, borne by that impossible Italian! He had a napkin across his arm—he was a servant.

Barring some of the band and the populace, I am doubtless the Sole Survivor, for Madame has for a number of years had a permanent engagement Above, and my faith in Divine Justice does not permit me to think that the servile wretch who cast down the mighty from their seat among the Sons of Hope was suffered to live out the other half of his days.

A dinner of seven in an old London tavern—a good dinner, the memory whereof is not yet effaced from the tablets of the palate. A soup, a plate of white-bait be-lemoned and red-peppered with exactness, a huge joint of roast beef, from which we sliced at will, flanked by various bottles of old dry Sherry and crusty Port—such Port! (And we are expected to be patriots in a country where it cannot be procured! And the Portuguese are expected to love the country which, having it, sends it away!) That was the dinner—there was Stilton cheese; it were shameful not to mention the Stilton. Good, wholesome, and toothsome it was, rich and nutty. The Stilton that we get here, clouted in tin-foil, is monstrous poor stuff, hardly better than our American sort. After dinner there were walnuts and coffee and cigars. I cannot say much for the cigars; they are not over-good in England: too long at sea, I suppose.

On the whole, it was a memorable dinner. Even its non-essential features were satisfactory. The waiter was fascinatingly solemn, the floor snowily sanded, the company sufficiently distinguished in literature and art for me to keep track of them through the newspapers. They are dead—as dead as Queen Anne, every mother's son of them! I am in my favorite rôle of Sole Survivor. It has become habitual to me; I rather like it.

Of the company were two eminent gastronomes—call them Messrs. Guttle and Swig—who so acridly hated each other that nothing but a good dinner could bring them under the same roof. (They had had a quarrel, I think, about the merit of a certain Amontillado—which, by the way, one insisted, despite Edgar Allan Poe, who certainly knew too much of whiskey to know much of wine, is a Sherry.) After the cloth had been removed and the coffee, walnuts and cigars brought in, the company stood, and to an air extemporaneously composed by Guttle, sang the following shocking and reprehensible song, which had been written during the proceedings by this present Sole Survivor. It will serve as fitly to conclude this feast of unreason as it did that:

THE SONG

Jack Satan's the greatest of gods,
And Hell is the best of abodes.
'Tis reached through the Valley of Clods
By seventy beautiful roads.
Hurrah for the Seventy Roads!
Hurrah for the clods that resound
With a hollow, thundering sound!
Hurrah for the Best of Abodes!

We'll serve him as long as we've breath—
Jack Satan, the greatest of gods.
To all of his enemies, death!—
A home in the Valley of Clods.
Hurrah for the thunder of clods
That smother the souls of his foes!
Hurrah for the spirit that goes
To dwell with the Greatest of Gods!

THE END

CPSIA information can be obtained
at www.ICGtesting.com
Printed in the USA
BVHW040901060123
655719BV00024B/1119/J

9 798888 303757